艺术类专业大学英语教程

主 编　倪　进

编 者　赵彦阳　刘　丹
　　　　万国瑞　邢国垣

下　册

南京大学出版社

图书在版编目(CIP)数据

艺术类专业大学英语教程. 下册 / 倪进主编. — 南
京 : 南京大学出版社,2011.8
 ISBN 978 - 7 - 305 - 08430 - 0

Ⅰ.①艺… Ⅱ.①倪… Ⅲ.①英语－高等学校－教材
Ⅳ.①H31

中国版本图书馆 CIP 数据核字(2011)第 101343 号

出版发行 南京大学出版社
社 址 南京市汉口路 22 号 邮 编 210093
网 址 http://www.NjupCo.com
出版人 左 健
书 名 艺术类专业大学英语教程(下册)
主 编 倪 进
责任编辑 蒋桂琴   编辑热线 025 - 83592655
照 排 南京南琳图文制作有限公司
印 刷 常州市武进第三印刷有限公司
开 本 787×1092 1/16 印张 14.5 字数 318 千
版 次 2011 年 8 月第 1 版 2011 年 8 月第 1 次印刷
ISBN 978 - 7 - 305 - 08430 - 0
定 价 34.00 元(配光盘)
发行热线 025 - 83594756
电子邮箱 Press@NjupCo.com
     Sales@NjupCo.com(市场部)

前　言

　　随着世界经济一体化进程速度的加快,随着我国市场经济改革的深入,我国艺术专业人士开始广泛地与国际进行交流。培养高水平艺术专业人员,扩展学生的艺术视野,迅速加强艺术类学生的专业英语知识是目前双语教学刻不容缓的任务。

　　由于历史原因,目前从事艺术专业研究的学者,外语水平不高影响了他们对艺术专业外文资料的理解和运用,导致一些研究难以深入,往往局限于"炒冷饭";另外,外语水平不高也妨碍了国内学者在研究领域与国际学术界之间进行通畅交流。随着改革开放的深入,这一状况必须尽快得到改变。培养既懂外语又懂艺术的研究型专业人才已刻不容缓。

　　开展艺术专业双语教学是扩大对外开放和实现教育面向世界和面向市场的需要。在艺术专业中实施双语教学,如何使学生在有限的学时中,做到专业知识与英语阅读共同提高,这在很大程度上依赖于教师的素质、学生的英语水平和合适的教材。

　　进入 21 世纪以来,随着中国全方位地与国际接轨,各行各业对英语这一国际语言的需求与日俱增,而对目标能力的追求已从原来的单向接受国外信息,即读写能力,变为直接参与交际,即听说的能力。原来以结构主义为指导所编写的教材已不能满足教学要求。近年来,国外各种新教学理论,如任务型语言教学理论、建构主义教学理论、认知心理学等被引入中国,从根本上改变了英语教材的面貌。但是,在新理论指导下编写的英语教材多半是综合类基础课教材,而多数特殊用途英语(ESP)教材,则依然遵循结构主义的老路,方法上以语法翻译法为主。ESP 教材在编写上不同于综合类教材,有其自身的特点和原则,其内容必须与既定的目标情景密切相关,与学生的专业相联系;ESP 教材也不是专业教材,不能完全按该专业的体系来编写,而应该在结合专业的同时按语言、语言教学和语言学习的规律来编写。

　　合适的教材是实施双语教学的物质前提。目前国内可以用于艺术双语教学的ESP 教材尚未见到,这就给艺术专业双语教学的正常开展造成极大的困难,艺术专业双语教材的编选也成了一个难题。即使对于国内较早实行双语教学的一些课程而言,在双语教材的选择上也一直存在分歧。我们认为,真正意义上的英汉双语教材必须遵循"内容第一、语言第二"的原则,也就是说,在选择教材时,首先要考虑内容的完整性和领先性,在满足这个要求的前提下选择语言浅易的版本。

　　本教材根据我国艺术专业知识的要求,收编了新颖、前沿的专业内容。学生可以了解国内外艺术及相关专业发展最新动态,从中汲取艺术精华,丰富创作灵感,迅速跟上世界专业潮流。

本教材在专门用途英语领域尝试运用最新语言教学理论,编写艺术类学生专用的教材,既满足艺术专业的特殊要求,又重点提升学生的综合语言能力,特别是听说能力。在上述编写理念的指导下,本教材主要有如下特点。

1. 合理把握难度,适应艺术类学生的现有水平

依据教育部高教司制定的《大学英语课程教学要求》来安排各级别教材的难度和词汇量,做到循序渐进,便于掌握。为便于学生抓住学习重点,特在本册书每课词汇表(New Words and Expressions)中用★、▲、△符号标注各级别词汇和短语:词汇和短语后没有标注的为四级,加★符号的为六级,加▲符号的为六级后,加△符号的为纲外词汇。

2. 选材方面突出艺术学科的特殊用途

功能语言学认为,ESP 实际上是一种语域变体,包含话语范围、话语基调、话语方式三个变量。从教材层面上,这主要体现在教材的语料组织和语料输入中。

2011 年,国务院学位委员会、教育部修订了《学位授予和人才培养学科目录(2011年)》,艺术学成为新的第 13 个学科门类,即艺术学门类,具体下设艺术学理论(1301)、音乐与舞蹈学(1302)、戏剧与影视学(1303)、美术学(1304)、设计学(可授艺术学、工学学位)(1305)共 5 个一级学科。长期以来,艺术学隶属于文学门类,与中国语言文学、外国语言文学、新闻传播学并列为一级学科。此次艺术学获批成为独立学科门类,标志着艺术学类毕业生将获取艺术学学位,而不是此前的文学学位。这一学科调整,将对我国艺术学学科发展产生重要的积极影响。

本教材的选材将充分考虑艺术学学科门类中的 5 个一级学科以及相近专业门类,兼顾各个门类艺术的学生。所选语料绝大多数来自英美人士使用的相关话语以及英美报刊和各种出版物中的相关真实语料,努力为艺术类学生营造逼真的情景语境。

3. 教材编排适应艺术类学生特点,多用图片等直观手段

心理学研究表明,在人的认知过程中,视觉信息占所有输入信息的 90% 以上,而视觉信息既是长时记忆的基础,其本身也是长时记忆的重要组成部分,人类语言能力中很大的一部分就是以视觉表象的形式存储于大脑中的。艺术类学生的思维方式更倾向于形象思维,图片等直观手段更符合他们的认知习惯。视觉信息是本教材的特色之一。

4. 一个单元围绕同一个主题综合听说读写译五项技能,不再另设听说教程

格式塔心理学强调对心理活动的整体感知,提出整体大于部分之和的观点。语言的学习是一个认知心理过程,也应强调对各种能力的整体把握,以达到事半功倍的效果。以前的教材一般分为《读写教程》和《听说教程》两大块,各自有自己的主题,彼此独立,缺乏统一性,本教材集听说读写译五项技能于一身,各部分围绕同一个主题展开,学生可以对各种能力做到整体认知、整体把握。中英语言信息共享,五种技能综合,文化和人际、学术交流技能融为一体,从而激发艺术类学生的英语学习积极性,真正提高学生英语应用能力和交际能力。

5. 以任务为主线,所有教学活动围绕任务展开,"做中学,学中做",学生在教师的指导下做到自主学习

根据建构主义教学理论,教师的作用已从传统的传递知识的权威转变为学生学习的辅导者,成为学生学习的高级伙伴或合作者。教师是意义建构的帮助者、促进者,而不是知识的提供者和灌输者。学生是意义建构的主动者,而不是知识的被动接收者和被灌输的对象。甚至监控学习和探索的责任也可逐渐由以教师为主转向以学生为主。使用本教材的学生学习完全自主,变"以学生为主体,教师为主导"为"以学生为中心,教师为辅导",即:在教师的指导和帮助下,学生自教自学,担当主要角色,班级设立评审委员会,由学生轮流担任委员,点评学生各项任务完成情况,教师退至幕后,仅提供组织、纠错、答疑等帮助,最终要使学生达到独立学习的目的。

6. 打破传统的课堂教学模式,教学场所跳出教室,直接进入真实的语境

在教学活动中可将学生带至博物馆、美术馆、工厂、画廊等与教学主题有关的场所,克服在课堂上模拟语境带来的心理不真实感。一般情况下,日常教学活动不可能总是安排在有关场所,但为了营造学习环境和氛围,有必要借助于信息技术,将实际场景虚拟化。这是一个有效的解决办法。

《艺术类专业大学英语教程》是我们在大学英语内容和课程体系改革方面所做的一次大胆尝试。本教材分上下两册,每册有 8 个单元。每个单元都由 Highlight, Warm-up tasks, Listening tasks, Reading tasks, Interactive tasks and Follow-up tasks 组成。各部分的具体编排如下。

1. Highlight

包括 Topic area, Structure, Skills 三项,以表的形式列出,让学生清楚所要掌握的语言知识和交际内容。

2. Warm-up tasks

1) 以一段与主题相关的听力材料引入本单元的主题,spot dictation 的形式既是一种听力训练,又可以使学生较为轻松地掌握大部分内容,从此开始逐渐进入本单元的主题。

2) 三到四幅与单元主题相关的精美图片展示了与主题相关的各个方面信息,为学生提供了很好的看图说话的素材。

3. Listening tasks

听力部分选取与单元主题相关的一个长对话和一篇短文,题型的设计力求多样化,既有选择题、判断题,又有便于课堂口语训练的回答题等题型。该部分的设计既可以使学生进行有针对性的听力训练,同时也可使学生对该主题有更深入的了解。

4. Reading tasks

阅读部分包括两篇与单元主题相关的文章,以便给学生提供更多关于该主题的资讯。Text A 作为仔细阅读(Reading in Detail),Text B 则作为泛读材料(Skimming and Scanning)。Text A 作为精读材料,包含有较多的核心词汇及重要词组和句型,以方便教师对学生进行相关的词汇、句型和翻译等语言技能的训练；Text B 篇幅相对稍长，以达到通过训练提高学生单位时间内更好地理解材料内容的目的。

课后练习包括阅读理解、回答问题、选词（词组）填空以及仿照例句翻译等，均针对历年来考试中出现的核心词汇进行设计，以帮助学生熟练掌握课文的关键词汇、词组及句型。值得一提的是其中一个有关 summary 的题型，既要求学生熟悉课文的内容，同时又要有较好的概括课文内容的能力，相信对学生的写作能力会是个很好的锻炼。

5. Interactive tasks

互动练习包括两个部分。第一部分提供两个紧扣交际主题的对话及两个情景对话的任务，学生可以通过模仿提供的范文进行口语练习。第二部分则包括一个团队活动的任务，教师可在课前将任务布置下去，学生以小组为单位进行准备以备单元结束时进行现场演示。

6. Follow-up tasks

该部分包括两个部分。第一部分是写作，主要是写作技巧的介绍，着重于四、六级和研究生英语入学考试短文写作讲解，如短文写作的四原则，如何进行段落的计划、段落的种类、段落的展开方法以及段落写作中应避免的问题等。具体的写作练习老师可以依据自己的教学要求自行确定。

第二部分则提供了一个有关单元主题的研究项目，学生同样以小组为单位尝试自选课题并进行研究。正如前文所说，教师在这个过程中要担当起一个引导者的角色，提供组织、纠错、答疑等帮助。

《艺术类专业大学英语教程》是集体科研和智慧的结晶，它的编写和出版得益于众多专业院校的专家和教授的热情关心、真诚帮助和悉心指导，特别是全国外语协会会长李霄翔教授在本书的策划、编写、出版等方面自始至终都给予编者以无私的帮助和指导，东南大学外国语学院和艺术学院给予编者以极大的支持。编者深知，如果没有他们的帮助和指导，要完成本套教材的编写是困难的。在此，编者向他们深表感谢！

英国著名语言学家塞缪尔·约翰逊（Samuel Johnson）曾感慨，编写词典的人是"unhappy mortals"（不幸的噍类），而作者深深体会到要真正写好书，写书人又何尝不是"unhappy mortals"呢？

"梅雨润兼旬，暑月不知夏。"今夜，思绪在江南初夏的丝雨里徜徉。深深呼吸这江南初夏夜晚的清凉空气，提笔写完本书的最后几句话。可是，我却感觉不到多少轻松。这套书送给读者的是快意还是其他？我说不好。也许就像李清照的词写的那样："随意杯盘虽草草，酒美梅酸，恰称人怀抱。"企盼使用者批评指正。

倪　进

2011 年 7 月 17 日于兰园

目　　录

Unit One　Chinese Painting

Highlight

Topic area	Structure	Skills
Classical styles of Chinese landscape painting The evolution of Chinese landscape painting Chinese Hand scrolls Some modern Chinese painting masters	evolve into in response to identify ... with face ... with serve to lie in allow for	Understanding the classical styles and format of Chinese landscape painting in relation to its appreciation Describing and discussing the evolution of Chinese landscape painting Discussing the greatness of modern Chinese painting masters

Warm-up Tasks

1 **Listen to the following passage and try to fill in the missing words and expressions.**

Many（1）_____ consider landscape to be the highest form of Chinese painting. The time from the Five Dynasties period to the Northern Song period is known as the "Great age of Chinese landscape". In the north, artists such as Jing Hao（荆浩）, Fan Kuan（范宽）, and Guo Xi（郭熙）painted pictures of（2）_____ mountains, using strong black lines, ink wash（墨染技巧）, and sharp dotted（遒劲有力的）（3）_____ to suggest（4）_____ stone. In the south, Dong Yuan（董源）, Ju Ran（巨然）, and other artists painted the rolling hills and rivers of their（5）_____ countryside in（6）_____ scenes done with（7）_____ rubbed（轻舒的）brushwork. These two kinds of scenes and（8）_____ became the（9）_____ styles of Chinese landscape painting. Usually, the purpose of such painting works was not to reproduce exactly the appearance of nature（realism）but rather to grasp an（10）_____ or atmosphere so as to catch the "rhythm" of nature.

2 **Look at the following Chinese landscape painting works and discuss the following questions with your partner.**

1. Try to study the given works of Chinese landscape painting. Do they match the classical styles of Chinese landscape painting? Why or why not?

2. What do you think are the major differences or similarities between the two works? Discuss them with reference to essential elements of Chinese painting

Travelers amid Mountains and Streams by Fan Kuan

The Xiao and Xiang Rivers by Dong Yuan

such as brushstroke, lines or ink wash.

3. Of the two pictures, which do you like better? Give your reasons.

Listening Tasks

Micro Listening Skills

3 **You will hear six sentences. Listen carefully and fill in the missing words.**

1. Whatever the art form, the essence of harmony _____ the same.

2. Painting should leave _____ for imagination.

3. There is the difference between active _____ and passive observation.

4. A plant is so ordinary but _____ at the same time.

5. Traditionally Chinese painting does not strive to be _____.

6. He or she has to desire to create something that is _____.

Dialogue

Du Pingrang: An Intriguing and Inspiring Artist[1]
—An Interview by Lily Pietryka

---

① This part cites information from http://en.artdu.com/news/html/? 4.html.

Du Pingrang

Lily Pietryka

Words & Phrases

tranquility /træŋˈkwɪlɪtɪ/ n.		宁静
vibrant /ˈvaɪbrənt/ adj.		振动的
chaotic /keɪˈɒtɪk/ adj.		混乱无序的
harmonically /hɑːˈmɒnɪkəlɪ/ adv.		调和地；和声地
essence /ˈesns/ n.		本质
portray /pɔːˈtreɪ/ vt.		描绘
innovate /ˈɪnəveɪt/ vt.		改革；革新
grandeur /ˈgrændʒə/ n.		庄严；伟大
strive /straɪv/ vt.		努力

4 Listen to the dialogue and choose the best answer to the following questions.

(   ) 1. How does Du Pingrang describe the sense of peace in his paintings?

      A. It is like philosophy.   B. It is like a mythology.

      C. It is like a symphony.   D. It is like psychology.

(   ) 2. Du's viewpoint about live objects for painting shows that _____.

      A. he doesn't want to set limits to the choice of them

      B. he doesn't want to choose them from imagination

      C. he doesn't want to understand them from observation

      D. he doesn't want to capture them in the universities

(   ) 3. According to Du, what is the major difference between Chinese paintings and the Western oil paintings?

      A. Traditionally Chinese paintings are more meaningful.

      B. Traditionally Chinese paintings are more understandable.

      C. Traditionally Chinese paintings are more liberal.

      D. Traditionally Chinese paintings are more formal.

(   ) 4. Which of the following is NOT true about Du's statement on a great artist's most important quality?

      A. Being creative.   B. Being innovative.

      C. Being thoughtful.   D. Being universal.

(   ) 5. About aspirations, Du does NOT emphasize the need to _____.

      A. show people beauty by painting

      B. express nature and life by painting

      C. reveal the power of truth and mind by painting

      D. earn fame and fortune by painting

5 Listen to the dialogue again and complete the following sentences with the information you have heard.

    1. In Du Pingrang's painting, the colors, the _____ and _____ come harmoniously together.

    2. Du chooses live objects from all _____. He wants to capture the _____ of nature.

    3. Traditional Chinese painters are more likely to explore _____ beyond _____.

    4. A great artist should portray something _____ what meets the eye.

    5. Du wants to show people through his painting the _____ of the human _____.

Passage

Reading Traditional Chinese Painting

Night-Shining White，by Han Gan（active 742—756，Tang Dynasty）

Words & Phrases

calligraphy /kəˈlɪgrəfɪ/ *n.*	书法
evolve /ɪˈvɒlv/ *vi.*	进化；发展
inscription /ɪnˈskrɪpʃən/ *n.*	题名
seal /siːl/ *n.*	印章

6 Listen to the passage and decide whether the following statements are true (T) or false (F).

_____ 1. The purpose of traditional Chinese painting is to grasp the special energy of nature.

_____ 2. A Chinese artist traditionally considers the use of color as something disturbing to his art.

_____ 3. Light and shadow are regarded by a traditional Chinese painter as good means of modeling.

_____ 4. The richness of traditional Chinese painting lies in its involvement of multiple art forms.

_____ 5. The "three perfections" in traditional Chinese art refer to life, force and spirit.

7 **Listen to the passage again and answer the following questions with the help of words and phrases provided below.**

1. What do we need to know to better appreciate a Chinese painting art?
   (*aim*, *capture*, *richness*, *integration*)

_____

2. What is the major aim of a traditional Chinese artist?
   (*outer appearance*, *inner essence*, *energy*, *life force*, *spirit*)

_____

3. How should we understand the richness of a traditional Chinese painting?
   (*integration*, *calligraphy*, *poetry*, *evolve*, *owners and admirers*, *add*, *inscriptions*, *seals*, *part of artistic expression*)

_____

4. What is special about the Chinese way of appreciating a traditional painting? Why is it also called *du hua*, "reading a painting"? What can you "read" in the above masterpiece, *Night-Shining White* by Han Gan?
   (*enter*, *dialogue*, *the past*, *experience*, *share*, *repeat*)

_____

Reading Tasks

Text A   Reading in Detail

Pre-reading Questions

1. What do you know about the evolution of Chinese landscape painting in history?
2. Do you admire some Chinese landscape painters and their works?
3. Do you think Chinese landscape paining is connected with the artist's inner aspirations?

Landscape Painting in Chinese Art[①]

By the late Tang Dynasty, landscape painting had evolved into an independent genre that embodied the universal longing of cultivated men to escape their worldly

---

① This text is adapted from the article with the same title by Charles Moffat at http://www. metmuseum. org/toah/hd/clpg/hd_clpg. htm; the pictures here are cited from the same website.

worries to commune with nature. Such images might also convey specific social, philosophical, or political convictions. As the Tang Dynasty disintegrated, the concept of withdrawal into the natural world became a major thematic focus of poets and painters. Faced with the failure of the human order, learned men sought permanence within the natural world, retreating into the mountains to find a sanctuary from the chaos of dynastic collapse.

Riverbank attributed to Dong Yuan

During the early Song Dynasty, visions of the natural hierarchy became metaphors for the well-regulated state. At the same time, images of the private retreat proliferated among a new class of scholar-officials. These men extolled the virtues of self-cultivation—often in response to political setbacks or career disappointments—and asserted their identity as literati through poetry, calligraphy, and a new style of painting that employed calligraphic brushwork for self-expressive ends. The monochrome images of natural objects such as old trees, bamboo, rocks created by these scholar-artists became emblems of retirement retreats in their character and spirit.

Under the Yuan Dynasty, when many educated Chinese were barred from government service, the model of the Song literati retreat evolved into a full-blown alternative culture. This disenfranchised elite transformed their estates into sites for literary gatherings and other cultural pursuits. These gatherings were frequently commemorated in paintings that, rather than presenting a realistic depiction of an actual place, conveyed the shared cultural ideals of a reclusive world through a symbolic shorthand in which a villa might be represented by a humble thatched hut.

Old Trees, *Level Distance*, by Guo Xi

Scholar by a Waterfall, by Ma Yuan

Because a man's studio or garden could be viewed as an extension of himself,   25
paintings of such places often served to express the values of their owner.

The Yuan Dynasty also witnessed the burgeoning of a second kind of cultivated
landscape, the "mind landscape". [①] The paintings of this kind embodied both learned
references to the styles of earlier masters and, through calligraphic brushwork, the
inner spirit of the artist. The scholar-artists tended to imbue their paintings with   30

① "mind landscape" 现常被用作元代赵孟頫《谢幼舆丘壑图》的英译名。但此处应指同时期钱选所持"士气"
画论以及倪瓒的"逸笔"、"逸气"画论。前者指以书法用笔的画技与画家清高品格的结合,后者则突出画家取法古
人时发挥自身个性神韵的重要性。可参阅葛路《中国画论史》第142—151页(北京大学出版社 2009 版)。

Twin Pines, *Level Distance*, by Zhao Mengfu

personal feelings. By evoking select antique styles, they could also identify themselves with the values associated with the old masters. Painting was no longer about the description of the visible world; it became a means of conveying the inner landscape of the artist's heart and mind.

35   During the Ming Dynasty, when native Chinese rule was restored, court artists produced conservative images that revived the Song metaphor for the state as a well-ordered imperial garden, while literati painters pursued self-expressive goals through the stylistic language of Yuan scholar-artists. Shen Zhou, the patriarch of the Wu School of painting centered in the cosmopolitan city of Suzhou, and his preeminent

Garden of the Unsuccessful Politician (*Zhuo Zheng Yuan* 拙政园), by Wen Zhengming

follower Wen Zhengming exemplified Ming literati ideals. Both chose to reside at home rather than follow official careers, devoting themselves to self-cultivation through a lifetime spent reinterpreting the styles of Yuan scholar-painters.

Morally charged images of reclusion remained a potent political symbol during the early years of the Qing Dynasty, a period in which many Ming loyalists lived in self-enforced retirement. Often lacking access to the important collections of old masters, loyalist artists drew inspiration from the natural beauty of the local scenery.

Images of nature have remained a potent source of inspiration for artists down to the present day. In Chinese landscape paintings, depictions of nature are seldom mere representations of the external world. Rather, they are expressions of the mind and heart of the individual artists— cultivated landscapes that embody the culture and cultivation of their masters.

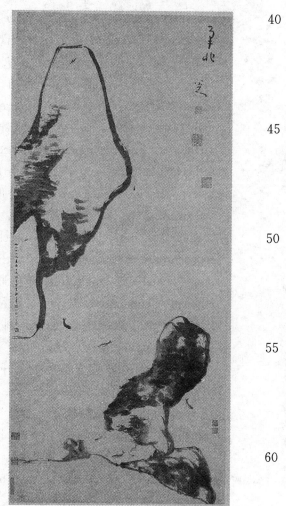

Fish and Rocks, by Bada Shanren(Zhu Da)

(685 words)

New Words and Expressions

commune△（**with**）/kəˈmjuːn/ *vt.*　communicate intimately 交换思想、意见～with nature 与大自然亲密交融;融入自然;寄情山水

conviction /kənˈvɪkʃən/ *n.*　a fixed or strong belief 信念

disintegrate▲ /dɪsˈɪntɪɡreɪt/ *vt.*　(cause to) break into parts or small bits （使）分解;碎裂;崩溃

withdrawal▲ /wɪðˈdrɔːəl/ *n.*　stopping one's participation in or use of; retreat; retirement 退隐

thematic△ /θiːˈmætɪk/ *adj.*　of, relating to, or being a theme 主题的

learned /ˈlɜːnɪd/ *adj.*　having great learning; knowledgeable; concerning knowledge or academic research 博学的;学术的

sanctuary△ /'sæŋktjʊərɪ/ *n.*   a place of refuge 避难所

hierarchy★ /'haɪərɑːkɪ/ *n.*   persons or things arranged in graded series 层次；等级

well-regulated /'wel'regjʊleɪtɪd/ *adj.*   well governed or ruled；put or maintained in order 治理得很好的；井然有序的

proliferate▲ /prəʊ'lɪfəreɪt/ *vt.*   increase or spread rapidly 增生；扩散

extol△ /ɪks'tɒl/ *vt.*   praise highly 赞美

virtue /'vɜːtjuː/ *n.*   moral excellence 美德

setback★ /'setbæk/ *n.*   a reverse or change from better to worse 挫折；退步

assert /ə'sɜːt/ *vt.*   declare 表明；主张；声称

self-expression /'selfɪks'preʃən/ *n.*   expression of one's own personality, feelings, or ideas，as through speech or art 自我表现；个性表现

monochrome△ /'mɒnəʊkrəʊm/ *n.*   the art of painting different shades by using a single color；of a single color 单色画法；单色

emblem△ /'embləm/ *n.*   symbol 象征

bar /bɑː/ *vt.*   keep out；exclude 排斥

full-blown /'fʊl'bləʊn/ *adj.*   fully developed or matured；having blossomed or opened completely 完全成熟的；盛开的

disenfranchise△ /ˌdɪsɪn'fræntʃaɪz/ *vt.*   （also disfranchise）deprive of a right or a privilege 剥夺权利或特权

transform /træns'fɔːm/ *vt.*   （～... into ... ）change markedly the appearance or form of 使……转变为……

commemorate★ /kə'meməreɪt/ *vt.*   honor the memory of with a ceremony 纪念

reclusive△ /rɪ'kluːsɪv/ *adj.*   seeking or preferring seclusion or isolation 隐遁的；隐居的

shorthand▲ /'ʃɔːthænd/ *n.*   method of speed writing or drawing 速记；速写

villa△ /'vɪlə/ *n.*   a country estate 别墅

thatch▲ /θætʃ/ *vt.*   cover with straw 覆盖茅草

burgeon△ /'bɜːdʒən/ *vi.*   begin to grow or blossom 萌芽

imbue▲ /ɪm'bjuː/ （with）*vt.*   fill or inspire ... with ... 用……（精神）浸染、感染

select /sɪ'lekt/ *adj.*   favored 精选的

identify /aɪ'dentɪfaɪ/ *vt.*   associate or affiliate （oneself）closely with a person or group 对……产生认同感；认为和……有联系

revive★ /rɪ'vaɪv/ *vt.*   （cause to）return to currency or notice （使）复兴；复苏

patriarch△ /'peɪtrɪɑːk/ *n.*   founder or venerable person 创始者；元老；掌门人

cosmopolitan▲ /ˌkɒzmə'pɒlɪtən/ *adj.*   belonging to or from all parts of the world or various places 世界性的；四通八达的

preeminent△ /prɪ(ː)'emɪnənt/ *adj.*   superior to or notable above all others；

outstanding 卓越的；突出的

exemplify /ɪɡˈzemplɪfaɪ/ *vt.*　illustrate by example 举例说明；体现

charge /tʃɑːdʒ/ *vt.*　fill or excite 充溢；激发

potent▲ /ˈpəʊtənt/ *adj.*　powerful or effective 有力的；有效的

loyalist△ /ˈlɔɪəlɪst/ *n.*　one who is faithful to a country, cause, government, sovereign or friend 忠臣；忠贞不贰的人

self-enforced /ˈselfɪnˈfɔːsɪd/ *adj.*　implemented by oneself on purpose; voluntary 故意的；主动自愿的

Proper Names

(Chinese) landscape painting	中国山水画
cultivated men	文人雅士
worldly worries	世俗纷扰
scholar-official	亦作 scholar-bureaucrats，意为士大夫
self-cultivation	自我修养
literati	（复数名词）文人
retirement retreat	隐退
calligraphic brushwork	书画风格
native Chinese rule	中原人的统治
court artists	宫廷画师
Wu School of Painting	吴门画派，亦简称"吴派"。发端于中国明代中期的宣德年间，其山水画之成就尤为突出，在艺术上较全面地继承了宋元以来的优秀传统，注重表现个人的节操和情怀，开创一代新风，取代受皇室赏识的宫廷院体和浙派而占据画坛主位，历时150多年，标志着文人士大夫画派的一段盛期。主要代表人物有沈周、文征明、唐寅、仇英等。

Comprehension

8 **Choose the best answer to each question with the information from the text.**

(　　) 1. According to the passage, by the late Tang Dynasty Chinese landscape painting had already become an independent genre that _____.

A. retreated into specific chaos because of the failure of natural world

B. communicated with the universe of cultivated men's nature

C. implied learned men's worries and hopes through images of nature

D. expressed the permanent focus of major poets and painters

(　　) 2. In early Song Dynasty the scholar-officials' virtues of self-cultivation were represented by all of the following EXCEPT _____.

A. their natural visions of employment by the well-regulated state

B. their artistic expression of mind in face of political failures

C. their increasing images of personal retreats into natural world

D. their simple-colored natural objects as symbols for their soul

(   ) 3. Landscape painting in the Yuan Dynasty _____.

A. symbolized the cultural ideals of the educated native Chinese

B. reflected the national oppression of the ruling Mongols

C. illustrated a well-developed culture of literati reclusion

D. All of the above.

(   ) 4. The "mind landscape" refers to the important thought of cultivated painting that stressed _____.

A. demonstrating the artist's own personality

B. expressing values in the styles of earlier masters

C. Both A & B.

D. the expression of an artist's stream of consciousness

(   ) 5. According to the passage, court artists and the literati painters were essentially different in that _____.

A. they earned salaries from different supplying sources in their lifetime

B. they pursued different poetic, calligraphic and painting styles

C. they both painted objects from nature yet with different purposes

D. they turned out either loyalists or traitors when their dynasty collapsed

9 **Complete the following summary with right words and expressions.**

In Chinese landscape painting, nature always remains an important _____ of the artist's mind and cultivation. Landscape painting in late Tang Dynasty was already an independent genre conveying social and philosophical convictions with the major theme of _____ into nature to escape worldly worries and chaos.

Such images of private retreat proliferated among the scholar-officials of the early Song Dynasty, who extolled their _____ of self-cultivation in response to political setbacks by painting _____ natural objects such as trees or rocks.

In the Yuan Dynasty, the Song literati retreat developed into a full-grown culture pursuit when many educated native Chinese were excluded from social and political participation. This culture often found its expression in _____ landscape symbolizing the artist's _____ mind. The idea of "_____" in this period involved following earlier masters' styles and expressing an artist's own _____ values.

The styles of Yuan scholar-painters were well inherited and developed in Ming

Dynasty. Disregarding official careers, the Wu school of painting _____ the literati ideals of self-cultivation by following the Yuan masterpieces. However, in the early Qing Dynasty, many painters as Ming loyalist turned to the local scenic beauty for _____.

10 **Discuss the following questions with the information from the text.**

1. Why was there the major thematic focus of withdrawal into nature in the landscape painting of late Tang Dynasty?

   (*failure, cultivated/learned men, conviction, escape*)

   _____

2. How did the "disenfranchised elite" of the Yuan Dynasty paint their estates? As far as the passage and history are concerned, what do you think were their reasons for doing so?

   (*symbolic, imply, pursuit, express, value*)

   _____

3. What was characteristic of Ming literati painters' art and life?

   (*follow, Yuan scholar-artists, official careers, self-cultivation*)

   _____

4. What kind of artists in the early Song Dynasty do you assume might be painting "the natural hierarchy" that "became metaphors for the well-regulated state"?

   _____

5. Consult some references on the social and political situations of the early Qing Dynasty. Try analyzing the "morally charged images of reclusion" in the painting by many Ming loyalists who "lived in self-enforced retirement".

   _____

Vocabulary & Structure

11 **Fill in the blanks with the words given below. Change the form where necessary.**

revive	convey	learned	metaphor	virtue
setback	assert	witness	pursue	exemplify

1. The help and rescue from all over the country quickly _____ the life of the disaster area.

2. The first decade of this century _____ great changes of the seaside town.

3. His father is a _____ professor but he appears very ignorant in many ways.

4. Jacky Chan's style has been well _____ by the amusing and intriguing scenes of his latest action film.

5. Among many of his _____ are courage, honesty, and loyalty.

6. Many workers in that country are on strike again to _____ their rights.

7. He was using the _____ "a sea of troubles" to refer to his difficult situation now.

8. To _____ success, we need better team work and more rational consideration.

9. Picasso's *Guernica* is believed to have _____ his angry outcry against the atrocities of the Fascists.

10. Their project suffered a severe _____ when the precious data of research had been lost during the internet virus infection.

12 **Complete the following sentences with phrases or expressions from the text.**

1. They decided to take measures _____ the recent external pressures.

2. He kept telling us how their small acting studio had _____ a theatrical company.

3. It is not always proper to _____ justice _____ punishment.

4. The foggy darkness in the forest _____ the trees _____ numerous ghost-like monsters.

13 **Translate the Chinese sentences into English by simulating the sentences chosen from the text.**

Chosen Sentences	Simulated Translation	Chinese Sentences
Faced with the failure of the human order, learned men sought permanence within the natural world.		面对死亡,小男孩显得异常镇定。
A man's studio or garden could *be viewed as* an extension of himself.		如果我们的克制被视作怯懦,后果将是非常严重的。(cowardice)
Paintings of such places often *served to* express the values of their owner.		朋友们的关心和体贴极大地缓解了他的悲伤和焦虑。(relieve)
The scholar-artists tended to *imbue* their paintings *with* personal feelings.		卓别林的幽默艺术充满了对被压迫者的深切同情。(profound)

(Continued)

Chosen Sentences	Simulated Translation	Chinese Sentences
Often ***lacking access to*** the important collections of old masters, loyalist artists drew inspiration from the natural beauty of the local scenery.		由于无法接近可靠的消息来源，她不得不求助于一些知名的朋友。（reliable）

14 **Rewrite each sentence with the word or phrase in brackets, keeping the same meaning. The first part has been done for you.**

1. Tourism will continue to be a lively industry in that country.

   Tourism will _____. （remain）

2. The public relations department launched a campaign to establish again the company's public popularity.

   A campaign _____. （restore）

3. Due to the recent terrorist attacks, panic grew and spread quickly among the city residents.

   Panic _____. （proliferate）

4. Represented in the painting is human beings' strong desire to seek permanent justice.

   The painting _____. （longing）

5. When he was a college student, he had the habit of doing physical workouts before going to bed every evening.

   While at college, he _____. （tend to）

Text B   Skimming and Scanning

Chinese Hand Scrolls[①]

Twin Pines Level Distance by Zhao Mengfu

---

① This text is adapted from the essay with the same title by Dawn Delbanco at http://www.metmuseum.org/toah/hd/chhs/hd_chhs.htm#slideshow9.

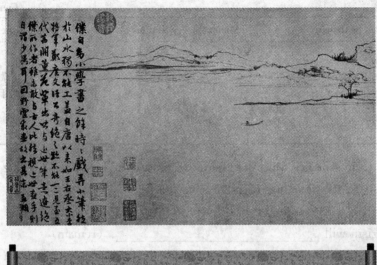

A significant difference between Eastern and Western painting lies in the format. (1) Unlike Western paintings, which are hung on walls and continuously visible to the eye, most Chinese paintings are not meant to be on constant view but are brought out to be seen only from time to time. This occasional viewing has everything to do with format.

A predominant format of Chinese painting is the hand scroll, a continuous roll of paper or silk of varying length on which an image has been painted, and which, when not being viewed, remains rolled up. Ceremony and anticipation underlie the experience of looking at a hand scroll. When in storage, the painting itself is several  layers removed from immediate view, and the value of a scroll is reflected in part by its packaging. Scrolls are generally kept in individual wooden boxes that bear an identifying label. Removing the lid, the viewer may find the scroll wrapped in a piece of silk, and, unwrapping the silk, encounters the hand scroll bound with a silken cord that is held in place with a jade or ivory toggle. After undoing the cord, one begins the careful process of unrolling the scroll from right to left, pausing to admire and study it, section by section, rerolling a section before proceeding to the next one.

The experience of seeing a scroll for the first time is like a revelation. As one 20
unrolls the scroll, one has no idea what is coming next: each section presents a new
surprise. Looking at a hand scroll that one has seen before is like visiting an old friend
whom one has not seen for a while. One remembers the general appearance, the
general outlines, of the image, but not the details. In unrolling the scroll, one greets
a remembered image with pleasure, but it is a pleasure that is enhanced at each 25
viewing by the discovery of details that one has either forgotten or never noticed
before.

Looking at a hand scroll is an intimate experience. Its size and format preclude a
large audience; viewers are usually limited to one or two. (2) Unlike the viewer of
Western painting, who maintains a certain distance from the image, the viewer of a 30
hand scroll has direct physical contact with the object, rolling and unrolling the scroll
at his/her own desired pace, lingering over some passages, moving quickly through
others.

The format of a hand scroll allows for the depiction of a continuous narrative or
journey: the viewing of a hand scroll is a progression through time and space—not 35
only the narrative time and space of the image, but also the literal time and distance it
takes to experience the entire painting. As the scroll unfurls, the narrative or journey
progresses. In this way, looking at a hand scroll is like reading a book: a viewer of
the scroll proceeds from section to section, just as a reader turns from page to page,
not knowing what to expect; in both painting and book, there is a beginning and an end. 40

Indeed, this resemblance is not incidental. The hand scroll format—as well as
other Chinese painting formats—reveals an intimacy between word and image. (3)
Many Hand scrolls contain inscriptions preceding or following the image: poems
composed by the painter or others that enhance the meaning of the image, or a few
written lines that convey the circumstances of its creation. Many hand scrolls also 45
contain colophons, or commentary written onto additional sheets of paper or silk that
follows the image itself. These may be comments written by friends of the artist or
the collector; they may have been written by viewers from later generations. The
colophons may comment on the quality of the painting, express the rhapsody (rarely
the disenchantment) of the viewer, give a biographical sketch of the artist, place the 50
painting within an art-historical context, or engage with the texts of earlier
colophons. And as a final way of making their presence known, the painter, the
collectors, the one-time viewers often "sign" the image or colophons with personal
seals bearing their names, these red marks of varying size conveying pride of
authorship or ownership. 55

Thus the hand scroll is both painted image and documentary history; past and present are in continuous dialogue. (4) Looking at a scroll with colophons and inscriptions, a viewer not only sees a pictorial representation but witnesses the history of the painting as it is passed down from generation to generation.

(735 words)

New Words and Expressions

hand scroll△ /hænd skrəʊl/ *n.* 中国画的卷轴(亦称手卷、横卷、轴卷、横轴、横看、手轴、卷子、行看子。字画装裱方式,横式装,是一种古老的装潢形式。卷轴体积较小,轻巧且宜收藏。但只能平放案头,不便张挂)

format /ˈfɔːmæt/ *n.* general style or arrangement of sth. 格式;样式;样式

from time to time once in a while; at intervals 时时;间或

predominant★ /prɪˈdɒmɪnənt/ *adj.* having the greatest importance, influence, or authority; prevalent 最重要的;最有权威的;最流行的

ceremony /ˈserɪmənɪ/ *n.* formal act prescribed by law, ritual, or convention 典礼;仪式

anticipation /ænˌtɪsɪˈpeɪʃən/ *n.* expectation; the act of getting prepared for or looking forward to 期待;预期

underlie▲ /ˌʌndəˈlaɪ/ *vt.* be the support or basis of; account for 成为……的根据、原因、支撑或基础

layer /ˈleɪə/ *n.* one thickness over or under another 层;层次

remove /rɪˈmuːv/ *vt.* move by lifting or taking off or away 移走;移开

in part partly; to some extent 部分地;在某种程度上

package /ˈpækɪdʒ/ *vt.* enclose in a wrapped or boxed object; bundle items together 包装

bear /beə/ *vt.* carry 具有

label /ˈleɪbl/ *n.* identification slip; identifying word or phrase 标签;标记

encounter /ɪnˈkaʊntə/ *vt.* meet unexpectedly 碰见;不期而遇

bind (bound, binding) /baɪnd/ *vt.* tie 捆扎

silken△ /ˈsɪlkən/ *adj.* smooth and lustrous; resembling silk in texture or appearance 柔软光亮的;质地外表像丝绸的

cord /kɔːd/ *n.* a slender and flexible string to tie, connect or support 带子;绳索

in place in the appropriate or usual spot, position or order 在适当的位置;有序

jade△ /dʒeɪd/ *n.* usually green gemstone 玉石

ivory★ /ˈaɪvərɪ/ *n.* a hard, smooth, yellowish-white substance composed primarily of dentin that forms the tusks of the elephant 象牙

toggle△ /ˈtɒgl/ *n.* a pin, rod, or crosspiece fitted or inserted into a loop in a rope, chain, or strap to prevent slipping, to tighten, or to hold an attached object 绳针;套索钉

undo /ˌʌnˈduː/ *n.*   untie, disassemble, or loosen 解开;拆卸;松开

section /ˈsekʃən/ *n.*   distinct part 部分

proceed /prəˈsiːd/ *vi.*   go forward or onward, especially after an interruption; continue 继续;继续前进

revelation★ /ˌreviˈleɪʃən/ *n.*   the act of revealing or disclosing 显示;揭露

enhance /ɪnˈhɑːns/ *vt.*   improve in value, beauty, or reputation 增进;提高

intimate /ˈɪntɪmɪt/ *adj.*   very close in distance or relationship; suggesting privacy 亲密的;涉及隐私的

preclude△ /prɪˈkluːd/ *vt.*   make impossible 排除;使……不可能

linger★ /ˈlɪŋgə/ *vt.*   be slow to leave or act 徘徊;逗留

allow for   take ... into consideration 考虑;顾及

narrative /ˈnærətɪv/ *n.*   a narrated account; a story 叙事;故事

literal★ /ˈlɪtərəl/ *adj.*   avoiding exaggeration, metaphor, or embellishment; factual; prosaic 精确的;平实的

unfurl△ /ʌnˈfɜːl/ *vt.*   unfold or unroll 展开;公开

resemblance★ /rɪˈzembləns/ *n.*   the state of resembling or being similar to 相似;类似

incidental /ˌɪnsɪˈdentl/ *adj.*   met by chance 偶然的

inscription▲ /ɪnˈskrɪpʃən/ *n.*   the act or an instance of inscribing or engraving 雕刻;铭刻

precede★ /priːˈsiːd/ *vt.*   be, go, or come ahead of 领先于;在……之前

circumstance /ˈsɜːkəmstəns/ *n.*   surrounding conditions 环境;详情;境况

colophon△ /ˈkɒləfən/ *n.*   an inscription (usually a page or more) placed usually on a painting or at the end of a book, giving facts or comments about its publication 画轴题记;书籍末页的版本记录

commentary★ /ˈkɒməntərɪ/ *n.*   explanation or interpretation 注释;解说词

rhapsody★ /ˈræpsədɪ/ *n.*   a state of elated bliss; ecstasy 一种得意的极快乐状态;狂喜

disenchantment★ /ˌdɪsɪnˈtʃɑːntmənt/ *n.*   the state of being free from illusion or false belief 觉醒;清醒

biographical★ /baɪəʊˈgræfɪkəl/ *n.*   containing, consisting of, or relating to the facts or events in a person's life 传记的

engage with   connect with 连接

Comprehension

15 Go over the text quickly and answer the following questions. For questions 1—7, choose the best answer from the four choices; for questions 8—10, complete the sentences with the information from the text.

(   ) 1. According to the passage, the difference in format between Chinese and Western painting reveals that _____.

     A. most Chinese paintings are shown to the viewers every now and then

     B. most Chinese paintings have no continuous meaning for their images

     C. most Chinese paintings show the significance of time and occasion

     D. most Chinese paintings are never hung up to satisfy the visitor's eye

(   ) 2. Which of the following is true about the outer appearance of a hand scroll?

     A. It is usually a long continuous roll of paper or silk with painted reflection on.

     B. It is usually stored in a jade or ivory box with an individual identifying mark.

     C. It is usually removed section by section right after the viewer has studied it.

     D. It is usually a roll of silk or paper properly wrapped and packaged in a box.

(   ) 3. The way a hand scroll is stored and packaged may show _____.

     A. how hard the owner works

     B. how pleasant the image is

     C. how precious the scroll is

     D. how serious the viewer is

(   ) 4. The way of appreciating a hand scroll involves all of the following EXCEPT _____.

     A. uncovering the lid of the container

     B. underlining the identifying label

     C. unrolling the scroll slowly with care

     D. untying the band around the scroll

(   ) 5. The author compares the experience of watching a hand scroll for a second time to _____.

     A. new pleasures with new discoveries

     B. new ceremonies with new greetings

     C. new surprises with new expectations

     D. new generations with new friendships

(   ) 6. Which is NOT true about the "intimate experience" in appreciating a hand scroll?

      A. The viewers closely contact the hand scroll itself.

      B. The viewers freely control their speed of appreciation.

      C. The viewers usually have very close relationships.

      D. The viewers frequently are a small group of people.

(   ) 7. The format of a hand scroll makes it impossible that _____.

      A. the viewer experiences how a story or a trip goes on in the painting

      B. the viewer appreciates in a gradual, progressive and continuous way

      C. the viewer unrolls the hand scroll bit by bit to anticipate new findings

      D. the viewer looks at the hand scroll while making his own art progress

     8. The hand scroll format shows an intimacy between _____ by inscribing poems or some written lines conveying the circumstances of its creation.

     9. The colophons may _____ on the quality of the painting, express the viewer's excitement, give a _____ sketch of the artist, place the painting within an art-historical _____, or engage with the texts of earlier colophons.

    10. The image or colophons of a hand scroll often go along with the personal _____ of its painter, collectors, or viewers; these red marks of varying size convey _____ of authorship or ownership.

Vocabulary & Translation

16 Fill in the blanks with the words given below. Change the form where necessary.

continuously	predominant	encounter	proceed	enhance
intimate	linger	depiction	literal	reveal

1. Their kindness and hospitality _____ greed(贪婪) and indifference.

2. For years Mary always remained her most _____ friend.

3. Hemingway's works are considered good _____ of human courage against death.

4. Green was becoming the _____ color in fashion design that year.

5. His efforts helped to _____ the efficiency of their cooperation.

6. The news story was a _____ account(记录) of the train accident last weekend.

7. With his dear wife gone forever, John often _____ in the coffee bar where they first met.

8. Profoundly(充分地) _____ in the painting is the merciful side of human nature.

9. The spokesperson _____ to explain the purpose of policy change this time.

10. During the wartime, their factory kept working _____ day and night to produce tanks.

17 Translate the underlined sentences in the text into Chinese.

1. Unlike Western paintings, which are hung on walls and continuously visible to the eye, most Chinese paintings are not meant to be on constant view but are brought out to be seen only from time to time.

_____

_____

_____

2. Unlike the viewer of Western painting, who maintains a certain distance from the image, the viewer of a hand scroll has direct physical contact with the object, rolling and unrolling the scroll at his/her own desired pace, lingering over some passages, moving quickly through others.

_____

_____

_____

3. Many hand scrolls contain inscriptions preceding or following the image: poems composed by the painter or others that enhance the meaning of the image, or a few written lines that convey the circumstances of its creation.

_____

_____

_____

4. Looking at a scroll with colophons and inscriptions, a viewer not only sees a pictorial representation but witnesses the history of the painting as it is passed down from generation to generation.

_____

_____

_____

Interactive Tasks

Pair Work

18 Read the sample dialogues carefully, and then complete the interactive tasks that follow.

Task 1

Sample dialogue

A portrait of Zhang Daqian

Ai Heng Lake by Zhang Daqian, splashed color on silk 1968

Zhang: Lisa, are you an admirer of Zhang Daqian? I heard you talk about him in class yesterday.

Lisa: Oh, yeah. In my eyes he himself is a legend of Chinese art. Look at this webpage! This is one of his masterpieces of landscape!

Zhang: In landscape he was a great inheritor of artists of as early as Tang and Song dynasties.

Lisa: What a grandeur the mountain carries!

Zhang: I also worship him for his strong and sharp brushwork. But magnificence was never his limit. He mastered various styles of Chinese painting.

Lisa: I can't agree more. As I know, he was also an expert in calligraphy, seal-carving(篆刻), poetry, and even drama and music. His art is so deeply rooted in Chinese cultural traditions.

Zhang: But he was never a conservative giant. His genius matches his open-mindedness. He never stopped learning and creating. Study his unique splashed color(泼彩) style of this landscape. You can even find Euro-American Impressionism(欧美印象主义) and Abstract Expressionism(抽象表现主义) here.

Lisa: Right. He traveled a lot and made friends all over the world. Even Picasso was impressed by his excellent art ...

Zhang: And his personality. That's where he impresses me most. Modesty, as well as creation was always part of his life and work.

Interactive task

A Portrait of Qi Baishi

A Painting of Shrimps by Qi Baishi

Two art students are talking about Qi Baishi's art. Qi's painting style is both traditional and innovative. He painted natural subjects just like many other Chinese artists, from animals to landscapes, yet in a way nobody else had achieved before. He once said, "The excellence of a painting lies in its being alike, yet unlike. Too much likeness flatters the vulgar taste; too much unlikeness deceives the world."

Role A: I think Qi Baishi is great, because his works fully represent Chinese painting tradition.

Role B: I like him, too. But I'm more interested in the freshness he brought to such familiar genres as birds, flowers as well as landscapes.

Task 2

Sample Dialogue

Portrait of Fu Baoshi studying in Japan

Lady of Xiang River by Fu Baoshi, 1954

Wang: Jennifer, we visited Fu Baoshi Memorial near our school. How do you like him?

Jennifer: Very much. I was completely fascinated with the poetic elegance in his painting. Look at this painting by him. The figures here are so vividly illustrated with sentiment. Do you like him, too?

Wang: Sure. I like his landscape more. In his works, you can find both delicacy and splendor. He was a keen observer as well as a skillful painter.

Jennifer: I agree. He drew inspiration from nature. His landscape painting reveals his strong passion and profound thinking.

Wang: Yeah. He kept traveling and learning widely all his life, and

A Portrait of Li Taibai by Fu Baoshi, 1963

he combined traditional methods with Western techniques and concepts.

Jennifer: That's true. But I think in his works you always find his personality typical of a Chinese literati painter. Both his natural objects and human figures signify the ideal and pursuit for a better life and world.

Wang: Absolutely. He integrates poetic imagery together with his unique painting techniques.

Jennifer: You got the key to his art. As I learned recently, he was such a learned scholar himself.

Wang: He was an excellent art historian. He wrote piles of books on art history. This is his *On the Evolution of Chinese Paintings*. It is a very good book for understanding Chinese art. Take a look at it.

Jennifer: Oh, thank you!

Wang: My pleasure. Let's talk more about him later.

Interactive task

A Portrait of Xu Beihong

A Galloping Horse by Xu Beihong, 1941

A and B are talking about Xu Beihong's painting style. A is a Chinese teacher of art. B is a foreign student studying Chinese painting in China. Xu Beihong was born in a family with very profound tradition of Chinese culture. His father was a famous scholar good at calligraphy, painting, and poetry and prose writing. And in early

Tian Heng and His Five Hundred Warriors by Xu Beihong, oil painting, 1930

years Xu used to travel and study art in many Western countries. He enriched Chinese painting with the notions and techniques he acquired about Western art, therefore, developed his own unique style of art.

Role A: Hi! I heard you have chosen Xu Beihong as the subject for your thesis study. I am his fan, too.

Role B: Oh! That's great. Xu Beihong has been my idol for so long. I already knew him even before I came to China. He understood Western art well, and he was a giant master of Chinese painting.

Group Work

19 **Work in groups to analyze the art of Chinese landscape painting.**

1. Form groups of 4 or 5 students.
2. Each group tries appreciating a Chinese landscape painting, ancient or modern. Identify the painter and the creation time. Discuss and analyze its style by using the checklist below.

Title, painter and creation time
Background of creation

	Brushwork
	Lines
	Ink wash
Style and features of art	Spaces
	Light and shade
	Objects of nature and human figures
	Inscriptions and seals
	Others
Possible themes	

3. After the discussion, a representative from each group makes a presentation to summarize their analysis on the painting's style.

Follow-up Tasks

Writing

段落长短

由于大学英语四、六级和研究生英语入学考试均有时间和字数的限制,因此段落的长短主要根据所论述内容的多少和字数要求而定。

一般来说,篇幅比例大致可作如下分配:

1. 短文开头段　应控制在 6 句话之内,以 4—5 句话为宜,约占全文篇幅的 15%—20%;

2. 短文主体段　应控制在 10 句话之内,以 6—8 句话为宜,约占全文篇幅的 60%—70%之间;

3. 结尾　应控制在 6 句话之内,以 4—5 句话为宜,占全文篇幅的 15%—20%。

段落的统一性

段落的统一性体现在整体一致、连贯和上下协调上。要达到统一性必须保持下面的四个统一:

1. 人称的统一　即当选定某个人称后,在段落的推展过程中要始终保持一致,不可随便中途更改;

2. 文体的统一　即应根据文章题材,采用某一种文体,或记叙文,或描写文,或论说文等,一经选定,则要始终保持统一;

3. 时态的统一　这一点在写作时应特别注意,不同的时态不能用于同一叙述中,

所以,掌握正确时态的运用是写好短文的重要方面;

    4. 主题的统一   段落中的每一个句子都要围绕着本段的主题展开。

Research Project

Work in groups of 4 or 5 students, and finish a research project based on the topic area of this unit. It involves lectures, seminars, team-based activities, individual activities, team presentation and a reflective summary.

Steps

1. Form a research group;
2. Decide on a research topic;
3. Work in groups to finish PPT slides;
4. Each member of the group gives oral presentation of his parts;
5. Hand in materials that include: Project Proposal (one for each team), Research Report (one for each team, 1 000 words), Summary (one for each person, 300 words), PPT (one for each team).

Research Methods

1. Field work: to generate the first-hand information
   - Questionnaires
   - Interviews (interpersonal, telephone, e-mail, door-to-door visit, etc.)
   - Observation
2. Desk work: to generate the second-hand information
   - Library: books and magazines
   - The Internet: Google the theme with the key words
   - Reading materials

Suggested Options

1. An investigation about art students' favorite master of traditional Chinese painting (*guohua*) in the 20th century.
2. What should be done by young Chinese artists to renovate traditional Chinese painting in today's world of globalization?

Tips for Options

1. For option 1, properly design a questionnaire for your survey. Clarify and mark the control group to collect your data. For example, your survey may

include such items as: freshmen of art school in XX university, male students, female students, Chinese art majors, or oil painting majors, etc.

2. For option 2, try to collect data by handing out a questionnaire or having interviews. Refer to concerned knowledge of statistics and try to maintain the validity and credibility of your investigation.

Unit Two   Western Sculpture

Highlight

Topic area	Structure	Skills
The concept of sculpture Auguste Rodin's *Burghers of Calais* The development of Greek sculpture	torn between ... and ... fit in well with as opposed to be entitled to subordinate ... to ...	Understanding sculpture Knowing the history and meanings of some best-known sculptures in the world Describing and discussing statues

Warm-up Tasks

1 **Listen to the following passage and try to fill in the missing words and expressions.**

Sculpture is (1) _____ artwork created by shaping or combining hard materials into required forms.

Sculptors often build small preliminary works called maquettes (雕塑设计模型) with materials such as plaster, wax, or clay. Then they have generally sought to produce works of art that are as (2) _____ as possible, working in durable and frequently expensive materials such as (3) _____ and marble. More rarely, (4) _____ materials such as gold, silver, and ivory are also used. More common and less expensive materials were used for sculpture for wider consumption, including glass, hardwoods and ceramics.

Sculptures are often painted, but commonly lose their paint to time. Many different painting techniques have been used in making sculpture, including (5) _____, gilding, and house paint.

Many sculptors seek new ways and materials to make art. Jim Gary used (6) _____ glass and automobile parts, tools, machine parts, and hardware. One of Pablo Picasso's most famous sculptures included (7) _____ parts. Alexander Calder and other modernists made spectacular use of (8) _____ steel. Since the 1960s, (9) _____ have been used as well. Some sculptures, such as ice sculpture, (10) _____ sculpture, and gas sculpture, are deliberately short-lived.

2 **Discuss the following questions about Western sculpture with your partner.**

1. The following pictures show some best-known sculptures in the world. Can you tell their names?

2. What else, such as the materials, the time of creation and the names of the sculptors, do you know about these sculptures?

3. Why did the sculptors choose to depict naked human bodies in their sculptures?

Listening Tasks

Micro Listening Skills

3 You will hear seven sentences. Each sentence contains one of the two words given to you. Listen carefully and choose the word you hear in each sentence.

1. A. rare   B. real
2. A. stir   B. spur
3. A. single   B. symbol
4. A. defined   B. designed
5. A. steel   B. still
6. A. instructed   B. constructed
7. A. erect   B. direct

Dialogue

A Chance to See Great Works

The Thinker by Auguste Rodin, 1902

Words & Phrases

showcase /ˈʃəuˌkeɪs/ vt.	陈列；展示
masterpiece /ˈmɑːstəpiːs/ n.	杰作
Auguste Rodin /ɔːˈɡʌst ˈrɒdən/	奥古斯特·罗丹
bronze /brɒnz/ n.	青铜
marble /ˈmɑːbl/ n.	大理石
Michelangelo /ˈmɪtʃɪlændʒɪˌləu/	米开朗基罗
the Renaissance /rɪˈneɪsns/	文艺复兴
replica /ˈreplɪkə/ n.	复制品

4 **Listen to the dialogue and choose the best answer to the following questions.**

(　　) 1. Why does the man tell the woman not to miss the exhibition?

      A. It's a rare chance to see great sculptures.

      B. Auguste Rodin himself will come.

      C. The exhibition will create quite a stir.

      D. The man has two tickets.

(　　) 2. Which of the following is true of *The Thinker*?

      A. It is made of bronze only.

      B. It is the symbol of philosophy.

      C. It depicts a man in great pain.

      D. It was made after Rodin himself.

(　　) 3. Which of the following is NOT true about *The Statue of David*?

      A. It was created by Michelangelo.

      B. It is Italy's national treasure.

      C. It's the first time that *The Statue of David* is exhibited abroad.

      D. The one to be on display is a replica.

(　　) 4. The following sculptures will be on display EXCEPT _____.

      A. *The Thinker*, *The Kiss*

      B. *Age of Bronze*, *The Statue of David*

      C. *The Kiss*, *Age of Bronze*

      D. *Venus de Milo*, *The Gates of Hell*

5 **Listen to the dialogue again and complete the following sentences with the information you have heard.**

1. The works of Western sculpture will be on display at _____.

2. Over _____ sculptures will be showcased in the Sculpture Hall.

3. *The Thinker* depicts a man in _____ while having a powerful

struggle _____.

4. *The Statue of David* was created during _____.

Passage

The Statue of Liberty

Words & Phrases

immigrant /ˈɪmɪgrənt/ *n.*	移民
colossus /kəˈlɒsəs/ *n.*	巨型雕像
spike /spaɪk/ *n.*	尖刺
Declaration of Independence	《独立宣言》
enlightenment /ɪnˈlaɪtnmənt/ *n.*	启蒙
framework /ˈfreɪmwək/ *n.*	构架
pedestal /ˈpedɪstl/ *n.*	底座

6 **Listen to the passage and decide whether the following statements are true (T) or false (F).**

_____ 1. *The Statue of Liberty* was the first thing that many immigrants saw of the USA.

_____ 2. The statue's face was modeled after the sculptor's mother.

_____ 3. The seven spikes on the crown symbolize the seven continents.

_____ 4. Gustave Eiffel was more famous for making the statue's steel framework than building the Eiffel Tower in Paris.

_____ 5. You can take the staircase inside the statue and walk up to the torch.

7 **Listen to the passage again and answer the following questions with the help of words and phrases provided below.**

1. Why did the French government give *The Statue of Liberty* to the USA?
   (*gift, birthday*)

   _____

2. How was the statue constructed?
   (*copper plates, steel framework*)

   _____

3. Why did the sculptor Bartholdi travel to the United States even before the arrival of the statue?
   (*location, President Grant*)

   _____

Reading Tasks

Text A   *Reading in Detail*

Pre-reading Questions

1. Do you want to become a hero?
2. Would you sacrifice your life for others in time of crisis?
3. What do you think a hero should behave before death?

A Monument to Civic Heroism[①]

The Burghers of Calais is one of Auguste Rodin's best-known sculptures. It was commissioned by the Municipal Council of Calais in 1884 and inaugurated a little more than a decade later. It is made of bronze and weighs about two tons. Each of the six burghers is slightly larger than life and about two meters tall. They all stand on the ground, which is cast as 20 to 30 centimeters high. The main figure in the group is Eustache de Saint-Pierre, an old man who was also the richest citizen in Calais.

The sculpture depicts an event that took place in 1347 and was part of the

5

_____

① This text is adapted from "Auguste Rodin's *The Burghers of Calais*" by Richard Swedberg in *Theory, Culture and Society* (SAGE), Vol. 22(2):45 – 67.

The Burghers of Calais by Auguste Rodin

Hundred Years' War① between England and France. King Edward Ⅲ had besieged the French town of Calais for nearly a year, and by early August its starved citizens

10　could no longer hold out. Edward Ⅲ then told the people of Calais that they would all be killed, unless six of its citizens presented themselves to him, dressed only in plain garments, with a rope around their necks, and with the keys to the city in their hands. Rodin's sculpture depicts the six citizens at the moment when they were about to leave Calais for the king's camp. Torn between their desire to stay alive and their

15　desire to save the lives of the other people in Calais, they slowly set out on their difficult journey.

　　Despite its ominous beginnings, the story ended well. Edward Ⅲ wanted them to be executed, but his pregnant wife persuaded him to spare them, believing that their deaths would be a bad omen for her unborn child. As a result of her efforts, the lives

20　of the burghers were saved.

Some forces for the creation of *The Burghers of Calais*

　　While Rodin's vision was no doubt the most important factor in the creation of *The Burghers of Calais*, one can say that two other forces were important as well: the Third Republic and the Municipal Council of Calais.

25　　　The Third Republic② made a huge effort to break with the royalist past of France and move the country in the direction of a modern nation for common people. Much of this desire for a decisive break with the past had to do with the humiliating defeat that

---

　　① The Hundred Years' War (1337—1453): a war started by a struggle for the French throne between England and France. It ended with England losing most of the land in France.

　　② The Third Republic(1870—1940): the republican government of France between the end of the Second French Empire in 1870 and the Vichy Regime after the invasion of France by the German Third Reich in 1940.

France had suffered in the war against Prussia in 1870[①]. The Prussian army had easily beaten the French army and then besieged Paris and brought it to its knees.

It is clear that *The Burghers of Calais* fitted in very well with the general ambitions of the Third Republic to create a new past for the nation. Rodin's sculpture depicted a famous incident from the history of France and one that involved a group of citizens, as opposed to the king and the nobles. The burghers had also sacrificed themselves for society, the collective representation of all the citizens. A common interpretation of Rodin's *Burghers of Calais* was that it represented a celebration of heroism, not in victory but in defeat. Calais may have lost the war against Edward Ⅲ, just as France had lost the war against Prussia in 1870; but its citizens had behaved like true heroes and deserved to be remembered.

But even if the Third Republic in several ways influenced the creation, it was the Municipal Council of Calais that paid for the statue. On 26 September 1884, the Municipal Council of Calais made a decision to commission a statue of Eustache de Saint-Pierre by a unanimous vote. That the decision was made at this particular point of time had much to do with its efforts to maintain its identity as a city. In the early 1880s it had been decided to merge Calais with the neighboring city of Saint Pierre, in order to create a new city in the Third Republic. The decision to commission a statue of Eustache was a way of affirming the identity and medieval past of Calais.

The Universal Appeal of *The Burghers of Calais*

Rodin, however, included six burghers in his sculpture. All of the burghers, as we know, were willing to give their lives for their city. But each of them reacted in a different way at the moment of departure. Some steeled themselves and held their bodies erect, while others were deep in despair, struggling with their fate, as evidenced by clasped hands and lowered heads. Rodin depicted the leader of the group, Eustache de Saint-Pierre, as its oldest member, and it is clear that Eustache was firmly determined to start the march to the king's camp. Some of the younger members, in contrast, kept in the background and were tormented by the idea of leaving their lives and their beloved.

And here we may finally have found a key to the universal appeal of Rodin's statue. The notion of sacrificing yourself for your own community is something that many people have as an ideal, but also something that they know would be very difficult to live up to in reality. Rodin's statue allows us to move from a state of certainty to a questioning of the soul.

---

①　Franco-Prussian War (19 July 1870—10 May 1871): a conflict between the Second French Empire and the Kingdom of Prussia. The complete Prussian victory brought about the final unification of Germany.

We may also note that Rodin in his sculpture rejected the image of the old-fashioned hero—one who faces death without batting an eyelid—and replaced him with six ordinary individuals who were all committed to sacrificing their lives, but

65 who were also human enough to fear and tremble before death. Old-fashioned heroism had given way to civic heroism.

The Burghers of Calais, in sum, appeals in a very powerful way to modern people. It does this because it conveys a hopeful message that heroes are ordinary people and that ordinary people under certain circumstances can become heroes. They

70 are like you or me—common people who stand directly on the ground, surrounded by other like-minded individuals, who all move forward together.

(979 words)

New Words and Expressions

burgher△/ˈbɜːgə/ *n.* ［old use］citizen ［旧用法］公民；市民

commission /kəˈmɪʃən/ *vt.* officially ask sb. to do sth., especially to produce a work of art 委托（某人做某事，尤指制作一件艺术品）

municipal★/mjuːˈnɪsɪpl/ *adj.* of a town with its own local government 市政的

council /ˈkaʊnsəl/ *n.* a group of people appointed to make laws or decisions 委员会

inaugurate★/ɪˈnɔːgjʊreɪt/ *vt.* open（a new building, etc.）with a special ceremony 为（新建筑）举行落成典礼

cast /kɑːst/ *vt.* make an object by pouring metal into a model 铸造

besiege▲/bɪˈsiːdʒ/ *vt.* surround a place with armed forces 包围

hold out maintain resistance 抵抗

ominous△/ˈɒmɪnəs/ *adj.* being a sign of sth. bad 不祥的

execute /ˈeksɪkjuːt/ *vt.* kill someone as a lawful punishment 处决

pregnant /ˈpregnənt/ *adj.* developing a baby in a female body 怀孕

omen△/ˈəʊmən/ *n.* a sign that sth. is going to happen in the future 预兆；征兆

humiliate▲/hjuːˈmɪlieɪt/ *vt.* make sb. feel ashamed and lose other people's respect 羞辱

sacrifice /ˈsækrɪfaɪs/ *vt.* give up sth. important or useful for a particular purpose 牺牲

deserve /dɪˈzɜːv/ *vt.* be worthy of a particular thing 应受；值得

unanimous★/juːˈnænɪməs/ *adj.* agreed by everyone 一致同意的

merge★/mɜːdʒ/ *vt.* become one 合并

affirm★/əˈfɜːm/ *vt.* declare positively 肯定；断言

appeal /əˈpiːl/ *n.* the power to make you feel attracted and/or interested 感染

力；吸引力

steel /stiːl/ *vt.*   harden 使坚硬

steel oneself△   get ready for sth. difficult 硬起心肠

evidence /ˈevɪdəns/ *vt.*   ［rare］prove by evidence ［罕］用证据证明

clasp★ /klɑːsp/ *vt.*   hold firmly 紧握

torment▲ /tɔːˈment/ *vt.*   make someone suffer pain or annoyance 折磨；使痛苦

ideal /aɪˈdɪəl/ *n.*   a belief in high or perfect standards 理想

live up to   reach someone's high standards 达到⋯⋯的高标准

not bat an eyelid△   show no surprise or fear 面不改色；泰然处之

be committed to△   be dedicated to 献身于，致力于(后接名词)

give way to   give place to 让位于；给⋯⋯让路

convey /kənˈveɪ/ *vt.*   communicate (a message, information, etc) 表达；传递

Proper Names

Calais /ˈkæleɪ/	加来(法国北部港口城市)
The Burghers of Calais	《加来义民》(罗丹作品)
Eustache de Saint-Pierre /ˈɜːstɑːʃ də ˈseɪn pɪeə/	厄斯塔什·德·圣皮埃尔(人名)
the Third Republic	(法兰西)第三共和国
Prussia /ˈprʌʃə/	普鲁士

Comprehension

8 **Choose the best answer to each question with the information from the text.**

(　　) 1. The six burghers set out to the king's camp in order to _____.

    A. surrender to King Edward Ⅲ

    B. give King Edward Ⅲ the key to the city

    C. open negotiations with King Edward Ⅲ

    D. save the lives of other people in Calais

(　　) 2. The king's wife persuaded the king not to kill the six burghers because she believed _____.

    A. their death would stir up a rebellion in Calais

    B. their death would be a bad omen for her unborn baby

    C. they were good people

    D. it was morally wrong to kill innocent people

(　　) 3. Rodin's *The Burghers of Calais* fit in well with the Third Republic's ambitions for all the following reasons EXCEPT that _____.

    A. It depicted a historical event

    B. It was an incident that involved common people

C. It created a new history for France

D. the burghers were committed to sacrificing their lives for the society

( ) 4. The Municipal Council of Calais made a decision to build a statue of Eustache because _____.

A. they worshiped ancient heroes

B. they wanted to maintain the identity of Calais as a city

C. they could afford it

D. they wanted to educate people with heroism

( ) 5. By putting the six burghers directly on the ground, Rodin intended to tell us _____.

A. heroes are merely ordinary people like you or me

B. heroes are easy to approach

C. heroes are as tall as common people

D. it's easy to be a hero

9 Complete the following summary with right words and expressions.

The Burghers of Calais is one of Auguste Rodin's best-known sculptures. It depicts an event that took place in _____. King Edward Ⅲ of England had _____ the French town of Calais for nearly a year, and its starved citizens could no longer _____. Edward Ⅲ then told the people of Calais that they would all _____, unless six of its citizens presented themselves to him. Rodin's sculpture depicts the six citizens at the moment when they were about to leave Calais for the king's camp.

While Rodin's _____ was no doubt the most important factor in the creation of *The Burghers of Calais*, one can say that two other forces were important as well: the _____ and the _____ of Calais.

We may also note that Rodin in his sculpture rejects the image of the _____ hero and replaces him with six _____ individuals. Old-fashioned heroism had given way to civic heroism.

The Burghers of Calais, in sum, appeals in a very powerful way to modern people. It does this because it conveys a hopeful message that _____ are ordinary people and that ordinary people under certain circumstances can become heroes.

10 Discuss the following questions with the information from the text.

1. What made the Third Republic decide to break with the royalist past of France?

(*defeat, Prussia*)

2. What was the common interpretation of Rodin's *Burghers of Calais*?
   (*heroism*, *defeat*)

   _____

3. How did these burghers react at the moment of departure?
   (*erect*, *despair*, *background*)

   _____

4. Would you stand out and join the burghers if you were then a citizen of Calais?
   Why or why not?

   _____

5. How would you treat the six burghers if you were King Edward Ⅲ?

   _____

Vocabulary & Structure

11 Fill in the blanks with the words given below. Change the form where necessary.

commission	inaugurate	affirm	besiege	execute
humiliate	sacrifice	unanimous	merge	convey

1. The _____ soldiers were resolved to fight to the last drop of blood.
2. We _____ that in its drive for modernization, China must adhere to the principle of self-reliance.
3. They paid me empty compliments which only _____ me.
4. Officers and men at the front were shedding their blood and _____ their lives.
5. The city library was _____ by the mayor last Monday.
6. Please allow me to _____ my best wishes and kindest regards to your family.
7. The traitor was sentenced to death and _____ immediately.
8. My friends finally _____ into the crowd and I lost sight of them.
9. The artist was _____ to paint a portrait of the late president.
10. Our products have obtained _____ approval.

12 Complete the following sentences with phrases or expressions from the text.

1. Our men must _____ for further attack.
2. How long can we _____ against these attacks?
3. The little girl's tears _____ laughter when she saw the clowns.
4. My parents make me feel that I've got to _____ their expectations.

13 **Translate the Chinese sentences into English by simulating the sentences chosen from the text.**

Chosen Sentences	Simulated Translation	Chinese Sentences
Torn between their desire to stay alive *and* their desire to save the lives of other people in Calais, they slowly set out on their difficult journey.		她在爱恨之间徘徊,夜不能寐。(fall asleep)
The Prussian army had easily beaten the French army and then besieged Paris and *brought it to its knees*.		他意志坚强,什么也不能使他屈服。(strong-minded)
It is clear that The Burghers of Calais *fitted in very well with* the general ambitions of the Third Republic to create a new past for the nation.		北京的新老建筑和谐衬托,相得益彰,令人惊叹。(architecture)
In the early 1880s it had been decided to *merge* Calais *with* the neighboring city of Saint Pierre.		为提高竞争力,他的公司和时代华纳合并。(competitiveness)
The old-fashioned hero is one who faces death *without batting an eyelid*.		罪犯表情木然地听着对他的宣判。(sentence)

14 **Rewrite each sentence with the word or phrase in brackets, keeping the same meaning. The first part has been done for you.**

1. If you don't repeat foreign words constantly, you will easily forget them.

   Foreign words are easily forgotten _____. (unless)

2. The criminal tried very hard to escape by digging a 50-meter tunnel.

   By digging a 50-meter tunnel, the criminal _____. (make an effort to)

3. What this novel portrays are not people who make decisions but those ordinary people.

   The novel depicts ordinary people in society, _____. (as opposed to)

4. You've got this stomachache largely because you ate the polluted food yesterday.

   Your stomachache _____. (have much to do with)

5. I could judge from her eyes that she didn't like me.

She didn't like me, _____. (as)

Text B   Skimming and Scanning

Greek Culture and Greek Sculpture[①]

About three thousand years ago there appeared on the shores and islands of the Aegean Sea a remarkably handsome and intelligent race. This race did not suffer itself to be mastered by a great religious conception like the Egyptians, nor by a vast social organization like the Persians. (1) In the place of a theocracy or a monarchy, the men of that race had an invention of their own, called the city, which, while sending forth branches, gave birth to others of the same description.

What was the life of this city like? In the city, a citizen performed little manual labor; he was generally supported by his subjects, and always served by slaves. The poorest citizen had one slave in his house. The citizen had few wants, and he passed the day in the open air.

How did he occupy himself? Serving neither king nor priest, he was free in the city. His occupation consisted largely of public business and war. In those days human life was not protected as it is in ours. Most of those cities were surrounded by barbarians and other hostile cities eager to prey upon them; the citizens were obliged to be under arms constantly; if not, enemies would soon have pitched their camps amid the ruins of battered walls and devastated temples. The results of war were cruel: a conquered city often ended in ruins; a wealthy noted man might one day see his house in ashes, his property pillaged, and his wife and daughters sold to brothels, while his sons and himself would be sold as slaves. With such perils before him it is natural for a man to be interested in affairs of state, and be qualified for battle.

In order to qualify themselves for these purposes, they developed a peculiar system of discipline. In those days, war was a combat between man and man. To ensure victory, the soldier must have the most resistant, strongest, and most agile body possible. To this end, Sparta, about the eighth century, set Greece an example with an efficient military system. Sparta itself was a camp without walls, situated amidst enemies and conquered people. So it was wholly military. Young men were enrolled, exercised, and accustomed to living together; they were divided into two

5

10

15

20

25

---

① This text is taken and adapted from *The Philosophy of Art* written by H. Taine (London: Bailliere, 1865).

rival bands, and fighting with the foot or the fist. They slept in the open air, bathed in the cool water, ate sparingly and badly, drank nothing but water, and endured bad weather. In other cities the discipline was undoubtedly less severe; nevertheless, despite its modifications, the same road conducted to the same end. Young people passed the greater part of the day in the gymnasia, wrestling, jumping, boxing, racing, pitching the discus, and fortifying their naked muscles. It was their aim to produce the most beautiful and the most capable bodies.

Discobolos by Myron

These peculiar customs of the Greeks gave birth to peculiar ideas. (2) In their eyes the ideal man was not the man of thought, but the naked man, the man of a fine stock, erect, well-proportioned, and accomplished in all physical exercises. On this account they were not afraid to expose it on solemn occasions. After the Battle of Salamis the tragic poet Sophocles, then fifteen years old, and known for his beauty, stripped himself in order to dance and chant before the trophy. One hundred years later Alexander, on passing through Asia Minor to contend with Darius Ⅲ, cast aside his garments and raced with his companions, for the purpose of honoring the tomb of Achilles. But the Greeks went still further; they considered the perfection of the human form as attesting divinity. In *Homer*, which is the Grecian Bible, the gods throughout possess human forms, flesh, red blood, instincts, passions, and pleasures, similar in every respect to our own, and to such an extent that heroes become the lovers of goddesses, and gods have children with mortal women. Between Olympus and the earth there is no yawning gulf; the gods descend and mortals ascend. If they surpass us it is because they are exempt from death, and they are stronger, handsomer, and happier than we are.

Out of this conception sculpture was born. We can distinguish every step of its progress. On the one hand, an athlete, once crowned in Olympics, was entitled to a statue; On the other hand, since the gods were only human forms, more serene and more perfect than others, it was natural to represent them by statues. The marble or bronze statue does not lend to the god muscles and bones which he does not possess, but represents the actual form of the god. A statue was good enough to be a truthful portrait of the god if it was the most beautiful.

The statue was now blocked out. But were the sculptors qualified to produce it?

Men in those days saw the naked body in the baths, in the gymnasia, in the sacred   65
dances and at the public games. They could distinguish and select the forms and
attitudes that denoted strength, health, and vigor; they tried their best to give the
statue such forms and place it in such attitudes. For three or four hundred years they
were thus correcting, purifying, and developing their ideas of physical beauty. It is
not surprising therefore that they finally discovered the ideal type of the human form.   70
When Nicholas of Pisa and other early modern sculptors at the end of the Gothic
period abandoned the meager, bony, and ugly forms, it was because they obtained
better ones from the Greek statues then in existence or excavated. (3) Today, if we,
forgetting our distorted or deformed bodies, wish to obtain accurate notions of a
perfect form, we are obliged to go to Greek statues, the monuments of a noble,   75
careless, gymnastic existence, for them.

Laocoon and His Sons

Not only is the form of the
statue perfect, but again, which is
unique, it embodies the artist's
conceptions. Unlike the moderns   80
who subordinate the body to the
head, the Greeks assigned to the
body a dignity of its own. They were
interested in a breast attesting sound
respiration, a trunk solidly resting   85
on the thighs, and a nervous supple
leg driving the body forward with
ease; they did not occupy themselves
solely with the breadth of a
thoughtful forehead, with the frown   90
of an irritated brow, or the turn of a
sarcastic lip. They could limit themselves to all conditions of perfect statuary, which
leaves the eye without an iris, and the face undisturbed by expression; which prefers
tranquility of characters to actions; which commonly employs a single tint, either of
marble or of bronze; which leaves the picturesque to painting; and which abandons   95
dramatic interest to literature. Sculpture, accordingly, became the central part of
Greek art; other forms were associated with it, or imitated it. When Rome, at a later
day, robbed the Greek world of its treasures, this vast city possessed a population of
statues almost equal to the number of its living inhabitants. Even at the present time,
after so many centuries of devastation, it is estimated that more than sixty thousand   100
statues have been excavated in Greece. (4) Never in history has the world seen such a

blooming period of sculpture, such a prodigious display of its flowers, so perfect, so enduring, so varied, and of such natural development.

(1 225 words)

New Words and Expressions

Persian△ /ˈpɜːʃn/ *n.* people living in Persia (now Iran) 波斯人

theocracy△ /θɪˈɒkrəsɪ/ *n.* the rule of a state by religious authority 神权统治

monarchy▲ /ˈmɒnəkɪ/ *n.* the rule of a state by a king or queen 君主统治

subject /ˈsʌbdʒɪkt/ *n.* a person under the authority or control of another 下人

barbarian△ /bɑːˈbeərɪən/ *n.* uncivilized or uncultured person 野蛮人

prey upon★ plunder 劫掠

brothel△ /ˈbrɒθl/ *n.* house at which prostitutes may be visited 妓院

peril▲ /ˈperəl/ *n.* serious danger 严重的危险

agile△ /ˈædʒaɪl/ *adj.* quick-moving 敏捷的

fortify▲ /ˈfɔːtɪfaɪ/ *vt.* strengthen sth. against attack 加强

stock /stɒk/ *n.* line of ancestry 血统；世系

strip /strɪp/ *vt.* undress 脱衣服

trophy▲ /ˈtrəʊfɪ/ *n.* sth. taken after much effort, especially in war or hunting 战利品

contend★ /kənˈtend/ *vi.* struggle 争斗

attest△ /əˈtest/ *vt.* be or give clear proof of 是……的证明

divinity△ /dɪˈvɪnɪtɪ/ *n.* the quality or state of being a god 神性

mortal★ /ˈmɔːtl/ *adj.* unable to live forever 终有一死的；凡人的

surpass★ /səˈpɑːs/ *vt.* do better than 超过；胜过

exempt★ /ɪgˈzempt/ *adj.* officially freed from a duty, service, or payment 被免除的

be entitled to be given the right to have sth. 有权享有

serene▲ /sɪˈriːn/ *adj.* completely calm and peaceful 宁静的；平静的

attitude /ˈætɪtjuːd/ *n.* the position in which someone is standing or sitting 姿态

purify★ /ˈpjʊərɪfaɪ/ *vt.* make sth. pure 净化

meager /ˈmiːgə/ *adj.* lacking in flesh 皮包骨的

subordinate★ /səˈbɔːdɪneɪt/ *vt.* put in a position of less importance 使……居于次要地位

supple△ /ˈsʌpl/ *adj.* bending or moving easily 伸屈自如的；灵活的

tint△ /tɪnt/ *n.* a pale or delicate shade of a color 浅色

inhabitant /ɪnˈhæbɪtənt/ *n.* a person who lives in a particular place 居民

Proper Names

the Aegean /iːˈdʒiːn/ Sea	爱琴海
Sparta /ˈspɑːtə/	斯巴达
the Battle of Salamis /ˈsæləmɪs/	萨拉米斯战役
Sophocles /ˈsɒfəkliːz/	索福克勒斯（人名）
Alexander /ˌælɪɡˈzɑːndə/	亚历山大（人名）
Asia Minor	小亚细亚
Darius Ⅲ	大流士三世
Achilles /ɑːˈkɪləs/	阿喀琉斯（人名）
Homer /ˈhəʊmə/	《荷马史诗》
Nicholas /nɪˈkəʊləs/	尼古拉斯（人名）
the Gothic period	哥特艺术时代

Comprehension

15 Go over the text quickly and answer the following questions. For questions 1—7, choose the best answer from the four choices; for questions 8—10, complete the sentences with the information from the text.

(　　) 1. A citizen in a Greek city performed little manual labor because _____.

    A. he occupied himself with public business and war

    B. he was not taught how to do it

    C. he was supported by his subjects and served by slaves

    D. he was supported by the government

(　　) 2. Why were the citizens under arms constantly?

    A. Because a failure in the war had cruel results.

    B. Because war was something very dangerous.

    C. Because they liked wars.

    D. Because they had nothing else to do.

(　　) 3. Sparta set Greece an example with _____.

    A. a perfect physical training system

    B. an advanced political system

    C. a peculiar system of discipline

    D. an efficient military system

(　　) 4. What was the ideal man in the eyes of the Greeks?

    A. The intelligent man.

    B. The noble-minded man.

    C. The naked man.

　　　　D. The wealthy man.

(　) 5. Alexander, on passing through Asia Minor, cast aside his garments and raced with his companions, for the purpose of _____.

　　　　A. showing how beautiful his body was

　　　　B. showing his respect for an ancient hero

　　　　C. showing how fast he could run

　　　　D. showing his strength to his enemies

(　) 6. *Homer* was used as an example to show _____.

　　　　A. Greeks made a divinity of the perfect human form

　　　　B. Greeks had no respect for gods

　　　　C. Greeks were familiar with gods

　　　　D. Greeks and gods looked alike

(　) 7. Greek statues were largely made to depict _____.

　　　　A. heroes and kings

　　　　B. ordinary citizens

　　　　C. wealthy men

　　　　D. Olympic winners and gods

　　8. For three or four hundred years Greek sculptors had been developing their ideas of physical beauty. Therefore, they finally discovered _____ _____.

　　9. Not only is the form of the statue perfect, but it embodies _____ _____.

　　10. Rome later robbed the Greek world of its treasures and found that the city possessed a population of statues almost equal to _____.

Vocabulary & Translation

16 **Fill in the blanks with the words given below. Change the form where necessary.**

prey	fortify	strip	contend	mortal
surpass	exempt	entitle	purify	subordinate

1. If we do not progress, we shall be _____ by many young people before long.

2. You should have declared that. Perfume is not _____ from import duty.

3. All the minority nationalities are _____ to appropriate representation.

4. The interests of the individual must _____ to those of the community.

5. After _____ himself with a bit wine, the farmer told his wife about the

ghost.

6. The water was _____ as soon as it was pumped up from the well.

7. Many people had their _____ remains buried in the churchyard after they died.

8. The oppressed peoples will never allow themselves to be _____ upon by any invaders.

9. Our football team is _____ with one from the next town for the championship.

10. It was so hot that the farmers _____ to the waist.

17 Translate the underlined sentences in the text into Chinese.

1. In the place of a theocracy or a monarchy, the men of that race had an invention of their own, called the city, which, while sending forth branches, gave birth to others of the same description.

   _____

   _____

   _____

2. In their eyes the ideal man was not the man of thought, but the naked man, the man of a fine stock, erect, well-proportioned, and accomplished in all physical exercises.

   _____

   _____

   _____

3. Today, if we, forgetting our distorted or deformed bodies, wish to obtain accurate notions of a perfect form, we are obliged to go to Greek statues, the monuments of a noble, careless, gymnastic existence, for them.

   _____

   _____

   _____

4. Never in history has the world seen such a blooming period of sculpture, such a prodigious display of its flowers, so perfect, so enduring, so varied, and of such natural development.

   _____

   _____

   _____

Interactive Tasks

Pair Work

18 Read the sample dialogues carefully, and then complete the interactive tasks that follow.

Task 1

Sample dialogue

Susan: We'll see the Acropolis in Athens soon!

Gerry: Yes. It's a very beautiful place.

Susan: Can you tell me something about the Acropolis in Athens?

Gerry: Sure. Acropolis means "highest city" in Greek. The one in Athens is the best known acropolis in the world.

Susan: How did it get started?

Gerry: For purposes of defense, early people naturally chose high ground, a hill in most cases, to build a new settlement. That's how it got started.

Susan: I've heard that carvings in Parthenon Temple are very successful.

Gerry: Yes. It was directed by a famous carver Phidias. Since the temple was dedicated to the Wisdom Goddess Athena, her statue was housed there. The decorative stonework was originally highly colored.

Susan: My wish to see Wisdom Goddess Temple becomes stronger and stronger.

Gerry: Don't worry! We'll get there right now.

Interactive task

Two young people are on the way to the Louvre Museum. Role A expects Role B to tell him/her more about the sculptures in the museum.

Role A: I'm very interested in the museum but know very little about it.

Role B: The Louvre Museum, housed in the Louvre Palace which began as a fortress built in the late 12th century under Philip Ⅱ, has a large collection of world-famous sculptures. Among them the best-known are *Venus de Milo*（米洛的维纳斯）, *Nike of Samothrace*（胜利女神）, *Rebellious Slave*（被缚的奴隶）, etc.

Task 2

Sample dialogue

Harry: Look. There's a cool new sculpture in the park.

Lisa: Where is it?

Harry: It's right ahead. Can't you see it?

Lisa: You mean the big mass of bronze?

Harry: Yeah. It's image of a naked woman. This is the head; these are legs.

Lisa: Let me see. Eh ... I can tell it's a woman. But it's quite out of shape; too fat, I'm afraid.

Harry: It's modernist sculpture, so a bit abstract. Such sculpture generally doesn't meet the public aesthetic standards.

Lisa: But what does it mean?

Harry: It's exaggerated image of a mother who is strong enough to bear and nurture the young. It shows us how great mothers are.

Lisa: Oh. I see. There's more to a sculpture than meets the eye.

Interactive task

Two young people are talking about a chair in the park that is shaped like a naked women getting down on her knees.

Role A: The chair is a cool sculpture of modernist trend, and it's hot.

Role B: Such a thing is foul, dirty and disgusting. It's an insult to women.

Group Work

19 Work in groups to depict a statue.

1. Form groups of 4 or 5 students.

2. Each group finds a statue. It can be classic or modern, outdoor or indoor. Give the name of the statue, find or draw a picture, and fill in the following chart:

What is the name?	What does it look like?	What does it mean?

3. A member of each group tells the class about the statue. Explain what it is like and what it means. Use the phrases below:

It is shaped like ...

It is formed by ...

It's made of ...

It gives the plain truth that ...

It conveys a message that ...

Follow-up Tasks

Writing

段落的种类

四、六级及考研英语作文通常由三个主要部分组成,通称三段式:开头部分(序论、引论或导论)、中间部分(正文或本论)、结尾部分(结论)。从结构上讲,开头部分称为引言段。中间部分称为正文或本论段,这部分可以根据需要写成一个或几个扩展段,但就考试而言,由于字数限制,用一个扩展段较好,少数的也有两个扩展段。结尾部分称为结论段。

古人常用"凤头猪肚豹尾"来形容写作,意思是开头要精彩亮丽,中间要充实丰富,结尾要响亮有力。

引言段

引言段用以揭示文章的主题,提出论点,引起读者注意和兴趣。好的引言段便于正文内容的展开。引言段不宜过长,应控制在 6 句话之内,以 4 至 5 句话为宜。过长易冲淡主题,达不到开宗明义、抓住读者注意力的效果。下面的引言段(1997 年 6 月六级作文题)就写得紧凑有力。

My View on Job-hopping

Job-hopping has been a hot topic in our modern society. Different people have different opinions towards job-hopping. Some people like to do one job in their whole life. They believe that whatever they do, they should stick to it, like it and be good at it. In their eyes, only by doing so can they be an expert in their fields and make more contribution to the society.

这段第一句"Job-hopping has been a hot topic in our modern society."便开门见山地表明文章的主题,接着说不同的人对 job-hopping 有不同的看法,有些人喜欢终身从事一种工作,因为他们认为不管做什么事,都要坚持不懈,做好做精才能对社会作出贡献。文字不多,但紧扣主题,把读者一步一步地引到对 job-hopping 的认识上。最后一句既总结了全段,又便于下面段落的进一步展开。

Research Project

Work in groups of 4 or 5 students, and finish a research project based on the topic area of this unit. It involves lectures, seminars, team-based activities, individual activities, team presentation and a reflective summary.

Steps

1. Form a research group;
2. Decide on a research topic;
3. Work in groups to finish PPT slides;
4. Each member of the group gives oral presentation of his parts;
5. Hand in materials that include: Project Proposal (one for each team), Research Report (one for each team, 1 000 words), Summary (one for each person, 300 words), PPT (one for each team).

Research Methods

1. Field work: to generate the first-hand information
   - Questionnaires
   - Interviews (interpersonal, telephone, e-mail, door-to-door visit, etc.)
   - Observation
2. Desk work: to generate the second-hand information
   - Library: books and magazines
   - The Internet: Google the theme with the key words
   - Reading materials

Suggested Options

1. A study of outdoor statues at home or abroad.
2. An introduction of a sculptor and his works.

Tips for Options

1. If you choose the first option, desk work is your major source of information. But you must also involve some first-hand information in your project. You can obtain such information with a camera.
2. For the second option, you may not necessarily choose very famous sculptors. Choose your own teacher or someone you know so that you can interview him or her very easily.

Unit Three   Modern Building

Highlight

Topic area	Structure	Skills
The concept of modern architecture Buckminster Fuller and the geodesic dome Adaptive reuse of historic buildings	spend ... doing have no alternative but ... pour in some ... with others taking as opposed to	Understanding modern architects' perceptions of buildings Describing and discussing some types of modern buildings Introducing an architect

Warm-up Tasks

1 **Listen to the following passage and try to fill in the missing words and expressions.**

Architecture is the art and science of designing buildings and other (1) _____ structures. Architecture is both the (2) _____ and product of planning, designing and constructing space that reflects (3) _____, social, and aesthetic considerations. It requires the manipulation and (4) _____ of material, technology, light, and shadow. Architecture also encompasses the pragmatic aspects of (5) _____ designed spaces, such as project planning, cost estimating and construction (6) _____. A wider definition may (7) _____ all design activity from the macro-level (urban design, landscape architecture) to the micro-level (construction details and furniture). In fact, architecture today may refer to the activity of designing any kind of (8) _____. Architectural works are often (9) _____ cultural and political symbols and as works of art. Historical (10) _____ are often identified with their surviving architectural achievements.

2 **Discuss the following questions about modern buildings with your partner.**

1. The following pictures show some great buildings in the world. Can you name them?
2. Which building do you like best? What is its style?
3. How are they different from traditional buildings?

Listening Tasks

Micro Listening Skills

3 **You will hear six sentences. Listen carefully and fill in the missing words.**

1. Tate Modern is a key _____ for London.

2. A visit to London isn't _____ without a trip to Tate Modern.

3. The interior of the old power plant was _____ into a great exhibition space.

4. Louis Kahn's architecture has several special _____.

5. The inside of the gallery shows Kahn's great _____.

6. Kahn also used geometric _____, including squares, circles and triangles.

Dialogue

Tate Modern

It is Lin's first visit to London. Her friend, Mary, who lives in London, invites her to visit the Tate Modern.

Words & Phrases

Tate Modern	泰特现代美术馆
landmark /ˈlændmɑːk/ n.	地标
transform /trænsˈfɔːm/ vt.	改变
the Pritzker Prize	普利兹克奖
exterior /eksˈtɪərɪə/ n.	外部；表面
interior /ɪnˈtɪərɪə/ n.	内部；里面
inspiration /ɪnspəˈreɪʃən/ n.	灵感
scale /skeɪl/ n.	规模
come alive	栩栩如生
spacious /ˈspeɪʃəs/ adj.	宽敞的
squeeze /skwiːz/ vi.	挤
elbow /ˈelbəʊ/ n.	肘部

clink /klɪŋk/ *vi.*	发出叮当声
airy /ˈeərɪ/ *adj.*	通风的

4 **Listen to the dialogue and answer the following questions.**

1. Where are the two speakers?

_____

2. When was Tate Modern completed?

_____

3. What is the Pritzker Prize?

_____

4. How does Mary feel about the museum?

_____

5. What makes Mary feel like dancing in the museum?

_____

5 **Listen to the dialogue again and complete the following sentences with the information you have heard.**

1. Tate Modern is Britain's _____ and located _____.
2. In Tate Modern, people can see _____ by artists such as Cézanne, Picasso and Dalí.
3. Mary thinks that it is not only a place for art, but also a place for people just _____. It's a great place to find _____ for the daily life.
4. Tate Modern has such a _____ that people can almost _____ in it.
5. Tate Modern is a _____. People don't pay to go in.

Passage

Louis Kahn

The National Assembly Building of Bangladesh

Words & Phrases

Louis Kahn /ˈluːɪs kɑːn/	路易斯·康(人名)
concrete /ˈkɒnkriːt/ n.	混凝土
geometric /dʒɪəˈmetrɪk/ adj.	几何的
apparent /əˈpærənt/ adj.	明显的
limestone /ˈlaɪmstəʊn/ n.	石灰岩
Bangladesh /bɑːŋɡləˈdeʃ/	孟加拉国
Dhaka /ˈdækə/	达卡(地名)
parliament /ˈpɑːləmənt/ n.	议会
solidity /səˈlɪdɪtɪ/ n.	坚固
heaviness /ˈhevɪnɪs/ n.	沉重
weightless /ˈweɪtlɪs/ adj	没有重量的
monumental /mɒnjəˈmentl/ n.	雄伟的

6 **Listen to the passage and choose the best answer to the following questions.**

(　　) 1. In his architecture, Kahn paid careful attention to the following aspects EXCEPT the _____.

      A. look and feel of the materials   B. use of sunlight

      C. indoor air quality   D. use of geometric shapes

(　　) 2. Kahn was heavily influenced by the _____.

      A. ancient Greek and Roman buildings

      B. classical Japanese buildings

      C. ancient Egyptian buildings

      D. Victorian buildings

(　　) 3. What materials did Kahn prefer to use in his works?

      A. Concrete, glass and metal.

      B. Wood, metal and concrete.

      C. Stone, brick and concrete.

      D. Glass, brick and wood.

(　　) 4. Which of the following public buildings is included in the project that Kahn designed in Dhaka?

      A. A church.   B. A gallery.

      C. A school.   D. A government center.

(　　) 5. Which of the following words can best describe the common feature of Kahn's buildings?

      A. Light.   B. Solid.

C. Elegant.   D. Complex.

7 **Listen to the passage again and decide whether the following statements are true (T) or false (F).**

        1. Many of Kahn's buildings use squares, circles and triangles.

        2. Kahn's later works were influenced by the industrial design of factory buildings.

        3. The surface of the Yale University Art Gallery is made of wood and stone.

        4. The materials Kahn used in his buildings distinguish him from the other famous architects of the period.

        5. The structures of Kahn's buildings usually look more modern than ancient.

Reading Tasks

Text A   Reading in Detail

Pre-reading Questions

1. What is your understanding of a nice building?
2. What do you know about Buckminster Fuller?
3. Have you ever seen or heard of a geodesic dome?

The Geodesic Dome—the House of the Future?[1]

Buckminster Fuller[2] was one of the most unusual thinkers of the twentieth century. During his long life, he discussed his idea about technology and human survival. He called his idea "dymaxion". He explained the word "dymaxion" as a method of doing more with less. Everything he did was guided by this idea. Although Buckminster Fuller invariably maintained that he was interested in almost everything, his life and work were dominated by a single issue: shelter and housing.

Fuller spent much of the early 20th century looking for ways to improve human shelter by applying modern technological know-how to shelter construction. His aim was to make shelter more comfortable, efficient, and more economically available to a greater number of people.

5

10

---

① This text is adapted from *Geodesic Domes* from www.bfi.org.

② Richard Buckminster Fuller (1895—1983): American inventor, futurist, architect, and author.

After acquiring some experience in the building industry and discovering the traditional practices and perceptions which severely limit changes and improvements in construction practices, Fuller carefully examined and improved interior structure equipment, including the toilet, the shower, and the bathroom as a whole. He studied
15 structure shells, and devised a number of alternatives each less expensive, lighter, and stronger than traditional wood, brick, and stone buildings.

In 1944, the United States suffered a serious housing shortage. Government officials knew that Fuller had developed a prototype family dwelling which could be produced rapidly, using the same equipment which had previously built war-time
20 airplanes. It could be installed anywhere, the way a telephone is installed, and with little additional difficulty. When one official flew to Wichita, Kansas to see this house built by Beech Aircraft and Fuller, the man reportedly gasped, "My God! This is the house of the future!"

Soon, unsolicited checks poured in from people who wanted to purchase this new
25 kind of house. However, Fuller was never able to get it into full production due to many obstacles at that time. He moved on to consider other innovations that could benefit humanity in the areas of structure and housing.

After the war, Fuller's efforts focused on the problem of how to build a shelter which is so lightweight that it can be delivered by air. Shelters should be mobile
30 which would require great breakthroughs in the weight-reduction of the materials. He began looking for the perfect shape and found it in nature. It is a fundamental principle of nature that a sphere is the smallest amount of material needed to enclose a given space. Certain carbon molecules, animal cells and soap bubbles are just a few examples of how nature takes advantage of the material efficiency of the sphere.

35 One of the ways Buckminster Fuller would use to describe the differences in strength between a rectangle and a triangle would be to apply pressure to both structures. The rectangle would fold up and be unstable but the triangle withstands the pressure and is much more rigid.
This principle together with his idea
40 of "doing more with less" directed his studies toward creating a new architectural design, the geodesic dome. Fuller discovered that if a spherical structure was created from
45 triangles, it would have unparalleled strength.

A geodesic dome is strong

enough to need no internal supports. The lack of internal support material combined with the maximized material efficiency of the building design add up to an approximately 30% reduction in materials compared to traditional box-style houses. 　50

Because of the minimized surface area-to-volume ratio, geodesic domes have a reduced exposure to the elements. Again, the spherical shape results in roughly 1/3 the surface area exposed to sun, wind and cold, minimizing the heating and cooling effect of weather on the internal temperature. Besides, the external shape of a geodesic dome allows wind to flow smoothly over the structure as opposed to blowing 　55 directly into a flat wall.

The spherical structure of a dome is one of the most efficient interior atmospheres for human dwellings because air and energy are allowed to circulate without obstruction. This enables heating and cooling to occur naturally. The efficient air circulation disperses cooled or heated air effectively and reduces energy consumption. 　60 The annual energy savings for a dome owner is 30% less than normal rectilinear homes according to the Oregon Dome Co. This is quite an improvement and helps save the environment from wasted energy. Domes have been designed by Fuller and others to withstand high winds and extreme temperatures as seen in the polar regions.

The structural integrity of geodesic domes helps to resist natural disasters. The 　65 natural wind resistance that makes geodesic domes energy efficient also allows them to resist hurricane and tornado damage, as severe winds are more likely to blow around the spherical structures than into them. Similarly, the balance between tension and compression of the geodesic dome structure is ideally suited to areas where earthquakes are a concern. Any stress placed on the dome is equally distributed 　70 among the network of triangles that makes up the building design, effectively dissipating the stress and preventing structural damage.

The minimal use of materials makes the domes lightweight, transportable and easily assembled. Many dome manufacturers offer various designs in geodesic dome housing with little assembly time required. Some houses can be assembled in less than 　75 a day with others taking up to six months. Many also come in dome kits that buyers can build themselves or with the help of friends.

Buckminster Fuller's first worldwide acceptance by the architectural community occurred with the 1954 Triennale where his cardboard dome was displayed for the first time and won the highest award. The Milan Triennale was established to stage 　80 international exhibitions which present the most innovative accomplishments in the fields of design, crafts, architecture and city planning. The theme for 1954 was *Life Between Artifact and Nature: Design and the Environmental Challenge* which fit in perfectly with Fuller's work.

85 Within a few years, Fuller's domes were showing up everywhere. The proliferation of the geodesic dome around the world moved it into its rightful position as a symbol of

90 developing humanity by doing more with fewer resources. Thus, geodesic domes are now employed for various tasks such as providing a more natural structure for children on

95 playgrounds, covering athletic stadiums, and being proposed for use

Disney's EPCOT Center

in future space construction. What's more, they are often the dominant symbols employed at major future-oriented expositions. When most people remember the 1967 Montreal World's Fair, the 1986 Vancouver World's Fair, or Disney's EPCOT

100 Center, the first image they recall is the geodesic dome.

  Buckminster Fuller dedicated his life to solving the problems of humanity, and the geodesic dome could be said to be his greatest achievement to that end. As a structure that is resource and energy efficient as well as structurally sound, the geodesic dome has potential to change the way the world looks at building design.

(1 118 words)

New Words and Expressions

geodesic△ /dʒiːəʊˈdesɪk/ *adj.* of the shortest possible line between two points on a sphere 测地线的

dome★ /dəʊm/ *n.* a rounded top on a building 圆屋顶；穹隆结构

invariably★ /ɪnˈveərɪəblɪ/ *adv.* always 总是

dominate /ˈdɒmɪneɪt/ *vt.* have the most important place(in) 在……中占首要地位；支配

know-how△ /nəʊˈhaʊ/ *n.* practical knowledge or skill 技术；实际知识

perception /pəˈsepʃn/ *n.* way of perceiving；view 观念；看法

devise /dɪˈvaɪz/ *vt.* plan or invent 计划；发明

alternative /ɔːlˈtɜːnətɪv/ *n.* possibility of choice between two or more things 抉择；可供选择的事物

prototype★ /ˈprəʊtətaɪp/ *n.* first form of anything 原型

dwelling★ /ˈdwelɪŋ/ *n.* house or flat 住所

reportedly△ /rɪˈpɔːtɪdlɪ/ *adv.* according to what is said 据报道；据说

gasp★ /gɑːsp/ *vi.* catch the breath suddenly and in a way that can be heard 喘气

unsolicited△ /ˈʌnsəˈlɪsɪtɪd/ *adj.* not looked for or requested 未被请求的

pour in give or send in a flow 大量地涌进

obstacle /ˈɒbstəkl/ *n.* sth. that stands in the way 障碍

innovation▲ /ɪnəʊˈveɪʃən/ *n.* act of innovating 创新

focus on center upon, concentrate on 致力于

breakthrough★ /ˈbreɪkˌθruː/ *n.* significant development or discovery 突破性进展；重要新发现

enclose /ɪnˈkləʊz/ *vt.* surround completely 围绕；围住

strength /streŋθ/ *n.* ability to withstand great force 牢度；强度

rectangle▲ /ˈrektæŋgl/ *n.* oblong shape 长方形；矩形

fold up bend; fail to support 弯曲；不能支撑

unstable /ʌnˈsteɪbəl/ *adj.* not firmly fixed and likely to fall 不稳固的；不结实的

withstand /wɪðˈstænd/ *vt.* resist or endure successfully 经受；承受

rigid /ˈrɪdʒɪd/ *adj.* physically unyielding or stiff 刚硬的；不弯曲的

spherical /ˈsferɪkəl/ *adj.* having the shape of a sphere 球形的；球面的

unparalleled△ /ʌnˈpærəˌleld/ *adj.* without parallel, equal, or match 无比的；无双的

internal /ɪnˈtɜːnəl/ *adj.* of, situated on, or suitable for the inside 内部的；里面的

maximize△ /ˈmæksɪˌmaɪz/ *vt.* make as high or great as possible 使增至最大限度

add up to amount to 总计达；总共是

approximately /əˈprɒksɪmɪtlɪ/ *adv.* almost but not quite exactly 近似地；大约

minimize★ /ˈmɪnɪmaɪz/ *vt.* reduce to the lowest degree or amount 把······减至最低

volume /ˈvɒljuːm/ *n.* size or quantity thought of as measurement of the space inside 体积；容积

ratio /ˈreɪʃəʊ/ *n.* quotient of two numbers or quantities 比例；比率

as opposed to as completely different ; in contrast 完全不同；对照

circulate /ˈsɜːkjʊleɪt/ *vi.* move or flow along a closed path; spread widely 流通；流传

obstruction▲ /əbˈstrʌkʃən/ *n.* act of being obstructed 阻碍；阻挡

circulation★ /sɜːkjʊˈleɪʃən/ *n.* flow of gas or liquid around a closed system 循环；流通

disperse★ /dɪsˈpɜːs/ *vt.* (cause to) scatter in different directions 疏散；驱散

rectilinear△ /rektɪˈlɪnɪə/ *adj.* characterized by straight lines 直线的

polar★ /ˈpəʊlə/ *n.* of or near either of the earth's poles 两极的；极地的

integrity★ /ɪnˈtegrɪtɪ/ *n.* state of wholeness 完整;完善

resist /rɪˈzɪst/ *vt.* stand firm against or oppose 阻挡;反抗

resistance /rɪˈzɪstəns/ *n.* force that slows or hampers movement 抵抗力

hurricane★ /ˈhʌrɪkən/ *n.* storm with a strong fast wind 飓风

tornado▲ /tɔːˈneɪdəʊ/ *n.* violent wind in the form of a very tall wide pipe of air that spins 龙卷风

tension /ˈtenʃən/ *n.* the amount of a force stretching sth. 张力;拉力

compression /kəmˈpreʃən/ *n.* the act of compressing or being compressed 压缩

ideally /aɪˈdiːəlɪ/ *adv.* in an ideal way 完美地;理想地

suited /ˈsjuːtɪd/ *adj.* suitable 适合的

distribute /dɪsˈtrɪbjuːt/ *vt.* share among the members of a particular group 分配;散发

dissipate★ /ˈdɪsɪpeɪt/ *vt.* scatter or break up (使)消散;消失

minimal★ /ˈmɪnɪməl/ *adj.* least possible quantity or degree 极少的;极小的

assemble /əˈsembl/ *vt.* fit or join together 装配;组装

assembly /əˈsemblɪ/ *n.* act of assembling 装配;组装

kit★ /kɪt/ *n.* a set of parts sold ready to be assembled 配套元件;成套用品

community /kəˈmjuːnɪtɪ/ *n.* group of people having common interests 社区;团体;界

cardboard▲ /ˈkɑːdbɔːd/ *n.* thick stiff paperlike material used for making boxes 硬纸板

stage /steɪdʒ/ *vt.* organize and carry out 展现;举行

innovative▲ /ˈɪnəʊveɪtɪv/ *adj.* marked by or given to innovations 革新的;创新的

accomplishment /əˈkɒmplɪʃmənt/ *n.* sth. completely and successfully done 成绩;成就

artifact△ /ˈɑːtɪfækt/ *n.* anything made by man 人工制品;手工艺品

fit in with (cause to) be suitable (to) 适合;与……一致

show up (cause to) be easily seen 出现;露面

proliferation▲ /prəʊˌlɪfəˈreɪʃən/ *n.* rapid increase or spreading 增殖

rightful△ /ˈraɪtfəl/ *adj.* right or proper 合法的;理应享有的

humanity★ /hjuːˈmænɪtɪ/ *n.* human beings generally 人类

dominant /ˈdɒmɪnənt/ *adj.* main or chief 统治的;支配的

oriented▲ /ˈɔːrɪentɪd/ *adj.* interested in or directed towards the thing specified 导向的;面向……的

dedicate★ /ˈdedɪkeɪt/ *vt.* devote oneself wholly to a special purpose or cause 致力于

Proper Names

Buckminster Fuller /bʌkˈmɪnstə ˈfʊlə/	巴克明斯特·福勒(人名)
Wichita /ˈwɪtʃɪtɑː/	威奇托（美国地名）
Kansas /ˈkænzəs/	美国堪萨斯州
Beech Aircraft	比奇飞机制造公司
Oregon Dome Co.	俄勒冈圆顶屋协会
the Milan Triennale	米兰三年展中心
the Montreal World's Fair	蒙特利尔世博会
the Vancouver World's Fair	温哥华世博会
EPCOT Center	艾波卡特主题公园(迪斯尼)

Comprehension

8 **Choose the best answer to each question with the information from the text.**

(　　) 1. Which of the following is NOT included in the Fuller's concern for buildings?

        A. Economy.　　　　B. Comfort.　　　　C. Beauty.　　　　D. Efficiency.

(　　) 2. The houses Fuller developed in 1944 _____.

        A. were produced on a large scale

        B. could be assembled easily

        C. solved the problem of housing shortage

        D. were made for pilots

(　　) 3. Geodesic domes are the most efficient structures ever created in terms of _____.

        A. labor cost　　　　　　　　B. heating cost

        C. material strength　　　　　D. material weight

(　　) 4. Which of the following statement about the geodesic dome is true?

        A. The balance between tension and compression helps to resist severe wind.

        B. The external dome shape contributes to the natural wind resistance.

        C. The geodesic dome has the most surface area per unit of volume per structure.

        D. The geodesic dome withstands more tension than compression.

(　　) 5. It is implied in the last paragraph that _____.

        A. architects should be concerned with a global vision

        B. the economy of means contributes little to the beauty in form

        C. the geodesic dome provides a new approach to building design

D. many other buildings are less structurally efficient than the geodesic dome

9 **Complete the following summary with right words and expressions.**

Fuller spent much of his life looking for ways to improve human _____. Everything he did was guided by the idea of _____. He improved _____ structure equipment, studied structure shells, and _____ a number of alternatives to traditional buildings. In 1944, the United States suffered a serious housing shortage. Fuller developed a prototype family dwelling which could be _____ anywhere easily.

After the war, Fuller focused on the problem of how to build lightweight and transpotable shelters. He discovered that if a _____ structure was produced from triangles, it would have unparalleled _____. Thus he created a new architectural design which provides maximum _____ with minimum structural effort. Buckminster Fuller's first worldwide acceptance by the architectural _____ occurred with the 1954 Triennale. Geodesic domes are now employed for diverse tasks. As a structure that is resource and energy efficient as well as structurally sound, the geodesic dome has _____ to change the way the world looks at building design.

10 **Discuss the following questions with the information from the text.**

1. What was Fuller's major goal with respect to human shelter and housing? (*comfortable, efficient, available*)

_____

2. What is the main feature of the geodesic dome? (*maximum, minimal*)

_____

3. How are geodesic domes used nowadays? (*diverse tasks*)

_____

4. What do you think of the geodesic dome?

_____

5. How will you apply Fuller's idea of doing more with less to practical issues or to your daily life?

_____

Vocabulary & Structure

11 **Fill in the blanks with the words given below. Change the form where necessary.**

withstand	assemble	interior	perception	devise
circulate	enclose	exposure	innovative	alternative

1. They _____ the parts and components into a car.

2. It is a city in southwestern Germany famous for _____ architecture.

3. The _____ of the building is magnificent and luxurious.

4. Scientists are working to _____ a means of storing this type of power.

5. I didn't have enough money to travel to Xinjiang, so I had no _____ but to stay at home this vacation.

6. Moderate exercise stimulates the _____ of blood.

7. Farmers often _____ their land with hedges.

8. Advertising affects the customer's _____ of a product.

9. The paint came off as the result of _____ to the rain.

10. Explorers usually have to _____ hardships.

12 **Complete the following sentences with phrases or expressions from the text.**

1. After the earthquake，$ 22 million in donations _____ by text message.

2. Many small victories _____ a big one.

3. Today we're going to _____ the question of homeless people.

4. Your description does not _____ my experience.

5. The pain in her stomach was so sharp that she _____.

13 **Translate the Chinese sentences into English by simulating the sentences chosen from the text.**

Chosen Sentences	Simulated Translation	Chinese Sentences
Fuller *spent* much of the early 20th century *looking for ways to* improve human shelter.		他花了大量的空余时间去寻找提高艺术表现力的方法。（artistic expression）
Soon, unsolicited checks *poured in from people who* wanted to purchase this new kind of house.		不久,那些看过那条电视广告的人们纷纷寄来了订单。（commercial，order）
After the war, Fuller's *efforts focused* on the problem of how to build a shelter which is so lightweight that it can be delivered by air.		毕业后,他集中精力研究如何保护当地的文物建筑。（conserve, heritage）

续表

Chosen Sentences	Simulated Translation	Chinese Sentences
The external shape of a geodesic dome allows wind to flow smoothly over the structure **as opposed to** blowing directly into a flat wall.		本文讨论的是民居建筑,而非商用建筑。(residential buildings, deal with)
Some houses *can be* assembled *in less than* a day *with others taking up* to six months.		有些菜十分钟不到就做好,而有些菜则要花个把小时。(prepare)

14 **Rewrite each sentence with the word or phrase in brackets, keeping the same meaning. The first part has been done for you.**

1. The young architect's aim is to build houses which most people can afford.
   The young architect's aim is to _____.
   (economically available)

2. There were all sorts of rumors in the air that dozens of people were dead in the fire.
   Rumors were _____. (circulate)

3. By using computers, people can get more information more quickly.
   Computers _____. (enable)

4. I'm afraid I can only ask my sister for help.
   I'm afraid I _____. (alternative)

5. Sports, not learning, seem to have the most important place in our school life.
   Our school life seems to _____. (dominate)

Text B   Skimming and Scanning

Old Buildings, New Uses

Adaptive reuse is a process that adapts buildings for new uses while retaining their historic features. When the original use of a structure changes or is no longer required, architects have the opportunity to change the primary function of the structure, while retaining some of the existing architectural details that make the building unique. An old factory may become an apartment building. A rundown church may find new life as a restaurant. And a restaurant may become a church. Nowadays there are many successful reuse projects around the world.

In Canada, especially in Vancouver, Toronto and Montreal, adaptive reuse has come to define the character of many neighborhoods, and even creates neighborhoods where none existed before. In Toronto, the Distillery District, a neighborhood in the city's southeast side, was entirely adapted from an old distillery. Vancouver's Yaletown, an upscale neighborhood established in the 1990s, is almost entirely re-used warehouse and other small-industrial structures and spaces.

Adaptive reuse covers a wide range of urban areas and building types. (1) <u>Urban waterfronts, historically used as points for industrial production and transport, are now selling points for home buyers and renters.</u> In Australia, there has been a number of projects to convert old silos into residential apartments. In the United States, especially in the Northeast and Midwest, formerly-industrial areas are being transformed into residential neighborhoods. Loft housing is one prominent result of the adaptive reuse projects.

The Stonehouse Distillery

The adaptation of old buildings presents a genuine challenge to architects and designers to find innovative solutions. As development pressures increase in our cities, more heritage buildings are being reused, producing some excellent examples of creative designs. One famous example of adaptive reuse is the Gallery of Modern Art for the Tate Museum in London. Designed by the Pritzker Prize winning architects Jacques Herzog and Pierre de Meuron, the museum was once a power station.

Ten years ago, the scene along London's South Bank was grim. Looming over the Thames River, the oil-fired Bankside Power Plant was a gargantuan expanse of ugly brown bricks and abandoned space. Designed in 1947 by Sir Giles Gilbert Scott, the plant shut down in 1981.

A number of architects submitted proposals for the new museum, but they planned to demolish much of the power house. Among the six finalists, Herzog & de Meuron was the only firm that suggested reusing a significant portion of the plant.

Left intact, the 500-foot-long turbine hall became a dramatic entrance for the museum. The industrial flavor of the building is reflected in the taupe walls and black steel girders. A new glass ceiling floods the austere space with natural light, creating an ideal environment for viewing art.

"It's a space you never could ever have achieved with a new building," says Rowan Moore, an architecture critic and author of *Building the Tate Modern*. "For one thing they'd never get the money for

Tate Modern Turbine Hall

it, but even if they did it would seem like a bombastic gesture because there's all this empty space here."

"Our strategy was to accept the physical power of Bankside's massive mountain-like brick building and to even enhance it rather than breaking it or trying to diminish it," Jacques Herzog and Pierre de Meuron said of their project. "This is a kind of Aikido strategy where you use your enemy's energy for your own purposes. Instead of fighting it, you take all the energy and shape it in unexpected and new ways."

Adaptive reuse of buildings has a major role to play in the sustainable global development. (2) When adaptive reuse involves historic buildings, environmental benefits are more significant, as these buildings offer so much to the landscape and identity of the communities they belong to.

One of the main environmental benefits of reusing buildings is the retention of the original building's "embodied energy". Embodied energy can be defined as the energy consumed by all of the processes associated with the production of a building, from the acquisition of natural resources to product delivery, including mining, manufacturing of materials and equipment, transport and administrative functions. By reusing buildings, their embodied energy is retained, making the project much more environmentally sustainable than entirely new construction. It is reported that the reuse of building materials usually involves a saving of approximately 95 per cent of embodied energy that would otherwise be wasted. In this context the reuse of heritage buildings makes good sense.

There are several financial savings and returns to be made from adaptive reuse of historic buildings. Embodied energy savings from not demolishing a building will only

increase with the predicted rise of energy costs in the future. (3) <u>While there is no</u>   85
<u>definitive research on the market appeal of reused heritage buildings, they have</u>
<u>anecdotally been popular because of their originality and historic authenticity.</u> In
Australia, a study that included four adaptive reuse sites revealed that the
sympathetic adaptive reuse plans have created commercially viable investment assets
for the owners.   90

Keeping and reusing historic buildings has long-term benefits for the communities
that value them. When done well, adaptive reuse can restore and maintain the
heritage significance of a building and help to ensure its survival. (4) <u>Rather than</u>
<u>falling into disrepair through neglect or being rendered unrecognizable, heritage</u>
<u>buildings that are sympathetically recycled can continue to be used and appreciated.</u>   95

The reuse of heritage buildings in established residential areas can provide the
community with new housing and commercial property opportunities. Location,
access and public transport availability will always attract developers. The size of the
sites and variety of buildings available for reuse mean that a good mix of dwelling
types can be offered, with broad appeal to buyers as a result.   100

Increasingly, communities, governments and developers are seeking ways to
reduce the environmental, social and economic costs of continued urban development
and expansion. People are realizing that the design of the built environment are vital
to their standard of living and their impact upon natural resources.

Heritage buildings have merged with more general environmental and quality-of-   105
life concerns in recent years. Communities increasingly recognize that future
generations will benefit from the protection of certain places and areas. People's
lifestyle is enhanced not just from the retention of heritage buildings, but from their
adaptation into accessible and useable places.

(1 037 words)

New Words and Expressions

adaptive△ /əˈdæptɪv/ *adj.*   having a capacity for adaptation 适合的;适应的
retain /rɪˈteɪn/ *vt.*   be able to hold or contain 保持;保留
define /dɪˈfaɪn/ *adj.*   determine the essential quality of 是……的特色,表明特征
distillery△ /dɪsˈtɪlərɪ/ *n.*   plant and works where alcoholic drinks are made by
distillation 酿酒厂
upscale△ /ˈʌpskeɪl/ *adj.*   appropriate for people with good incomes 高档的
warehouse★ /ˈweəhaʊs/ *n.*   a storehouse for goods and merchandise 仓库;货栈
silo△ /ˈsaɪləʊ/ *adj.*   a cylindrical tower used for storing silage 筒仓
residential /rezɪˈdenʃəl/ *adj.*   used or designed for residence 住宅的

prominent /'prɒmɪnənt/ *adj.*　noticeable 显著的；突出的

genuine /'dʒenjuɪn/ *adj.*　actual or real 真的；真实的

grim★ /grɪm/ *adj.*　harsh and unpleasant 阴森的；令人畏惧的

loom★ /luːm/ *vi.*　appear very large or occupy a commanding position 赫然耸起

gargantuan△ /gɑː'gæntʃʊən/ *adj.*　huge and bulky 巨大的；庞大的

submit /səb'mɪt/ *vt.*　send（application or proposal）for judgment or consideration 提交

proposal /prə'pəʊzəl/ *n.*　sth. proposed 提议；设计

demolish▲ /dɪ'mɒlɪʃ/ *vt.*　destroy completely 摧毁；拆毁（大建筑物）

finalist△ /'faɪnəlɪst/ *n.*　contestant who reaches the final stage of a competition 决赛选手

portion /'pɔːʃən/ *n.*　part 部分

intact★ /ɪn'tækt/ *adj.*　undamaged in any way 完整无缺的

turbine /'tɜːbɪn/ *n.*　an engine or motor in which the pressure of a liquid or gas drives a special wheel 涡轮

flavor /'fleɪvə/ *n.*　distinctive quality or atmosphere 特色

taupe△ /təʊp/ *adj.*　greyish brown 褐色的

girder△ /'gɜːdə/ *n.*　a beam made usually of steel 梁；钢架

austere▲ /ɒs'tɪə/ *adj.* severely simple 朴素的；无装饰的

critic /'krɪtɪk/ *n.*　professional judge of art，music，or literature 评论家

bombastic△ /'bɒmbæstɪk/ *adj.*　ostentatiously lofty in style 夸大的；言过其实的

diminish★ /dɪ'mɪnɪʃ/ *vt.*　decrease in size，extent，or range 减少；缩小

gesture /'dʒestʃə/ *n.*　sth. done as an indication of intention 姿态；表示

enhance /ɪn'hæns/ *vt.*　make better or more attractive 提高；加强；增加

aikido△ /aɪ'kiːdəʊ/ *n.*　a Japanese form of self-defence and martial art ［日］合气道（日本的一种自卫拳术，利用对方的力以取胜）

sustainable /sə'steɪnəbl/ *adj.*　capable of being sustained 可持续的

landscape /'lændskeɪp/ *n.*　an expanse of scenery that can be seen in a single view 景观

retention★ /rɪ'tenʃən/ *n.*　the act of retaining sth. 保留；保持

embody★ /ɪm'bɒdɪ/ *vt.*　include as part of a whole 包含；包括

acquisition /ækwɪ'zɪʃən/ *n.*　the act of acquiring sth. 获得

mining△ /'maɪnɪŋ/ *n.*　act of extracting ores or coal from the earth 采矿（业）

administrative /əd'mɪnɪˌstreɪtɪv/ *adj.*　of or relating to the control and direction of affairs 管理的

heritage★ /'herɪtɪdʒ/ *n.*　anything that has been carried over from the past 遗产；继承物

make sense be a wise course of action 有意义；言之有理

definitive★ /dɪˈfɪnətɪv/ *adj.* clearly defined or formulated 明确的

appeal /əˈpiːl/ *n.* the power to attract, please, or interest people 吸引力

anecdotal▲ /ænɪkˈdəʊtl/ *adj.* based on casual observations or indications rather than rigorous or scientific analysis 趣闻的；传闻的

originality /əˌrɪdʒəˈnælɪtɪ/ *n.* the quality of being new and original 独创性

authenticity★ /ɔːθenˈtɪsətɪ/ *n.* the quality of being true 真实性

sympathetic /sɪmpəˈθetɪk/ *adj.* likable and appealing 让人喜欢的；支持的

viable△ /ˈvaɪəbəl/ *adj.* capable of life or normal growth and development 可实施的；能自行生长的

asset /ˈæset/ *n.* property 资产；财产

render /ˈrendə/ *vt.* cause to become 使成为；使变得

unrecognizable /ʌnˈrekəgnaɪzəbl/ *adj.* changed or damaged so much that it is hard to recognize 无法识别的

Proper Names

Toronto /təˈrɒntəʊ/	多伦多（加拿大）
the Distillery District	古酿酒厂区（地名）
Vancouver /vænˈkuːvə/	温哥华（加拿大）
Yaletown /jeɪlˈtaʊn/	耶鲁镇（地名）
Jacques Herzog /ʒɑːk ˈhɜːzɒg/	雅克·赫尔佐格
Pierre de Meuron /piːeə dəˈmɜːrɒn/	皮艾尔·德·穆龙
Sir Giles Gilbert Scott /sɜː dʒaɪlz ˈgɪlbət skɒt/	贾尔斯·吉尔伯特·司哥特爵士

Comprehension

15 **Go over the text quickly and answer the following questions. For questions 1—7, choose the best answer from the four choices; for questions 8—10, complete the sentences with the information from the text.**

(　　) 1. Which of the following adaptive reuse is not mentioned in the text?

    A. A warehouse was reused as a gallery.

    B. A church was adapted into a restaurant.

    C. A power plant was converted into a museum.

    D. A distillery was transformed into a neighborhood.

(　　) 2. The buildings in the Yaletown are mainly adapted from _____.

    A. an old distillery   B. an old power plant

    C. an old warehouse   D. an old railroad terminal

(　　) 3. What did Jacques Herzog and Pierre de Meuron do with the power plant?

          A. They relocated the power plant.

          B. They retained much of the power house.

          C. They demolished the exterior shell of the power plant.

          D. They adapted the inner walls.

(   ) 4. What is NOT true about the turbine hall of Tate Modern?

          A. It was damaged or impaired in some way.

          B. It became an entrance for the museum.

          C. It is about 500 feet in length.

          D. It is very impressive.

(   ) 5. The original building's "embodied energy" refers to _____.

          A. the energy that was consumed in the process of acquiring natural resources

          B. the available energy that was used in the work of making a building

          C. the sum total of the energy necessary for the manufacturing of materials and equipment

          D. all the energy embodied in the building materials

(   ) 6. When a building can no longer function with its original use, a new use through adaption may preserve its _____.

          A. building materials   B. heritage significance

          C. exterior walls   D. original design

(   ) 7. By saying that "the reuse of heritage buildings makes good sense", the author means that _____.

          A. it makes people feel good   B. it is understandable

          C. it is not practical   D. it is a wise course of action

      8. Adaptive reuse of buildings plays an important role in the _____.

      9. One environmental benefit of reusing buildings is that _____.

     10. Developers will always be attracted by the location, _____ in established residential areas.

Vocabulary & Translation

16 Fill in the blanks with the words given below. Change the form where necessary.

genuine	retain	transform	primary	submit
appeal	involve	merge	acquisition	enhance

   1. Lifelong learning is the ongoing _____ of knowledge or skills.

   2. My boss shows _____ interest in my work.

   3. With this method the salmon _____ its flavor and texture.

   4. The last forty years have seen the country has _____ from a peasant

economy to a major industrial power.

5. They decided to _____ the two companies into one.

6. These changes in the business _____ the interests of all owners.

7. Applicants should _____ their applications as early as possible.

8. The _____ task of the chair is to ensure the meeting runs smoothly.

9. Bright geometrics _____ the appearance of the cloth.

10. The editorial work has always had a great _____ to me as I have some ability in writing and editorial work.

17 Translate the underlined sentences in the text into Chinese.

1. Urban waterfronts, historically used as points for industrial production and transport, are now selling points for home buyers and renters.

_____

_____

_____

2. When adaptive reuse involves historic buildings, environmental benifits are more significant, as these buildings offer so much to the landscape and identity of the communities they belong to.

_____

_____

3. While there is no definitive research on the market appeal of reused heritage buildings, they have anecdotally been popular because of their originality and historic authenticity.

_____

_____

4. Rather than falling into disrepair through neglect or being rendered unrecognisable, heritage buildings that are sympathetically recycled can continue to be used and appreciated.

_____

_____

Interactive Tasks

18 Read the sample dialogues carefully, and then complete the interactive tasks that follow.

Task 1

Sample dialogue

Lin: Look at these buildings!

Wang: Nice, aren't they? They are residential apartments.

Lin: I can't believe my eyes. Do you mean that they are used for residence?

Wang: That's right. People live in them. Look at these big cylinders, these big windows. Do they remind you of anything?

Lin: I just feel they look very special, so different from the box-style buildings. Maybe they are the works of some famous architect?

Wang: Not exactly. These buildings were transformed from some silos built in 1970s. Kind of adaptive reuse.

Lin: What is a silo?

Wang: A silo is a structure to store bulk materials. In agriculture, farmers use them to store grain.

Lin: It must be very exciting to live in these towers! They offer uninterrupted views.

Wang: Well, that's just how I see it.

Interactive task

Two students are talking about a new art gallery. The art gallery was converted from an old warehouse.

Role A: The building looks very special and so different from the galleries I know.

Role B: It was originally an old warehouse built in 1970s. A warehouse usually has a huge space.

Task 2

Sample dialogue

Lin: Wang, look at this picture. Isn't this building great?

Wang: That's not my cup of tea.

Lin: Then, what's your idea of a nice building?

Wang: I like the kind of building which is very impressive at first glance. For example, a geodesic dome.

Lin: The kind of building that looks like a ball? I think it's a little bit simple.

Wang: Beauty lies in the simplistic. It appeals to me very much. The image of the dome always reminds me of the future world. What's more, they are very efficient buildings. They can save a lot of energy and materials.

Lin: They may be very efficient. But it seems to me that the sloping interior walls are not very comfortable.

Wang: Oh, that's a problem. But you know, everything has two sides.

Lin: Well, that's the thing. Nothing is perfect in this world.

Wang: People may like geodesic domes. Or people may dislike them. But geodesic domes are there to stay.

Interactive task

Two young people are talking about skyscrapers. One thinks that skyscrapers are modern while the other argues that they cause problems.

Role A: Skyscrapers may look great, but many of them make city life unpleasant. They block sunlight from reaching the streets. The large numbers of people who work or live in these skyscrapers crowd the sidewalks and streets below.

Role B: I like the kind of building which is absolutely modern. Skyscrapers are fantastic. They are the landmark of a developed city.

Group Work

19 Work in groups to discuss about a modern building.

1. Form groups of 4 or 5 students.

2. Each group finds a modern building that they enjoy most. Fill in the following chart:

What is the name of the building? Where is it located?	Who is the architect? What is his design philosophy?	What is its style? Why do you like it?

3. A member of each group introduces the building to the rest of the class.

Follow-up Tasks

Writing

正文段

正文段是接引言段之后的主体段落，是文章的重要部分。它针对引言段所提出的主题思想，进行具体的阐述和论证，是表达思想、澄清事实的地方。正文段的长短，取决于作者所要表达内容的多少。但由于受到考试时间和篇幅的限制，作文正文段应控制在 10 句话之内，以 6—8 句话为宜，约占全文篇幅的 65%—80%之间。正文段和其他段一样都有一个中心思想，以指引和贯穿全段。请看 1997 年考研作文题"Good Health"正文段：

Good Health

There are many ways to keep fit. Clean air and water, nutritious food, moderate activity, a little walk in the sunshine, and a good night's sleep; the key here is persistence. Moreover, we should pay attention to spiritual well-being, for spiritual well-being is as important as physical well-being. We understand that healthy people are happier than unhealthy people. Likewise, happy people are healthier than unhappy people. Therefore, if we want to improve our health, we must face the life with smiles.

此段针对引言段提出的"健康的重要性"，写了保持身体健康的种种方法。

Research Project

Work in groups of 4 or 5 students, and finish a research project based on the topic area of this unit. It involves lectures, seminars, team-based activities, individual activities, team presentation and a reflective summary.

Steps

1. Form a research group;
2. Decide on a research topic;
3. Work in groups to finish PPT slides;
4. Each member of the group gives oral presentation of his parts;
5. Hand in materials that include: Project Proposal (one for each team), Research Report (one for each team, 1 000 words), Summary (one for each

person, 300 words), PPT (one for each team).

Research Methods

1. Field work: to generate the first-hand information
   - Questionnaires
   - Interviews (interpersonal, telephone, e-mail, door-to-door visit, etc.)
   - Observation
2. Desk work: to generate the second-hand information
   - Library: books and magazines
   - The Internet: Google the theme with the key words
   - Reading materials

Suggested Options

1. An introduction to an influential Chinese modern architect.
2. An exploration into the impact of tall buildings on big cities.

Tips for Options

1. For Option 1, it is suggested that you first make a survey among architecture students to find out the architect they most appreciate. Then collect information on the architect's life and career, especially his important works, philosophy, and contributions to Chinese modern architecture.
2. For Option 2, in addition to collecting the second-hand information, you can also design a questionnaire to investigate about people's attitude towards high-rise buildings in big cities.

Unit Four   Designing

Highlight

Topic area	Structure	Skills
The concept and different areas of design Two traditions of industrial design Principles of fashion design	range from ... to ... have ... in common for all ... ... one's way out of ... see to it that ...	Understanding design Describing and discussing different products of design Designing a product

Warm-up Tasks

1 **Listen to the following passage and try to fill in the missing words and expressions.**

Designing is the (1) _____ that lays the basis for the making of every object or system in our world. It is the process of originating and developing a plan for a product, structure, symbol, or component with (2) _____. In a broader way, it means (3) _____ arts and engineering. The final product of designing can be anything from (4) _____ to clothing to cars. Even virtual concepts such as corporate identity (the philosophy of a corporation) and cultural traditions such as celebration of certain holidays are sometimes designed.

Designer is a term used for people who work professionally in one of the various design areas, such as a(n) (5) _____ designer, (6) _____ designer or (7) _____ designer. Designing often requires a designer to consider the (8) _____, functional, and many other aspects of an object or a process, which usually requires considerable research, thought, modeling, interactive adjustment, and re-design. With such a broad definition, there is no universal language or unifying (9) _____ for designers of all disciplines. This allows for many different philosophies and (10) _____ toward the subject.

2 **Discuss the following questions about design with your partner.**

1. Design can be classified into different areas such as web design, garden design or packaging design. Can you name any other areas of design?
2. The following pictures show products of design in different areas. Can you put

them into their areas?

Graphic symbols from the US National Park Service   iPod *Apple*

Handbag *Chanel*

3. How do products of design affect your life?

Listening Tasks

Micro Listening Skills

3 You will hear seven sentences. Each sentence contains one of the two words given to you. Listen carefully and choose the word you hear in each sentence.

1. A. logo   B. local
2. A. suit   B. sue
3. A. color   B. corner
4. A. cave   B. creative

5. A. pin   B. pink

6. A. catches   B. scratches

7. A. display   B. disagree

Dialogue

Never Learn from Pepsi

Words & Phrases

Pepsi /'pepsɪ/	百事(美国公司名)
graphic designer	平面设计师
logo /'ləʊgəʊ/ *n.*	徽标
prototype /'prəʊtətaɪp/ *n.*	原型；样品
sue /sjuː/ *vt.*	起诉；控告
infringement /ɪn'frɪndʒmənt/ *n.*	侵犯；侵害
start from scratch	从零开始

4 Listen to the dialogue and decide whether the following statements are true (T) or false (F).

_____ 1. The new logo doesn't work because it isn't as beautiful as that of Pepsi's.

_____ 2. The logo of Pepsi is protected by law.

_____ 3. The law department thinks the new logo violates Pepsi's copyright.

_____ 4. The new logo can be modified to differentiate from that of Pepsi's.

_____ 5. The only purpose of designing a more creative logo is to avoid violating copyright.

5 Listen to the dialogue again and complete the following sentences with the information you have heard.

1. The problem with the new logo is that it is _____.

2. Pepsi would _____ if they came out with something even close to the design of Pepsi's.

3. The law department determined it would be _____ to place this design on their products.

4. The final decision from the law department is that they have to _____.

Passage

The Folding Plug

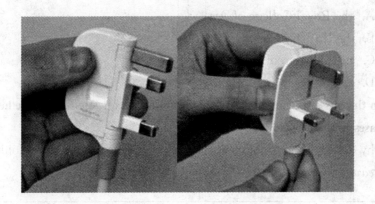

Words & Phrases

laptop /ˈlæpˌtɒp/ *n.*	便携式电脑
prestigious /presˈtɪdʒɪəs/ *adj.*	有声望的
beat off	击败
the British Insurance Product Award	英国生命保险设计大奖
scratch /skrætʃ/ *vt.*	抓破；划破
ingenious /ɪnˈdʒiːnɪəs/ *adj.*	（指物）制作精巧的
shortlisted /ˈʃɒtˌlɪstɪd/ *adj.*	入围的

6 Listen to the passage and choose the best answer to the following questions.

(　　) 1. Which of the following is NOT mentioned about the three-pin British plug?

　　　A. It's big and heavy.

　　　B. It's quite safe.

　　　C. It has changed little since 1947.

        D. It scratches the laptop and other things in the bag.

(   ) 2. Min-Kyu Choi(崔铭九) won _____ on 17 March 2010.

        A. the London Design Award

        B. the Design Museum Award

        C. the British Insurance Product Award

        D. the Royal Art College Award

(   ) 3. Min-Kyu Choi's folding plug is _____ thick when folded.

        A. less than one centimeter

        B. between one and two centimeters

        C. about two centimeters

        D. more than two centimeters

(   ) 4. The plug and all the shortlisted designs will be on display at _____ until 31 October.

        A. the Royal College of Art

        B. the British Museum

        C. the Museum of London

        D. the Design Museum

7 **Listen to the passage again and answer the following questions with the help of words and phrases provided below.**

    1. Why did Min-Kyu Choi come up with the idea of designing a folding plug?

        (*heavyweight*, *ultra-light*, *scratch*, *traveling*)

        _____

    2. How can one use the folding plug?

        (*turn*, *pin*, *open*, *cover*)

        _____

    3. What do you think are the advantages of the folding plug?

        _____

Reading Tasks

Text A   *Reading in Detail*

Pre-reading Questions

    1. Have you ever seen or heard of any industrial designers?

    2. What do you think of industrial design? Can it be called an art?

3. What convenience does a well-designed industrial product, like an electric razor, bring to you?

Industrial Design, a Business or an Art[①]?

Industrial designers in the world fall into two traditions. Those in the United States knowingly or unknowingly try their best to follow in the footsteps of Raymond Loewy[②], a French-born designer who made industrial design a business as important as advertising. Earning his money initially as a freelance with jobs ranging from window displays to fashion magazine illustrations, Raymond Loewy was soon building up one of the most successful design businesses in the world. By the end of the 1940s Loewy's achievements had already brought him such recognition that he appeared on the cover of *Time* magazine under the headline "Designer Raymond Lowey. He streamlines the sales curve".

And in Europe, there is the other tradition of industrial design, perhaps best personified by Dieter Rams[③] and William Morris, who view industrial design as an art. Unlike William Morris, Rams believes in the potential of industrial production. But both Morris and Rams have a sense of good taste, and a rejection of ugliness, in common. As a precocious teenager, Morris refused to set foot inside the Crystal Palace at London's Great Exhibition of 1851, so convinced that he would find nothing inside but machine-made junk. Rams is the man who used to walk in the

Cover picture from *Time* Magazine of 31 October, 1949

5

10

15

20

25

---

① This text is adapted from "The Children of Raymond Loewy" written by Deyan Sudjic (*Metropolis Magazine*, March 2009, New York).

② Raymond Lowey (1893—1986): France-born American designer and engineer who made great achievements in the field of industrial design, a pioneer of streamlined form.

③ Dieter Rams (1932   ): German industrial designer who had been chief designer of Braun for more than 30 years.

woods around his home with a sack to collect the garbage—visual pollution in his delicate eyes—that he found on the way and took it back to the dump.

30   For all their apparent differences, both Loewy and Rams are in fact doing the same thing—using design as a means of giving material objects meanings, different meanings, but still meanings. Loewy was brilliant at presenting himself as the personification of glamour. He built a replica of his studio in the Metropolitan Museum of Art. He posed, lolling on the footplate of one of his streamlined

35 locomotives for the Pennsylvania Railroad. He turned the Gestetner duplicating machine from an unattractive office standby into the iMac of its day.

Loewy's design embodied the view of consumption developed by Earnest Elmo Calkins, the man who created the contemporary advertising industry. Calkins and the American marketing pioneers in the 1930s had been determined to persuade the world

40 to consume its way out of the Depression[①]. "Goods fall into two classes, those which we use, such as motor cars, and safety razors, and those which we use up, such as tooth paste, or soda biscuits," Calkins wrote in 1932. "Consumer engineering must see to it that we use up the kind of goods we now merely use." And while we may have convinced ourselves that we are a generation too sophisticated to fall for planned

45 obsolescence[②], the truth is that we have never been so deluged with stuff that is calculated to seduce us into acquiring it. And in a world in which every government is now desperate to persuade its citizens to start borrowing and spending, it's not hard to see how design is again called on to carry out a similar task: to persuade us to buy

---

    ① The Depression: a severe worldwide economic depression in the decade before World War Ⅱ. It was the longest, most widespread, and deepest depression of the 20th century.

    ② Planned obsolescence: the process of a product becoming obsolete or non-functional after a certain period or amount of use in a way that is planned or designed by the manufacturer.

things we don't necessarily need.

It's possible that we now see the two traditions coalescing in the design work of　50
Apple Inc. [①] Designers in Apple learned the good taste developed by Rams, and put it
to work in smart electronics. For example, they used the elder designer's Braun
calculator as the calculator interface of the first-generation iPhone. But at the same
time, Apple has taken us back to the idea of planned obsolescence in a way that would
gladden Calkins's heart. Every 18 months, there is a better, sharper, smarter, new　55
Mac that makes the last one, and all the costly peripherals that came with it,
redundant.

Braun calculator and its iPhone version

In essence, both traditions use design to show us the objects that shape our daily
lives. These objects are calculatingly designed to achieve an emotional response from
consumers. They can be beautiful, witty, ingenious, and sophisticated, but they can　60
also be crude, banal, and inferior. The designer tries to use design to make objects
that are cheap to mass-produce look valuable, to make them look masculine or
feminine, and to make them look up-to-date. That is what design has always done in
one way or another. What has really changed is our relationship to our possessions.
They are losing their ability to grow old with us. Polycarbonate looks great fresh out　65
of the box, but as soon as it starts to interact with human skin, it begins to blemish.
When my cell phone has spent a month or two in my pocket, it looks as if it has
developed psoriasis.

----

① Apple Inc.: an American multinational corporation that designs and manufactures consumer electronics
products. The company's best-known products include Macintosh computers, iPod, iPhone and iPad.

70

But my first Nikon SLR aged with dignity. As the black paint began to chip, it revealed little glimpses of the brass body beneath, like denim fading to the texture of cashmere. I still have my father's portable typewriter; the keys are rusted together, the ribbon is tattered, and it will never compose another letter. But I can't bring myself to part with it. It lasted him half a lifetime. I change laptops every 18 months, and I don't see my daughter ever keeping one of them on her top shelf.

(855 words)

New Words and Expressions

fall into　be classified as 分成

freelance▲ /ˈfriːˌlæns/ *n.*　a self-employed person, especially a writer or artist 自由职业者

illustration /ˌɪləˈstreɪʃn/ *n.*　a picture in a book or magazine 插图

streamline★ /ˈstriːmlaɪn/ *vt.*　make more efficient 提高效率

streamlined★ /ˈstriːmlaɪnd/ *adj.*　having a shape that offers least resistance to the flow of air, water, etc. 流线型的

personify△ /pəˈsɒnɪfaɪ/ *vt.*　be a striking example of a quality 为……的实例；为……的化身

personification△ /pəˌsɒnɪfɪˈkeɪʃn/ *n.*　striking example of a quality 化身；活例

precocious△ /prɪˈkəʊʃəs/ *adj.*　(of a child) too grown up（儿童）早熟的

junk★ /dʒʌnk/ *n.*　old useless things 废旧杂物

delicate /ˈdelɪkeɪt/ *adj.*　sensitive 灵敏的

glamour★ /ˈglæmə/ *n.* special quality of charm, beauty and excitement 魅力

replica△ /ˈreplɪkə/ *n.*　a close copy of a painting or other work of art 复制品

loll△ /lɒl/ *vi.*　hang loosely 松弛地垂下

locomotive★ /ˌləʊkəˈməʊtɪv/ *n.*　a railway engine 火车机车

depression /dɪˈpreʃn/ *n.*　a period of reduced business activity and high unemployment 经济萧条期

see to　give care and thought to 注意；留心

fall for　be cheated by 受……的骗；上……的当

deluge△ /ˈdeljuːdʒ/ *vt.*　come down on (sb. or sth.) like a great flood 如洪水涌至（某人或某物）

seduce▲ /sɪˈdjuːs/ *vt.*　persuade (sb.) to do wrong 引诱（某人）犯错误

desperate /ˈdespərɪt/ *adj.*　violent and not caring about danger 拼命的

coalesce△ /ˌkəʊəˈles/ *vi.*　come together 合并

interface△ /ˈɪntəfeɪs/ *n.*　surface common in two areas 界面

take sb. back to△　bring memory of an earlier period to sb. 使某人回想或追忆

peripheral▲ /pəˈrɪfərəl/ n.　electronic equipment connected by cable to a computer（计算机的）外围设备

redundant★ /rɪˈdʌndənt/ adj.　no longer needed for a particular purpose 多余的

banal△ /bəˈnæl/ adj.　commonplace; uninteresting 平庸的；无趣味的

masculine★ /ˈmæskjʊlɪn/ adj.　having the qualities that are considered typical of a man 有男子特征的

feminine★ /ˈfemənɪn/ adj.　having the qualities that are considered typical of a woman 女性化的

polycarbonate△ /pɒlɪˈkɑːbəneɪt/ n.　聚碳酸酯

interact /ˈɪntəˈrækt/ vi.　act on each other 相互作用；相互影响

blemish△ /ˈblemɪʃ/ vi.　spoil the beauty or perfection of sth. 玷污

psoriasis△ /səˈraɪəsɪs/ n.　牛皮癣；银屑病

glimpse /glɪmps/ n.　a quick look at sth. 一瞥

denim△ /ˈdenɪm/ n.　a strong cotton cloth which is often blue 蓝色斜纹粗棉布

cashmere△ /ˈkæʃmɪə/ n.　fine soft wool of Kashmir goats of Asia 喀什米尔羊毛

tattered△ /ˈtætəd/ vt.　old and torn 破烂的

Proper Names

Raymond Loewy /ˈreɪmənd ˈləʊwɪ/	雷蒙·罗维（人名）
Dieter Rams /ˈdiːtə ˈræms/	迪特尔·拉姆斯（人名）
William Morris /ˈwɪlɪəm ˈmɔrɪs/	威廉·莫里斯（人名）
the Crystal Palace	水晶宫
the Metropolitan Museum of Art	大都会艺术博物馆
the Pennsylvania Railroad	宾夕法尼亚铁路公司
Gestetner /dʒesˈtenə/	基士得耶（英国办公设备制造商）
iMac /ˈaɪˈmæk/ n.	一体式电脑（苹果公司产品）
Ernest Elmo Calkins /ˈɜːnɪst ˈelmɒ ˈkælkɪnz/	厄内斯特·埃尔默·凯尔金斯（人名）
planned obsolescence /ɒbsəˈlesns/	有计划的淘汰
Braun /braʊn/	博朗（德国电器制造商）
iPhone /ˈaɪfəʊn/ n.	智能移动电话（苹果公司产品）
Mac /mæk/ n. (=Macintosh)	麦金托什电脑（苹果公司产品）
Nikon SLR (single-lens reflex)	尼康单镜头反光相机

Comprehension

8 **Choose the best answer to each question with the information from the text.**

(　　) 1. We can infer from the passage that _____.

　　　　A. industrial design is merely a business

    B. industrial design is a pure art

    C. industrial design is both a business and an art

    D. industrial design is more of a business than of an art

( ) 2. Which of the following is NOT true about Raymond Loewy?

    A. He was a successful designer and businessman.

    B. He never cared the beauty of industrial products.

    C. He appeared on the cover of *Time* magazine.

    D. His major concern was to promote the sales.

( ) 3. By saying "different meanings, but still meanings", the author indicates that the two designers _____.

    A. were doing the same thing in different ways

    B. had different purposes in their design work

    C. explained their design work in different ways

    D. agreed with each other in most cases

( ) 4. Which of the following is an example of "planned obsolescence"?

    A. We use up our tooth paste faster than before.

    B. Designers use design to make cheap objects look valuable.

    C. The design of Braun calculator is used in iPhone.

    D. When a new Mac appears on the market, the old one becomes useless.

( ) 5. The author's purpose in the last paragraph is to tell us _____.

    A. products in the past were better designed

    B. products of today are of poor quality

    C. products of today are designed to last shorter

    D. we must love our fathers

9 **Complete the following summary with right words and expressions.**

  Industrial designers in the world fall into two traditions. Those in the United States follow in the footsteps of Raymond Loewy who made industrial design a _____. And in Europe, there is the other tradition of industrial design personified by Dieter Rams and William Morris, who view industrial design as a(n) _____. For all their apparent _____, both Loewy and Rams are in fact doing something _____—using design as a means of giving material objects _____. Loewy's design embodied the view of _____ developed by Earnest Elmo Calkins, the so-called planned obsolescence.

  We now see the two traditions _____ in the design work of Apple Inc. Designers in Apple learned the _____ developed by Rams. But at the same time, Apple has adopted the idea of planned obsolescence.

  In essence, both traditions use design to show us the objects that _____ our daily lives. What has really changed is our relationship to our possessions. They are losing their ability to _____.

10 **Discuss the following questions with the information from the text.**

1. What is the difference between Raymond Loewy and Dieter Rams?
   (*business, art*)

   _____

2. Why did William Morris refuse to enter the Crystal Palace?
   (*junk*)

   _____

3. How did the two traditions of industrial design coalesce in Apple Inc. ?
   (*taste, planned obsolescence*)

   _____

4. Why does the author keep his father's typewriter while his daughter never keeps his used laptop?

   _____

5. Do you prefer an up-to-date product that lasts shorter or an old-fashioned but long-lasting product? Why?

   _____

Vocabulary & Structure

11 **Fill in the blanks with the words given below. Change the form where necessary.**

freelance	streamline	junk	delicate	depression
seduce	desperate	redundant	interact	glimpse

1. The new assembling line will make 10% of the work-force _____.
2. Today, many people take _____ jobs for the attraction of flexibility.
3. We use the foreign language as a tool to communicate and _____ with others.
4. The economic _____ hits building industry badly.
5. He caught a _____ of her before she disappeared into the crowd.
6. The state commercial banks will be urged to improve their management systems, _____ organizational structures and staff, and to improve services.
7. The prisoners became _____ in their attempt to escape.
8. My grandfather put all broken furniture and other _____ in the attic.
9. This substance is almost undetectable with even the most _____ instruments.

10. The young officer was _____ by the offer of money into betraying his own country.

12 Complete the following sentences with phrases or expressions from the text.

1. He must have been pretty gullible to _____ that old trick

2. Cook was claimed to be the first European to _____ in Australia.

3. This machine is out of order; get a mechanic to _____ it.

4. Yellow flowers of rape always _____ my childhood in the countryside.

13 Translate the Chinese sentences into English by simulating the sentences chosen from the text.

Chosen Sentences	Simulated Translation	Chinese Sentences
Those in the United States knowingly or unknowingly try their best to *follow in the footsteps of* Raymond Loewy.		我们不可以盲目效仿国际惯例。（blindly, international practices）
But both Morris and Rams *have* a sense of good taste, and a rejection of ugliness, *in common*.		我娶了她是因为我们俩有许多共同的兴趣和爱好。（interest, hobby）
For all their apparent differences, both Loewy and Rams are in fact doing the same thing.		他虽然遇到许多挫折,可是意志仍旧那样坚强。（setback, determination）
Calkins had been determined to persuade the world to consume *its way out of* the Depression.		影星很艰难地从大群影迷中挤出去。（jostle, fans）
That is what design has always done *in one way or another*.		为抗击自然灾害,各行各业的人们以这样或那样的方式提供援助。（natural disaster, all lines of work）

14 Rewrite each sentence with the word or phrase in brackets, keeping the same meaning. The first part has been done for you.

1. There are three categories for the environmental problems.

The environmental problems _____. (fall into)

2. Wealthy Singapore and impoverished Cambodia have totally different living standard.

Living standards _____. (range from ... to)

3. The only thing the enemy could do was to surrender.

The enemy _____. (nothing but)

4. An equality before the law must be ensured among all people.

We must _____. (see to it that)

5. It was difficult for them to believe the news.

They could not _____. (bring oneself to)

Text B Skimming and Scanning

Principles of Fashion Design

(1) The principles of fashion design are not always taught, discussed in critiques or consciously employed, but they exist nonetheless. Designers may not consciously think of these principles as they work, but when something is wrong with a design, they are able to analyze the problem in terms of proportion, balance, rhythm, emphasis, or harmony (the first four principles work together to create the ultimate   5
goal of harmony). These principles are flexible, always interpreted within the context of current fashion.

Proportion

Proportion is simply the pleasing interrelationship of the size of all parts of the garment. When conceiving a style, the designer must consider how the silhouette is to   10
be divided with lines of construction or detail. These lines create new spaces, which must relate in a pleasing way. Generally, unequal proportion is more interesting than equal. Many mathematical formulas have been proposed as guidelines, but the best results come from practice in observing and analyzing good design, for standards of proportion change with fashion cycles.   15

The height and width of all parts of a design must be compared. Individual sections of a garment, such as sleeves, pockets, and collar, must all relate in size to each other as well as to the total silhouette. A jacket's length and shape must work with the length and shape of the skirt or pants.

Background space is just as important as the detail or shapes within it. A large,   20
bold shape against a plain background is dramatic. Areas broken into small shapes suggest daintiness. Therefore, smaller space divisions are used for teens and juniors and fewer divisions for dramatic evening wear. Each detail or shape within the silhouette should complement the whole.

The spacing of trimmings, pleats, and tucks must have meaning in relation to the   25
total design. Trimmings must not be too heavy or too light, too large or too small to harmonize with the space around them as well as with the feeling of the garment. Ideally, the trim on a smaller space should be narrower than the trim on a larger area.

Every line, detail, or trim changes the proportion because it breaks up the space.

30 Concepts of proportion vary with each new fashion direction. Proportion sometimes follows natural body divisions and sometimes creates its own divisions. Designers continually experiment with subtle variations in proportion, changing with the evolution in silhouette and line.

Balance

35 (2) <u>As a design principle, the term "balance" is used most often in reference to horizontal relationships, or the relationship of one side of the garment to the other.</u> A garment should look stable and not lopsided. If the design composition is the same on both sides, then the design is considered symmetrical or following the natural bisymmetry of the body, just as we have two eyes, two arms, and two legs. Symmetrical balance is the easiest, most logical way to achieve stability because it takes no experimentation. Used in most apparel, it gives a conservative feeling. Even slight deviations, when minor details such as pockets are not exactly alike on both sides, are considered approximate

Symmetrical Balance

50 symmetry. A sensitive use of fabric, rhythm, and space relationships is needed to keep a design from being boring.

To achieve a more exciting, dramatic effect, asymmetrical balance can be used. Examples are side closings and one-shouldered evening dresses. Though asymmetrical design composition is not identical on both sides of a garment, it still must be stable.

55 It is a matter not of actual weight but of visual effect. A small, unusual, eye-catching shape or concentrated detail on one side can balance a larger, less imposing area on the other side. Striking line, color, or texture can appear to balance larger masses of less significance. The means of achieving asymmetrical balance are infinite and subtle, giving the designer more freedom of expression but requiring imagination,

60 experimentation, and sensitivity. Technically, asymmetrical designs require separate pattern shapes for the right and left sides that cannot be reversed when cutting. Because of the design and technical skills required, fewer asymmetrical than symmetrical garments are produced.

Rhythm

65 Rhythm, or a sense of movement, is necessary to create interest in a design. We

can see rhythm of lines and shapes in the repetition of pleats, gathers, and tiers, and in rows of trimmings, bands, or buttons. The sense of movement must be felt, even if implicitly or subtly. There are various ways to use rhythm.

70

Graduation is the gradual increasing or decreasing of space divisions. A focal point is often created as the series comes closer and closer together. (3) <u>For examples, sequins on an evening dress can be heavily encrusted at the hem but fade in number as they travel up in garment.</u> Gathers could be full in the centre of the yoke, but diminishing towards the side. Since the eye tracks the different degrees of change through the design, graduation can be used as a way of drawing attention towards or disguising body features.

75

80

Asymmetrical Balance

Continuous line movement is often used in draped garments, whose soft fabrics hang in gathers or folds. The folds and the shadows they create make the rhythmic lines, which flow from one side to another without a distracting break.

85

In radiation, the least used rhythmic pattern, all the lines originate from a central point. This creates movement around the center, which attracts attention and becomes the focal point. A sunray-pleated skirt is a good example of this.

Emphasis

Emphasis is a dominant focal point or center of interest in a garment. It could be anything that you focus on, from a horizontal stripe, a belt, jewel, to contrasting color. This point is the central theme; the rest of the garment is of secondary importance. Such a focal point can be achieved by means of color, significant shapes, lines coming together, details, or contrast.

90

95

Garments with no focal point are weak and boring. On the other hand, there should never be more than one main center of interest. Two or more would be confusing and displeasing because the eye becomes overly stimulated. Spotty use of

100

details—especially those of equal importance, such as pockets—is distracting. Such distractions should be removed and the dominant design feature strengthened.

105 **Harmony**

Harmony is simply the condition in which all the elements and principles of design work together successfully. It is the perfect combination of fabric, color, line, and silhouette and the correct use of

110 balance, proportion, rhythm and emphasis.

(4) Consistent visual effect can be achieved while the design and its theme work together harmoniously. A beautiful design results from a well-developed theme. For example, if the theme of a design is dramatic, the

115 design should have a bold statement of line, and exaggerated silhouette, large space divisions, strong contrast of bright or dark colors, large prints and extreme textures.

Of course, there are infinite ideas in fashion design. However, the design

120 principles must be thought of in relation to the garment. Knowing how to use these principles helps you view designs objectively. They are usually the key to why a design does or doesn't work.

(1 174 words)

New Words and Expressions

nonetheless★ /ˌnʌnðə'les/ *adv.* in spite of that 尽管如此

ultimate /'ʌltɪmət/ *adj.* the highest or most significant 终极的；根本的

silhouette△ /ˌsɪlu:'et/ *n.* the outline of a solid figure （人的）整体廓形

formula /'fɔ:mjʊlə/ *n.* a group of letters, signs, or numbers expressing a general scientific law or rule 公式

guideline /'gaɪdlaɪn/ *n.* rule or instruction about how sth. should be done 指导方针；准则

daintiness△ /'deɪntɪnɪs/ *n.* the quality of being pretty and neat 娇美；俏丽

trimming△ /'trɪmɪŋ/ *n.* sth. added to the main thing, often for decoration 装饰物

harmonize with△ go together well with 与……协调

evolution /ˌi:və'lu:ʃn/ *n.* process of gradual development 渐进

stable /'steɪbl/ *adj.* not easily moved, upset, or changed 稳定的；稳固的

lopsided△ /ˌlɒp'saɪdɪd/ *adj.* with one side lower than the other 一边高一边低的

apparel△ /ə'pærəl/ *n.*　[old use]clothing [旧用法]服装

conservative /kən'sɜːvətɪv/ *adj.*　opposed to change 保守的

deviation★ /ˌdiːvɪ'eɪʃn/ *n.*　instance of turning aside or away 偏差；偏离

symmetry★ /'sɪmətrɪ/ *n.*　quality of harmony or balance between parts 对称

implicitly /ɪm'plɪsɪtlɪ/ *adv.*　without being clearly expressed 含蓄地；暗示地

sequin△ /'siːkwɪn/ *n.*　tiny metal disc used for ornament on a dress （衣服装饰）小金属圆片

encrust△ /ɪn'krʌst/ *vt.*　cover with a crust of ornamental material 覆以装饰性外层

diminish★ /dɪ'mɪnɪʃ/ *v.*　make or become less （使）减少

disguise /dɪs'gaɪz/ *vt.*　conceal 隐藏

draped△ /dreɪpt/ *adj.*　covered in folds of cloth 成褶而下垂的

theme /θiːm/ *n.*　topic 主题

consistent /kən'sɪstənt/ *adj.*　in agreement 一致的

Proper Names

symmetrical balance	对称平衡
asymmetrical balance	不对称平衡
evening dress	晚礼服
sunray-pleated skirt	阳光百褶裙

Comprehension

15 Go over the text quickly and answer the following questions. For questions 1—7, choose the best answer from the four choices; for questions 8—10, complete the sentences with the information from the text.

(　　) 1. The best proportion of a garment comes from _____.

    A. mathematical formulas

    B. the designer's experience

    C. observing and analyzing good design

    D. world's top designers

(　　) 2. Smaller space divisions are generally used in the clothes for _____.

    A. teens and juniors　　　　　　B. adults

    C. young women　　　　　　　　D. babies

(　　) 3. What is true about symmetrical balance?

    A. It does not even allow very slight differences on both sides of a garment.

    B. It still needs more experimentation to prove its stability.

    C. It refers to the vertical relationships of different parts in a garment.

D. It follows the natural bisymmetry of the body.

(　　) 4. Why do manufacturers produce more symmetrical garments than asymmetrical garments?

A. Because consumers like symmetrical garments better.

B. Because asymmetrical garments don't look stable.

C. Because asymmetrical garments are more difficult to produce.

D. Because symmetrical garments are much cheaper.

(　　) 5. Which of the following is NOT a way to use rhythm?

A. Continuous line movement.　　　　B. Division.

C. Graduation.　　　　D. Radiation.

(　　) 6. Graduation can be used to draw attention towards or disguise body features because _____.

A. eyes track changes through design　　B. eyes are stimulated by it

C. it is a dynamic process　　　　D. it is very obvious

(　　) 7. Which of the following is an example of radiation?

A. A one-shouldered evening dress.　　B. A sunray-pleated skirt

C. A draped garment.　　　　D. A jacket.

8. Two or more focal points in a garment would be confusing and displeasing because the eye _____.

9. Harmony is simply the condition in which all the elements and principles of design _____.

10. _____ can be achieved while the design and its theme work together harmoniously.

Vocabulary & Translation

16 Fill in the blanks with the words given below. Change the form where necessary.

ultimate	guideline	harmonize	evolution	stable
conservative	symmetry	diminish	disguise	consistent

1. Measures have been taken to _____ friction.

2. Bilateral _____ is almost universal among animals.

3. Hard work is the _____ source of success.

4. For _____ investors, the best choice is to buy government bonds only.

5. The cottages _____ well with the landscape in the countryside.

6. The old man remained _____ in his opposition to anything new.

7. In the course of _____, some birds have lost the power of flight.

8. The alloy, with _____ performance and low processing cost, is widely

used in industry.

9. The factory tries to _____ its failure in false statements.

10. The government has issued _____ on increase in wages and price.

17 Translate the underlined sentences in the text into Chinese.

1. The principles of fashion design are not always taught, discussed in critiques or consciously employed, but they exist nonetheless.

_____

_____

2. As a design principle, the term "balance" is used most often in reference to horizontal relationships, or the relationship of one side of the garment to the other.

_____

_____

3. For examples, sequins on an evening dress can be heavily encrusted at the hem but fade in number as they travel up in garment.

_____

_____

4. Consistent visual effect can be achieved while the design and its theme work together harmoniously.

_____

_____

Interactive Tasks

Pair Work

18 Read the sample dialogues carefully, and then complete the interactive tasks that follow.

Task 1

Sample dialogue

Peter: Hi, I already finished the design of this handle. What are your comments?

Judy: Oh, I like the shape very much. If you can replace the plastic part with copper, it will be better.

Peter: That's easy. But you know copper costs a lot. That will leave the manufacturer with little profit.

Judy: That's true. But you can turn to something cheaper. Say wood. Wood costs a little more than plastic, but looks a lot better.

Peter: I thought about wood. But wood costs almost as much as copper.

Judy: How come?

Peter: Wood is not expensive. But to make it into special shapes, you need extra equipment. That adds to the cost.

Judy: Sounds like we have to use plastic. But I still feel the handle made of plastic looks rather humble.

Peter: Don't worry. We use the ABS plastic. It looks as good as copper, and is even more resistant to force.

Judy: Oh, I see.

Interactive task

Two people are talking about a car logo which was designed by Role A.

Role A: The car logo must be silver in color.

Role B: The silver color is rather dull. Red or pink may look better.

Task 2

Sample dialogue

Clerk: Hi, lady. What kind of car are you looking for?

Linda: Well. My parents and my husband's parents like traveling with us. So, together with my own family, we always have seven people traveling together. But I can't find a proper car.

Clerk: What about our Honda Odyssey? It's big and comfortable enough to transport your big family.

Linda: Really? Let me take a look.

Clerk: Please look at the interior of the car. With three rows of seats, Odyssey is quite large inside. Who says seven people can't be seated comfortably in one car?

Linda: It looks great!

Clerk: The seats are well designed. The third-row seats can be folded into the floor with one hand. Two chairs in the second row can be moved in all directions, or removed altogether.

Linda: So I can put a lot of things inside. Is the car easy to drive?

Clerk: Odyssey has made a lot of design improvements to make driving easier. The gearshift lever is placed in the dashboard where it doesn't block cabin space and is easier to shift. Switches for operating the power doors and windows sit on a flat surface to the left of the steering wheel so they can be found without fumbling.

Linda: I think Odyssey is the perfect car for my family. Can I have a test drive now?

Clerk: Yes. Here's the key.

Interactive task

A customer is talking about an Audi car with a sales clerk.

Role A: I'm looking for a car which is comfortable and powerful enough for business use.

Role B: The Audi A8 car is good enough for business purpose. It is powered by a 3. 7 liter V8 engine and has a 6-speed automatic transmission with a manual mode. The A8 is available with standard luxury amenities, including dual-zone climate control, wood and leather interior trim, and 14-way power and heated seats.

Group Work

19 **Work in groups to design your own products.**

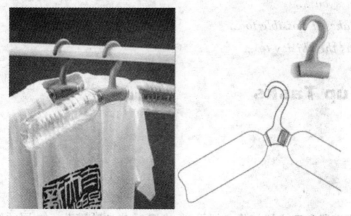

1. Form groups of 4 or 5 students.
2. Each group finds or thinks of a new product. It can be serious or silly, useful or useless. Give your product a name, draw it, and write what it does in the following chart:

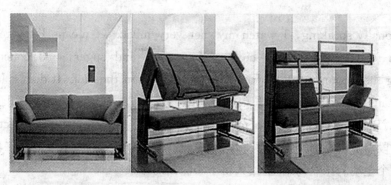

What is it called?	What does it look like?	What does it do?

3. A member of each group tells the class about the new design. Explain what it does and how it works. Use the phrases below.

It allows you to ...

It enables you to ...

It lets you ...

It makes it possible to ...

It has the ability to ...

Follow-up Tasks

Writing

结论段

　　文章的引言段和正文段好像一棵果树，春夏时节枝叶繁茂。结尾的结论段好比金秋时节的累累硕果。一个好的结尾不但给读者留下美好、深刻的印象和强有力的感染力，而且会给读者以无穷的回味和深思。结论段的长短应控制在 6 句话之内，以 4—5 句话为宜，占全文篇幅的 15%—20%。请看 1997 年考研作文题"Good Health"结论段：

　　Personally speaking, I watch my diet very much. It means I try to avoid all processed foods, avoid foods high in fat, salt, and sugar, and concentrate on increasing the amount of fresh fruits and vegetables in the diet. It does a lot of good to my health. Furthermore, I devote part of my time to doing regular physical exercises. Believe it or not, "doctor" and "medicine" never exist in my dictionary.

　　这一段写了个人的实践和感受，与第一段有联系，但又不完全重复第二段的内容，最后以一个生动的比喻句结尾，给人留下了深刻的印象。

Research Project

Work in groups of 4 or 5 students, and finish a research project based on the topic area of this unit. It involves lectures, seminars, team-based activities, individual activities, team presentation and a reflective summary.

Steps

1. Form a research group;
2. Decide on a research topic;
3. Work in groups to finish PPT slides;
4. Each member of the group gives oral presentation of his parts;
5. Hand in materials that include: Project Proposal (one for each team), Research Report (one for each team, 1 000 words), Summary (one for each person, 300 words), PPT (one for each team).

Research Methods

1. Field work: to generate the first-hand information
   - Questionnaires
   - Interviews (interpersonal, telephone, e-mail, door-to-door visit, etc.)
   - Observation
2. Desk work: to generate the second-hand information
   - Library: books and magazines
   - The Internet: Google the theme with the key words
   - Reading materials

Suggested Options

1. The history and present condition of the industrial design.
2. A study of a designer and his or her designing works.

Tips for Options

1. If you choose the first option, desk work is your major source of information. But you must also involve some first-hand information in your project. You can obtain such information with a camera or through observation of some new products.
2. For the second option, you may not necessarily choose very famous designers. Choose your own teacher or someone you know so that you can obtain first-hand information very easily.

Unit Five   Beijing Opera

Highlight

Topic area	Structure	Skills
Renowned Beijing Opera performers Performing art of Beijing Opera Development of Beijing Opera	succeed not only in ... but in ... as an old saying goes ... thus doing ... ensure that ...	Understanding performing art of Beijing Opera Discussing the history and future of Beijing Opera

Warm-up Tasks

1 **Listen to the following passage and try to fill in the missing words and expressions.**

Beijing Opera is perhaps the most (1) _____ form of theater in the world, (2) _____ singing, dialogue, pantomime, and acrobatics. The classical Beijing Opera is amazing (3) _____ it combines so many forms, which in Western drama are usually (4) _____. Some plays are comprised mainly of music and singing, while in others pantomime, battle scenes and acrobatics are given (5) _____.

When most people watch a Beijing Opera performance for the first time they are attracted by the (6) _____ with its brilliant colors, the strange wonderful (7) _____ masks as well as the rich costumes and acrobatic battles. Make-up is an (8) _____ element in shaping a character for the performer's mask can fully express a character's personality and (9) _____. A knowledgeable theatergoer can (10) _____ identify many characters by their makeup.

2 **Discuss the following questions about Beijing Opera with your partner.**

1. What do you know about the origin of Beijing Opera?
2. These days many foreigners have fallen for Beijing Opera. What do you think of this phenomenon?

Listening Tasks

Micro Listening Skills

3 You will hear six sentences. Listen carefully and fill in the missing words.

1. In addition to its presence in Mainland China, Beijing Opera has _____ to many other places.

2. Beijing Opera has enormous _____ and stars like Mei Lanfang.

3. Beijing Opera performers these days are searching for ways to attract younger _____.

4. Beijing Opera follows other traditional Chinese arts in _____ meaning, rather than accuracy.

5. The length and internal _____ of Beijing Opera plays is highly variable.

6. The form was extremely popular in the Qing Dynasty and has come to be regarded as one of the cultural _____ of China.

Dialogue

Make-up in Beijing Opera

Words & Phrases

make-up *n.*	脸谱
lead /liːd/ *n.*	角色
loyalty /ˈlɔɪəltɪ/ *n.*	忠诚
distinguish /dɪsˈtɪŋgwɪʃ/ *vt.*	辨别
clown /klaʊn/ *n.*	丑角
uprightness /ˈʌpraɪtnɪs/ *n.*	正直

4 Listen to the dialogue and choose the best answer to the following questions.

(　　) 1. Which of the following is NOT included in the four main types of character in Beijing Opera according to the conversation?

　　A. The female lead. 　　　　　　B. The clown.

　　C. The painted face. 　　　　　　D. The old lead.

(　　) 2. Which of the following is true according to the conversation?

　　A. The actress looks younger than her real age.

　　B. The actress looks older than her real age.

　　C. The actress looks as old as her real age.

　　D. The actress looks like the famous actor Mei Lanfang.

(　　) 3. How does the painted face differ the characters?

　　A. By different gestures. 　　　　B. By different voices.

　　C. By different costumes. 　　　　D. By different colors.

(　　) 4. What does the "red" on the painted face stand for?

　　A. Loyalty. 　　　　　　　　　　B. Disloyalty.

C. Uprightness.   D. Passion.

5 **Listen to the dialogue again and fill in the blanks with the information you have heard.**

1. The make-up in Beijing Opera is an _____ in itself.

2. Mei Lanfang used to play the role of a young female lead until he was _____.

3. They paint their faces in different patterns with different colors to _____.

4. The make-up seems _____ the performance.

Passage

A Foreigner Was Attracted by Beijing Opera

Words & Phrases

troupe /tru:p/ *n.*	剧团
costume /'kɒstju:m/ *n.*	服装
interpreter /ɪn'tɜ:prɪtə/ *n.*	翻译
fabled /'feɪbəld/ *adj.*	虚构的
graciously /'greɪʃəslɪ/ *adj.*	亲切地
elaborate /ɪ'læbəreɪt/ *adj.*	复杂的

6 **Listen to the passage and decide whether the following statements are true (T) or false (F).**

_____ 1. My introduction to Beijing Opera happened in 1980 when I paid my first visit to Beijing.

_____ 2. When I attended the opening night performance, the facial make-up was the only thing that attracted me.

_____ 3. At a post-performance party, I was invited to have a Chinese dinner with the performers.

_____ 4. I was glad to have an opportunity to watch performers' rehearsal backstage.

_____ 5. Li Yuanchun had been performing the role of Monkey King for less than 40 years.

7 Listen to the passage again and answer the following questions with the help of words and phrases provided below.

1. What did I do when I was invited backstage the next evening?
   (*photos*, *makeup*, *costumes*)

   _____

2. What did Li Yuanchun, the famous performer, graciously allow me to do?
   (*detail*, *process*)

   _____

3. Why did I present Mr. Li and the Beijing Opera school with some photos on my first visit to Beijing?
   (*benefit from*)

   _____

Reading Tasks

Text A Reading in Detail

Pre-reading Questions

1. What do you think of the statement that Beijing Opera is facing a crisis as young people tend to seek what is new and fashionable?
2. Which one do you prefer, Beijing Opera or pop music? Why?
3. What measures can be taken to revive Beijing Opera?

Mei Lanfang, the Great Master of Dramatic Art

Any introduction to Beijing Opera would be incomplete without mentioning Mei Lanfang. Born on October 22, 1894, in a family of Beijing Opera in Jiangsu, Mei started his training as a Beijing Opera actor at the age of eight and made his stage debut when he was 10 years old. During his stage life, he reformed the traditions of
5   the past with his own creations, shaping a style of his own and giving birth to the Mei Lanfang School. Mei's stage career spanned five decades, during which he played more than 100 female roles, ranging from emperor's concubines to female generals and goddesses. He succeeded not only in portraying each role, but in creating a role that would be the model for succeeding generations.
10   As an old Chinese saying goes, "It takes an actor ten years of work for one moment of triumph." Mei Lanfang built his legend by paying persistent efforts.

Unit Five Beijing Opera

Never denying that he was a student without great talent, Mei just strived his whole life to achieve artistic perfection through practice. His teacher once commented that Mei showed little promise due to his lack-luster eyes. To change this, he exercised them persistently by practicing gazing at the movements of an incense flame in a dark room, flying kites and staring at them drifting in a blue sky, and feeding pigeons in order to look at them soaring higher and higher until they disappeared into the clouds. Thanks to his efforts, he successfully transformed his dull peepers into a pair of bright, keen, highly expressive eyes.

As an outstanding Beijing Opera representative serving as a link between the past and the future, Mei Lanfang was a pioneer who made innovations in a abroad range of areas such as music, dressing, and performance. Mei was the first to introduce *erhu*, a two-stringed musical instrument, to the Beijing Opera orchestra. Today, more than 60 years since its debut, *erhu* has become one of the main instruments used to accompany Beijing Opera. An article in *China Culture* mentioned that Mei would also create different dances that would give audience a better insight into the character he played. In *Conqueror Xiang Yu Bids Farewell to His Concubine*, the character's bravery, grace and beauty were expressed through a sword dance. In *The Fairy Scattering Flowers*, Mei attached two long silk ribbons to his body and created a dance originating from ancient frescoes. The many dances he created form the great legacy that he left to Beijing Opera.

Highly accomplished at singing, dancing, and acting, the three main components of the traditional Chinese opera, Mei Lanfang turned himself into a performer of almost all types of the female roles and thoroughly broke the rigid distinction between *qingyi*, the graceful female, and the vivacious young female *huadan*. The *qingyi* usually walks in a sedate fashion, with one hand on her stomach and the other hanging at one side. Such a character was only asked to excel in singing, while the *huadan* was expected to show lively facial expressions and gestures. Mei Lanfang, who was adept at both, redefined female roles by combining the two perfectly. After many years of effort he enabled the *dan* to take an extremely important position in Beijing Opera, with a clear-cut role for new comers to follow and develop.

Mei Lanfang was also the first artist to introduce Beijing Opera to an overseas audience, winning international recognition and fame across the globe. He visited

countries such as Japan, the United States, and the former Soviet Union, where his
50 performance was applauded.

Mei visited Japan on three occasions where, during the first visit in 1919, he was praised as an outstanding performer of the Oriental arts. In 1930, Mei Lanfang embarked on a successful US tour. There his exotic but exquisite performances fascinated both public and academic circles, making them realize that Beijing Opera
55 was a theatrical form of great literary and artistic value. Despite the Great Depression, the tickets for the week-long performances were sold out in three days. Mei's performances were truly a great success. Drama critic Justin Brooks Atkinson[1] once wrote in the *New York Times*: "You may feel yourself vaguely in contact, not with the sensation of the moment, but with the strange ripeness of centuries." Mei
60 received two honorary doctorates from the University of Southern California and Pomona College, making him the first operatic doctor in Chinese history. American art critics hailed him, commenting that east is east, west is west, but the twins, which had never met before were perfectly combined in Mei
65 Lanfang's performance. Five years later, Mei Lanfang had another stage success in the former Soviet Union, where he won the praise of such dramatic masters as Stanislavsky[2] and Meyerhold[3].

Throughout his life Mei Lanfang made
70 outstanding contributions in promoting cultural exchanges between China and foreign countries. The performing art of the Chinese traditional theatre represented by Mei Langfang is now recognized as one of the three world
75 contemporary main systems of performing art.

Mei Lanfang had been a patriot all through his life and is highly respected by the people. When the Japanese invaded China, Mei Langfang was trapped in the district occupied

---

① Justin Brooks Atkinson (1894—1984): American theater critic. He worked for *The New York Times* from 1925 to 1960.

② Stanislavsky (1863—1938): Russian actor and theater director. He made great contribution to modern European and American realistic acting.

③ Meyerhold (1874—1940): Russian theater director, actor and theatrical producer. His provocative experiments dealing with physical being and symbolism in an unconventional theater setting made him one of the seminal forces in modern theater.

by the enemy. The commander of Japanese army ordered him to perform for them and appointed him to a high rank official position. With righteousness, Mei refused the temptation and threat from the enemy and grew a moustache to show his ideal, thus enduring an impoverished life until the war ended in 1945.

Age was never a barrier for Mei Lanfang. Even in his 60s, he could still play a female warrior. Right up until the time of his death, he managed to preserve the splendor of his art, playing roles with the same vitality he did as a young man.

80

85

90

For a century, Mei Lanfang was a household name in China. His most enduring legacy was his son and disciple Mei Baojiu, who reinterpreted his father's roles and ensured that the Mei Lanfang School would thrive for another generation.

(1 016 words)

New Words and Expressions

debut▲ /'deɪbuː/ n.   a person's first appearance or performance in a particular capacity or role 崭露头角

give birth to   initiate; give rise to 引起；产生

span /spæn/ vt.   extend across (a period of time)持续(一段时间)

range /reɪndʒ/ vi.   vary or extend between specified limits(在一定幅度或范围内)变动

concubine△ /'kɒŋkjʊˌbaɪn/ n.   a woman who lives with a man but has lower status than his wife or wives 妾；姨太太

goddess△ /'gɒdɪs/ n.   a female deity 女神

portray★ /pɔː'treɪ/ vt.   depict (sb. or sth.) in a work of art or literature 描述；刻画

triumph /'traɪəmf/ n.   the state of being victorious or successful 获胜；成功

strive★ /straɪv/ vt.   make great efforts to achieve or obtain sth. 努力

promise /'prɒmɪs/ n.   the quality of potential excellence 前途

incense▲ /'ɪnsens/ n.   a gum, spice, or other substance that is burned for the sweet smell it produces 香

soar /sɔː/ vi.   fly or rise high in the air 高飞；翱翔

thanks to△   as a result of; due to 幸亏;因为

transform /træns'fɔːm/ *vt.*   make a thorough or dramatic change in the form, appearance, or character of 改变

peeper△ /'piːpə/ *n.*   a person's eyes 眼睛

representative /ˌreprɪ'zentətɪv/ *n.*   an example of a class or group 代表

innovation★ /ˌɪnəʊ'veɪʃən/ *n.*   the action or process of innovating 革新

instrument /'ɪnstrʊmənt/ *n.*   a tool or implement 仪器

orchestra /'ɔːkɪstrə/ *n.*   a group of instrumentalists 乐队

insight /'ɪnsaɪt/ *n.*   the capacity to gain an accurate and deep intuitive understanding of a person or thing 洞察力

fresco△ /'freskəʊ/ *n.*   a painting done on a wall or ceiling 壁画

legacy▲ /'legəsɪ/ *n.*   an amount of money or property left to someone in a will 遗产

accomplished△ /ə'kɒmplɪʃt/ *adj.*   highly trained or skilled in a particular activity 技术娴熟的

rigid /'rɪdʒɪd/ *adj.*   not able to be changed or adapted 僵化的

distinction /dɪs'tɪŋkʃən/ *n.*   a difference or contrast between similar things or people 不同;差异

vivacious△ /vɪ'veɪʃəs/ *adj.*   (especially of a woman) attractively lively and animated (尤指妇女)活泼的

sedate△ /sɪ'deɪt/ *adj.*   calm, dignified, and unhurried 稳重的

excel▲ /ɪk'sel/ *vi.*   be exceptionally good at or proficient in an activity or subject 擅长

gesture /'dʒestʃə/ *n.*   an action performed to convey one's feelings or intentions 姿态

be adept at△   be good at 擅长

combine /kəm'baɪn/ *vt.*   unite; merge 结合

clear-cut△ /'klɪə'kʌt/ *adj.*   sharply defined; easy to perceive or understand 轮廓清晰的

recognition /ˌrekəg'nɪʃən/ *n.*   acknowledgement of sth's existence, validity, or legality 承认;认可

applaud /ə'plɔːd/ *vt.*   show strong approval of; praise 表示强烈赞同;赞扬

embark on△   begin (a course of action) 开始从事

exotic★ /ɪg'zɒtɪk/ *adj.*   originating in or characteristic of a distant foreign country 具有异国情调的

exquisite★ /'ekskwɪzɪt/ *adj.*   extremely beautiful and, typically, delicate 优美的;精致的

academic /ˌækəˈdemɪk/ *adj.*   of or relating to education and scholarship 学术的

vaguely /ˈveɪɡlɪ/ *adv.*   uncertainly 含糊地；不明确地

doctorate▲ /ˈdɒktərɪt/ *n.*   the highest degree awarded by a university faculty or other approved educational organization 博士学位

operatic△ /ˌɒpəˈrætɪk/ *adj.*   characteristic of opera 歌剧的

represent /ˌreprɪˈzent/ *vt.*   be a specimen or example of；typify 代表

patriot★ /ˈpeɪtrɪət/ *n.*   a person who vigorously supports his country and is prepared to defend it against enemies or detractors 爱国者

invade /ɪnˈveɪd/ *vt.*   （an armed force）enter（a country or region）so as to subjugate or occupy it（指军队）入侵

trap /træp/ *vt.*   have（sth.）held tightly by sth. so that it cannot move or be freed（尤指身体某部位等）被卡住

appoint /əˈpɔɪnt/ *vt.*   assign a job or role to（sb.）任命

righteousness△ /ˈraɪtʃəsnɪs/ *n.*   being morally right 正直

temptation /tempˈteɪʃən/ *n.*   a desire to do sth. ，especially sth. wrong or unwise 诱惑

endure /ɪnˈdjʊə/ *vt.*   suffer（sth. painful or difficult）patiently 忍耐（痛苦，困难）

impoverished△ /ɪmˈpɒvərɪʃt/ *adj.*   poor 穷困的

barrier /ˈbærɪə/ *n.*   a fence or other obstacle that prevents movement or access 障碍物

splendor△ /ˈsplendə/ *n.*   magnificent and splendid appearance 光辉

vitality△ /vaɪˈtælɪtɪ/ *n.*   the state of being strong and active；energy 生动性；活力

disciple△ /dɪˈsaɪpəl/ *n.*   a follower or pupil of a teacher，leader，or philosophy 学生

thrive /θraɪv/ *vi.*   prosper；flourish 繁荣；旺盛

Proper Names

Justin Brooks Atkinson /ˈdʒʌstɪn brʊks ˈætkɪnz/ 　贾斯丁·布鲁克斯·阿特金森（人名）

Stanislavsky /ˌstænɪsˈlɑːvskɪ/ 　斯坦尼斯拉夫斯基（人名）

Meyerhold /ˈmaɪəˌhəʊld/ 　梅耶荷德（人名）

Comprehension

8 **Choose the best answer to each question with the information from the text.**

(　　) 1. According to the first paragraph, which of the following is NOT true?

A. Mei Lanfang set up a school to train students.

        B. Mei Lanfang made his stage debut in 1904.

        C. Mei Lanfang shaped a style of his own.

        D. Mei Lanfang played many female roles in his stage career.

(   ) 2. Mei Lanfang's great achievement mainly resulted from _____.

        A. his unique insight into Beijing Opera

        B. his teacher's instruction

        C. his great talent

        D. his persistent practice

(   ) 3. Mei Lanfang made innovations in a abroad range of areas except _____.

        A. introducing *erhu* to Beijing Opera

        B. creating dances to portray roles

        C. breaking the rigid distinction between *qingyi* and *huadan*

        D. emphasizing facial expressions

(   ) 4. Traditionally, *qingyi* was only asked to _____.

        A. be good at singing

        B. show lively facial expressions

        C. show lively gestures

        D. walk in a vivacious fashion

(   ) 5. As for Mei Lanfang's overseas performance, which of the following is NOT true?

        A. It was fascinated by public but criticized by academic circles.

        B. It was hailed by American critics.

        C. It promoted cultural exchanges.

        D. It made him the first operatic doctor in Chinese history.

9 Complete the following summary with right words and expressions.

    Mei Lanfang was born in a family of Beijing Opera in Taizhou, Jiangsu Province. He started his training as a Beijing Opera actor at the age of eight and made his stage _____ when he was 10 years old. During his five-decade stage career, Mei played more than 100 female roles which ranged from emperor's _____ to female _____ and goddesses. As a student without great talent, Mei built his legend by paying persistent efforts. Mei Lanfang made _____ in a broad range of areas such as music, dressing and performing skill in Beijing Opera. He turned himself into a performer of almost all types of the female roles and thoroughly broke the rigid _____ between *qingyi* and *huadan*. After many years of effort he enabled the Dan to take an extremely important position in Beijing Opera, with a _____ role for new comers to inherit and develop. Mei was also the first artist to introduce Beijing Opera to an overseas audience. Mei's performances were truly a great success in numerous countries like Japan, U. S. and the former Soviet Union, where he won international _____ and fame. Mei Lanfang had been a _____ all through his life and is highly respected by the people. Age was never a _____ for Mei Lanfang and he always managed to preserve the splendor of his art. His son Mei Baojiu ensured that the Mei Lanfang School would _____ for another generation.

10 **Discuss the following questions with the information from the text.**

1. What are Mei Lanfang's main contributions to the performing art of Beijing Opera?

   (*reform, shape, give birth to*)

   _____

2. How did Mei Lanfang successfully transform his dull peepers into a pair of bright, keen, highly expressive eyes?

   (*persistent efforts*)

   _____

3. How did Mei Lanfang redefine female roles in Beijing Opera?

   (*break, combine*)

   _____

4. What effect did Mei Lanfang's overseas performance produce?

   (*recognition, fame*)

   _____

5. What do you think of the future of the Mei Lanfang School?

   _____

Vocabulary & Structure

11 **Fill in the blanks with the words given below. Change the form where necessary.**

strive	transform	innovation	attach	originate
accomplished	applaud	represent	appoint	thrive

1. He came to the Britain in 1976, already _____ in the English language.
2. The university constantly _____ for excellence in its teaching and research.
3. The decision to save the company has been warmly _____ by the board.
4. He seems to have been miraculously _____ into a first-class player in NBA.
5. A business is unlikely to _____ without good management.
6. For purposes of litigation, an infant must be _____ by an adult.

7. She believed she had come up with one of the greatest _____ of modern times.

8. The newly-released film _____ from a short story.

9. He was _____ director of human resources department.

10. He made certain that the trailer was securely _____ to the van.

⓲ Complete the following sentences with phrases or expressions from the text.

1. The scientist's experiments _____ a new treatment.

2. I stopped the car very quickly _____ the good brakes.

3. One whose Chinese is poor usually finds it difficult to _____ English.

4. Therefore, in order to achieve modernization, we must _____ learning from other countries.

5. He is about to _____ a new business venture.

⓳ Translate the Chinese sentences into English by simulating the sentences chosen from the text.

Chosen Sentences	Simulated Translation	Chinese Sentences
Any introduction to Beijing Opera *would be incomplete without mentioning* Mei Lanfang.		不涉及过去十年的统计数据，这些记录是不完整的。（statistics, incomplete）
He succeeded *not only* in portraying each role, *but* in creating a role that would be the model for succeeding generations.		他不仅事业有成，而且在家庭生活方面也很出色。（career, family life）
As an old Chinese saying goes, "It takes an actor ten years of work for one moment of triumph."		正如俗话说的那样，诚实为上策。（best policy）
With righteousness, Mei refused the temptation and threat from the enemy and grew a moustache to show his ideal, *thus enduring* an impoverished life until the war ended in 1945.		他有责任感，因此成为了组织的领导。（sense of responsibility）
His most enduring legacy was his son and disciple Mei Baojiu, who reinterpreted his father's roles and *ensured that* the Mei Lanfang School would thrive for another generation.		我们与专家协作以确保统一的设计能贯穿整个开发过程。（cooperatively, a cohesive design）

14 **Rewrite each sentence with the word or phrase in brackets, keeping the same meaning. The first part has been done for you.**

1. His stage career began in 1945 and ended in 1964, lasting for nearly 20 years.

    His stage career _____. (span)

2. The organization offers free help to young people between the ages of 11 and 18.

    The organization offers free help to young people _____

    _____. (range)

3. For all your quality of potential excellence in music, your lack of practice is keeping you back.

    You _____ but your lack of practice is keeping you back. (promise)

4. They made the research in order to have an accurate and deep understanding of labor market processes.

    The objective of their research is to _____. (insight)

5. People still have the right to pursue their happiness when they are aged.

    _____ in one's pursuit of happiness. (barrier)

Text B   *Skimming and Scanning*

Beijing Opera, the Quintessence of Chinese Culture

Among the hundreds of forms of opera throughout China, Beijing Opera has the greatest influence and is therefore regarded as a national form. The accompanying music, singing and costumes are all fascinating and artistic. (1) Full of Chinese cultural facts, the opera presents to the audience an encyclopedia of Chinese culture as well as unfolding stories, beautiful paintings, exquisite costumes, graceful gestures and acrobatic fighting.   5

Beijing Opera was born when the "Four Great Anhui Troupes" brought Anhui opera, or what is now called Huiju, to Beijing in 1790, for the birthday of the Qianlong Emperor. Beijing Opera was originally staged for the court and came into the public later. In 1828, some famous Hubei troupes came to Beijing. They often   10 jointly performed in the stage with Anhui troupes. The combination gradually formed Beijing Opera's main melodies.

Beijing Opera is not actually a monolithic form, but rather a combination of many

older forms. However, the new form also introduced its own innovations. The vocal
15　requirements for all of the major roles were greatly reduced for Beijing Opera.
Perhaps most noticeably, true acrobatic elements were introduced with Beijing Opera.
The form grew in popularity throughout the 19th century and the Anhui troupes
reached their peak of excellence. Beginning in 1884, the Empress Dowager Cixi
became a regular patron of Beijing Opera. The popularity of Beijing Opera has been
20　attributed to the simplicity of the form, with only a few voices and singing patterns.

Beijing Opera was initially an exclusively male pursuit. The Qianlong Emperor
had banned all female performers in Beijing in 1772. The appearance of women on the
stage began unofficially during the 1870s. Female performers began to impersonate
male roles and declared equality with men. (2) By 1894, the first commercial venue
25　showcasing female performance troupes appeared in Shanghai, encouraging other
female troupes to form, which gradually increased in popularity.

Beijing Opera performers utilize four main skills. The first two are song and
speech. The third is dance-acting including pure dance, pantomime, and all other
types of dance. The final skill is combat played by both acrobatics and fighting with
30　all manner of weaponry.

Beijing Opera follows other traditional Chinese arts in emphasizing meaning,
rather than accuracy. The highest aim of performers is to put beauty into every
motion. Indeed, performers are strictly criticized for lacking beauty during training.
Additionally, performers are taught to create a synthesis between the different aspects
35　of Beijing Opera. The four skills of Beijing Opera are not separate, but rather should
be combined in a single performance. One skill may take precedence at certain
moments during a play, but this does not mean that other actions should cease. Much
attention is paid to tradition in the art form, and gestures, settings, music, and
character types are determined by long held convention. In other words, symbolism
40　prevails in Beijing Opera. The stage of Beijing Opera knows no limit in space or time.

It can be the setting for any action. For example, walking in a large circle always symbolizes traveling a long distance, and a character straightening his or her costume and headdress means that an important character is about to speak.

The character roles in Beijing Opera are divided into four main types according to the sex, age, social status, and profession of the character. *Sheng* refers to male roles. *Sheng* is subdivided into *laosheng* (middle-aged or old men), *xiaosheng* (young men)and *wusheng* (men with martial skills). *Dan* refers to female roles. Like *sheng*, *dan* is also subdivided into various types. *Qingyi* is a woman with a strict moral code; *huadan* is a vivacious young woman; *wudan* is a woman with martial skills and *laodan* is an elderly woman. *Jing* refers to the roles with painted faces. They are usually warriors, heroes, statesmen, or even demons. *Jing* can be further divided into *wenjing* (civilian type) and *wujing* (warrior type). *Chou*, or clown, is a comic character and can be recognized at first sight for his special make-up (a patch of white paint on his nose). Usually, white patches of varying shapes and sizes are used to further distinguish roles of different character. These clowns are definitely not rascals, and in most cases they play roles of wit, alertness, and humor. It is these characters who keep the audience laughing, and improvise quips at the right moments to ease tension in some serious plays.

45

50

55

In Bejing opera, facial painting shows the characer's age, profession and personality by using different colors. Each color symbolizes a certain characteristic: red for loyalty and uprightness, black for a rough, stern or honest nature, yellow for rashness and fieriness, white for a cunning and deceitful character, gold and silver for gods and demons. In Beijing Opera, over one thousand painted facial patterns are used. Each pattern lies in his ability to make subtle and interesting changes within the fixed facial pattern.

60

65

The costumes in Beijing Opera impress the audience with their bright colors and

magnificent embroidery. Some of the costumes used in the present performances have a resemblance to the fashion of the Ming Dynasty. Due to the scarcity of props in Beijing Opera, costumes take on added importance. The use of colors indicate different
70 social status: yellow for the imperial family, red for high nobility, red or blue for upright men, white for old officials, and black for each role. A student usually wears a blue gown, a general wears padded armor, and an emperor wears a dragon robe. Besides exquisite clothes and headdresses, jewelry girdles for men and hair ornaments for women are also used in Beijing Opera. (3) Shoes may be high or low soled, the
75 former being worn by characters of high rank, and the latter by characters of low rank or acrobatic characters.

During the second half of the 20th century, Beijing Opera witnessed a steady decline in audience numbers. This has been attributed both to a decrease in performance quality and an inability of the traditional opera form to capture modern
80 life. Furthermore, the archaic language of Beijing Opera required productions to utilize electronic subtitles, which prevented the development of the form. The influence of Western culture has also left the younger generations impatient with the

slow pacing of Beijing Opera. In response, Beijing Opera began to see reform starting in the 1980s. (4) <u>Such reforms have taken the form of creating a school of performance theory to increase performance quality</u>, utilizing modern elements to <u>attract new audiences, and performing new plays outside of the tradition.</u> With such reforms, Beijing Opera is expected to revive in the 21st century.

(1 117 words)

New Words and Expressions

quintessence△/kwɪnˈtesəns/ *n.*　the aspect of sth. regarded as the intrinsic and central constituent of its character 精髓

encyclopedia▲/enˌsaɪkləʊˈpiːdjə/ *n.*　a book giving information on many subjects 百科全书

acrobatic△/ˌækrəˈbætɪk/ *adj.*　performing, involving, or adept at spectacular gymnastic feats 杂技的

melody★/ˈmelədɪ/ *n.*　a sequence of single notes that is musically satisfying 曲调

monolithic△/ˌmɒnəˈlɪθɪk/ *adj.*　large, powerful 庞大的；大一统的

vocal★/ˈvəʊkəl/ *adj.*　of or relating to the human voice 声音的；嗓音的

patron★/ˈpeɪtrən/ *n.*　a customer, especially a regular one 顾客（尤指老主顾）

attribute to　regard sth. as being caused by 把……归因于

initially /ɪˈnɪʃəlɪ/ *adv.*　at first 最初；开始

exclusively /ɪksˈkluːsɪvlɪ/ *adv.*　to the exclusion of others；only；solely 仅仅；专门地

impersonate△/ɪmˈpɜːsəˌneɪt/ *vt.*　pretend to be (another person) as entertainment 扮演；模仿

commercial /kəˈmɜːʃəl/ *adj.*　concerned with or engaged in commerce 商业的

venue△/ˈvenjuː/ *n.*　the place where sth. happens, especially an organized event 举办地点；举办场所

utilize /ˈjuːtɪlaɪz/ *vt.*　make practical and effective use of 利用

pantomime△/ˈpæntəˌmaɪm/ *n.*　a dramatic entertainment in which performers express meaning through gestures 哑剧；童话剧

combat /ˈkɒmbət/ *vt.*　take action to reduce, destroy, or prevent (sth. bad or undesirable) 与……战斗

synthesis★/ˈsɪnθɪsɪs/ *n.*　combination or composition 综合

precedence△/ˈpresɪdəns/ *n.* the condition of being considered more important than sb. or sth. else 优先权

symbolism△/ˈsɪmbəlɪzəm/ *n.* symbolic meaning attributed to natural objects or facts 象征意义

prevail /prɪˈveɪl/ *vi.* prove more powerful than opposing forces 占优势

symbolize△ /ˈsɪmbəˌlaɪz/ *vt.* be a symbol of 象征

straighten△ /ˈstreɪtn/ *vt.* make tidy or put in order again 整理；清理

headdress△ /ˈheddres/ *n.* an ornamental covering or band for the head 头饰

martial▲ /ˈmɑːʃəl/ *adj.* warlike 战争的；尚武的

statesman★ /ˈsteɪtsmən/ *n.* a skilled, experienced, and respected political leader or figure 政治家

demon△ /ˈdiːmən/ *n.* a cruel, evil, or destructive person 恶棍

comic /ˈkɒmɪk/ *adj* causing or meant to cause laughter 滑稽的

wit /ˈwɪt/ *n.* keen intelligence 才智

alertness△ /əˈlɜːtnɪs/ *n.* the state of being watchful for possible danger 警惕

improvise△ /ˈɪmprəˌvaɪz/ *vt.* create and perform (music, drama, or verse) without preparation 即席创作表演

quip△ /ˈkwɪp/ *n.* a witty remark 妙语；俏皮话

rashness△ /ˈræʃnɪs/ *n.* a lack of careful consideration of the possible consequences of an action 轻率，莽撞

fieriness△ /ˈfaɪərɪnɪs/ *n.* a passionate, quick-tempered nature 激情；脾气火爆

deceitful△ /dɪˈsiːtfʊl/ *adj.* deceiving or misleading others 欺诈的

subtle /ˈsʌtl/ *adj.* so delicate or precise as to be difficult to analyse or describe 微妙的；难以描述的

magnificent /mæɡˈnɪfɪsənt/ *adj.* impressively beautiful, elaborate 华丽的

embroidery▲ /ɪmˈbrɔɪdərɪ/ *n.* the art or pastime of embroidering cloth 刺绣；绣花

resemblance★ /rɪˈzembləns/ *n.* the state of resembling or being alike 相似；相像

scarcity△ /ˈskeəsɪtɪ/ *n.* insufficiency for the demand 缺乏；不足

imperial /ɪmˈpɪərɪəl/ *adj.* of or relating to an emperor 皇帝的

gown /ɡaʊn/ *n.* a long dress worn on formal occasions 长礼服

girdle△ /ˈɡɜːdl/ *n.* a belt or cord worn round the waist 腰带；腰绳

ornament /ˈɔːnəmənt/ *n.* a thing used or serving to adorn sth. but usually having no practical purpose 装饰品

witness /ˈwɪtnɪs/ *vt.* see (an event) take place 目击

subtitle△ /ˈsʌbˌtaɪtl/ *n.* captions displayed at the bottom of a cinema or television screen that translate or transcribe the dialogue or narrative 字幕

Comprehension

15 Go over the text quickly and answer the following questions. For questions 1—7, choose the best answer from the four choices; for questions 8—10, complete the

sentences with the information from the text.

(　　) 1. Among the hundreds of forms of opera throughout China, Beijing Opera is regarded as a national form due to its _____.

    A. most enormous influence   B. longest history

    C. largest audience   D. unique performing skills

(　　) 2. The most striking innovation that Beijing Opera introduced was _____.

    A. graceful gestures   B. acrobatic elements

    C. facial paintings   D. exquisite costumes

(　　) 3. The popularity of Beijing Opera has resulted from _____.

    A. its simple form   B. its monolithic form

    C. the court's appreciation   D. its acrobatic fighting

(　　) 4. According to paragraph 6, which of the following is NOT true?

    A. Beauty is highly valued in Beijing Opera.

    B. The four skills of Beijing Opera are usually separate in a single performance.

    C. The stage of Beijing Opera can be the setting for any action.

    D. Meaning, rather than accuracy, has the priority in Beijing Opera.

(　　) 5. The roles in Beijing Opera fall into four main types according to _____.

    A. the sex, age, educational background, and personality of the character

    B. the sex, age, marital status, and profession of the character

    C. the sex, age, personality, and profession of the character

    D. the sex, age, social position, and profession of the character

(　　) 6. Clowns can be further distinguished through _____.

    A. costumes they wear

    B. patches of varying colors and shapes on their noses

    C. white patches of different shapes and sizes on their noses

    D. patches of varying colors and sizes on their noses

(　　) 7. Costumes are vital in Beijing Opera because _____.

    A. props are scarce

    B. they have bright colors and magnificent embroidery

    C. they indicate roles' personality

    D. they reflect the fashion of some dynasty

    8. Different colors of costumes in Beijing Opera suggest _____.

    9. The influence of imported culture has made the younger generations ____

    _____.

   10. Some reforms have been made to help Beijing Opera _____

    _____.

Vocabulary & Translation

16 **Fill in the blanks with the words given below. Change the form where necessary.**

exclusively	utilize	precedence	prevail	symbolize
improvise	deceitful	magnificent	scarcity	witness

1. He _____ a song about the baseball team's victory.

2. The needs of the patient take _____ over those of the doctor.

3. Easter eggs _____ the renewal of life.

4. The past decade has _____ a sharp increase in the scope of the electronic media.

5. The film star has a ski slope reserved _____ for him.

6. The interior layout of the palace is _____.

7. The _____ of fresh water is worrying the explorer.

8. A _____ peace is more hurtful than an open war.

9. Visitors are interested in the custom _____ over the whole area.

10. The hostess will _____ the leftover ham bone to make soup.

17 **Translate the underlined sentences in the text into Chinese.**

1. Full of Chinese cultural facts, the opera presents to the audience an encyclopedia of Chinese culture as well as unfolding stories, beautiful paintings, exquisite costumes, graceful gestures and acrobatic fighting.

_____

_____

2. By 1894, the first commercial venue showcasing female performance troupes appeared in Shanghai, encouraging other female troupes to form, which gradually increased in popularity.

_____

_____

3. Shoes may be high or low soled, the former being worn by characters of high rank, and the latter by characters of low rank or acrobatic characters.

_____

_____

4. Such reforms have taken the form of creating a school of performance theory to increase performance quality, utilizing modern elements to attract new audiences, and performing new plays outside of the tradition.

_____

_____

Interactive Tasks

Pair Work

18 Read the sample dialogues carefully, and then complete the interactive tasks that follow.

Task 1

Sample dialogue

James: I went to see Beijing Opera last night. It's fantastic!

Li Hao: That's great. What repertoire did you see?

James: I don't remember the name of it. But the story is about a defeated king and his concubine who killed herself.

Li Hao: That must be *The King Bid Farewell to His Concubine*.

James: That's it! It's really a moving story.

Li Hao: It is amazing that you can understand Beijing Opera.

James: Thanks. Actually, I understand it with the help of English lines shown beside the stage.

Li Hao: Of course you need translations. As a Chinese, I cannot make out what performers are singing all the time.

James: That's for sure. However, without translation, I can also enjoy the beautiful facial paintings and costumes, and the wonderful acrobatics.

Li Hao: You bet.

Interactive task

A Chinese and a foreigner are talking over a Beijing Opera show. It seems that the foreigner falls in love with Beijing Opera and manages to understand it.

Role A: Beijing Opera is so enchanting. I want an opportunity to learn something further about it.

Role B: There is a selective course, which may help you understand Beijing Opera better.

Task 2

Sample dialogue

Li Na: Diana, Have you ever seen a Beijing Opera?

Diana: Of course. Beijing Opera is kind of a symbol of Chinese culture. I suppose every foreigner would manage to see one.

Li Na: Definitely. What do you think of Beijing Opera?

Diana: Well, it is a fascinating art and at the same time an abstract art.

Li Na: So it is. Beijing Opera synthesizes music, drama, dancing, and acrobatics along with very elaborate costumes and a minimum of props, according to traditions and customs dating back as far as the twelfth century.

Diana: Oh, I don't know that! You guys are lucky to have such wonderful heritage.

Li Na: Yes, we are. But there are not many fans of Beijing Opera left. Many people are worried about its future.

Diana: That is a common problem for all classic arts across the globe. But I believe there will always be some people who like it and pass it on to the next generation.

Li Na: So do I. Listen, let's go to see a Beijing Opera together some time!

Diana: That's a great idea!

Interactive task

A Chinese and his foreign friend are talking over Beijing Opera and its future.

Role A: It is difficult to find young people these days with an enthusiasm for Beijing Opera.

Role B: That is a common problem for all classic arts across the globe. Beijing Opera won't die.

Group Work

19 **Work in groups to design your own interview.**

In an interview on TV, one or two renowned Beijing Opera performers, an art critic and a host hold a discussion on what measures will be taken to revive Beijing Opera.

1. Form groups of 3 or 4 students.

2. Each group finds some measures as to how to revive Beijing Opera. Fill in the following chart first.

What is the measure?	Why do you propose such a measure?	What problem does it solve?

3. A member of each group tells the class about the measure.

4. All groups share the measures proposed by other groups and play the interview in front of the whole class.

Follow-up Tasks

Writing

段落展开的方法

引言段展开的方法

引言段是文章的开头部分,一般都开门见山、直截了当地引出主题句,然后根据文章的体裁特点,用不同的方法展开。引言段不宜过长,以免冲淡主题。引言段展开的方法主要有以下五种。

1. 开门见山,直截了当提出观点,用简洁的语言直陈主题,吸引读者注意力。请看 2001 年研究生入学考试作文题"Love Is a Bright Lamp in Darkness" 引言段:

Love Is a Bright Lamp in Darkness

Among all the worthy feelings of mankind, love is probably the noblest. It is of the utmost importance to the human beings. As is depicted in the picture, a lamp in the darkness seems very bright. And love is just a lamp that is brighter in darker places. People in darker places need more light than ordinary people. Maybe just a thread of light will call forth their strength and courage to step out of their difficulties.

文中开门见山地提出,"在人类所有珍贵的情感中,爱是最高贵的"。

2. 描写背景,引入主题。例如:

Mysteries of Migration

Winter weather comes with its extreme coldness and low supply of food. Since most animals cannot survive in it, they either sleep through it or migrate.

文章一开头就用冬天的严寒和食物的短缺为背景,引出主题思想:动物的冬眠与移栖。

3. 提出问题,引起思考。提出与主题相关的问题,激发读者的兴趣,然后自问自答地来阐明主题。请看六级 1996 年 1 月作文题"Why I Take the College English Test Band 6" 引言段:

Why I Take the College English Test Band 6

Why do I take the CET-6? First of all, I like the challenge. Secondly, passing

CET-6 can stimulate me to study English harder so as to improve my English. Finally, I'm very interested in English, and I never give up any chance like this. In one word, taking CET-6 brings me only good.

上面这一段第一句就向读者提出问题：我为什么要参加大学英语六级考试？从而引起读者的思考，然后自问自答地阐明自己的观点。这样的展开段落方式，将会给读者留下无穷的回味。

4. 强调主题思想的重要性。例如：

Friendship

One of life's pleasures is friendship. And one of life's sorrows is the loss of such relationship. There are three common causes for lost friendship: betrayal, boredom, and distance.

上段中作者一上来就点名全文主题，引人入胜，以达到一笔破题的目的，然后在下文中再围绕这一主题进行发挥，加以详细描述、分析、论证。

5. 叙事入手，引出主题。例如：

What Causes Waves

Waves are beautiful to look at, but they can destroy ships at sea, as well as houses and buildings near the shore. What causes waves? Most waves are caused by winds blowing over the surface of the water. The sun heats the earth, causing the air to rise and the winds to blow. The winds blow across the sea, pushing little waves into bigger and bigger ones.

上文从叙述"大海中的波浪看起来美丽、壮观，但当它发起怒来会翻船、倒屋、令人可畏"为开端，引出主题 What causes waves，然后提出"波浪的形成是风吹日晒的结果"的看法。

写引言段应避免的问题

良好的开端是成功的一半，古人把文章的开端比喻为"凤头"，可见开端的重要性。大多数考生都希望通过写好开篇段落，给阅卷人以良好的印象，吸引住他们的注意力。但是，在具体的写作中，开头似乎很难。上文已介绍了几种常见的开端法，不过实际写作时要因人而异、因题而异，最聪明的做法最好是开门见山，直接切题，少兜圈子，少说废话。具体应避免以下四种：(1) 开头离题太远，(2) 抱歉或埋怨，(3) 内容空泛无物，(4) 不言自明的陈述。

另外，引言段一定要考虑文章的读者，确定用什么语气，选择何种表达方式，用正式用语还是非正式用语等。

Research Project

Work in groups of 4 or 5 students, and finish a research project based on the topic area of this unit. It involves lectures, seminars, team-based activities, individual activities, team presentation and a reflective summary.

Steps

1. Form a research group;
2. Decide on a research topic;
3. Work in groups to finish PPT slides;
4. Each member of the group gives oral presentation of his parts;
5. Hand in materials that include: Project Proposal (one for each team), Research Report (one for each team, 1 000 words), Summary (one for each person, 300 words), PPT (one for each team).

Research Methods

1. Field work: to generate the first-hand information
   - Questionnaires
   - Interviews (interpersonal, telephone, e-mail, door-to-door visit, etc.)
   - Observation
2. Desk work: to generate the second-hand information
   - Library: books and magazines
   - The Internet: Google the theme with the key words
   - Reading materials

Suggested Options

1. An investigation on university students' attitude to Beijing Opera.
2. An introduction to a renowned Beijing Opera performer.

Tips for Options

1. If you choose to investigate university students' attitude to Beijing Opera, firstly you need to work out a questionnaire. Then, hand them out and collect the data. Meanwhile, you are encouraged to have some interviews with your schoolmates.
2. If you try to introduce a renowned Beijing Opera performer, you need to seek relevant information on the Internet. Your introduction may cover the performer's performing style, classical repertoire, etc.

Unit Six Movie

Highlight

Topic area	Structure	Skills

International movie stars
New technology employed
  in producing *Avatar*
Stages in movie production
	be supposed to do ...
	indicate that ...
	be prior to
	make it possible for someone
	  to do ...
		Understanding the process of movie
		  production
		Discussing the elements in movie
		  industry

Warm-up Tasks

1 **Listen to the following passage and try to fill in the missing words and expressions.**

Film encompasses individual motion pictures, the field of film as a (n) (1) _____ , and the motion picture industry. Films are produced by recording (2) _____ from the world with cameras, or by creating images with animation techniques or visual (3) _____ .

Films are cultural artifacts created by specific cultures, which (4) _____ those cultures, and, in turn, affect them. Film is (5) _____ to be an important art form, a source of popular (6) _____ and a powerful method for education. Some films have become popular (7) _____ attractions by using dubbing or subtitles that translate the dialogue.

The (8) _____ of the name "film" comes from the fact that photographic film has historically been the primary (9) _____ for recording and displaying motion pictures. A common name for film in the United States is movie, while in Europe the term "cinema" is (10) _____ .

2 **Discuss the following questions about movie with your partner.**

1. Have you ever seen *Harry Potter*? Talk about your feelings on this movie if you have seen it; otherwise, share one of your favorite movies with your partner.

2. The following pictures show two international stars. Share with others what you know about them.

Listening Tasks

Micro Listening Skills

3 **You will hear five sentences. Listen carefully and fill in the missing words.**

1. Movies are widely used in education, _____ as teaching aids.

2. The idea may come from someone's _____ or from an existing book or play.

3. Movies have a _____ history, compared to such art forms as music and painting.

4. Hollywood is generally considered the motion-picture _____ of the world.

5. The high price has made the public more _____ in its movie going.

Dialogue

Perfect Date Movie

Andrews and Frank are discussing a scientific way to choose the perfect date movie.

Words & Phrases

violent /ˈvaɪələnt/ *adj.*	暴力的；暴行的
stimulate /ˈstɪmjʊleɪt/ *vt.*	刺激；激励
unconscious /ʌnˈkɒnʃəs/ *adj.*	未察觉的
hormone /ˈhɔːˌməʊn/ *n.*	（生理）荷尔蒙；激素
progesterone /prəʊˈdʒestərəʊn/ *n.*	孕酮
testosterone /tesˈtɒstərəʊn/ *n.*	睾丸激素

4 **Listen to the dialogue and complete the following sentences with the information you have heard.**

1. According to Andrews, there might be some _____ for why romantic movies are good for dates.

2. The study mentioned in the dialogue suggested that watching the romance stimulated the viewers' unconscious desires for _____.

3. The viewers who watched the romantic movie experienced _____ in

progesterone levels.

4. The reaction to the violent movie seemed to depend on the amount of testosterone _____ before watching the movie.

5. The study helps explain _____.

5 Listen to the dialogue again and answer the following questions.

1. What is decreased in men when they watch a romantic movie?

_____

2. How did women with lower testosterone levels feel when watching a violent movie?

_____

3. At the end of the dialogue, what does Andrews suggest on the ideal date movie?

_____

Passage

Developing a Feature Film

Words & Phrases

feature film	故事片
screenwriter /ˈskriːnˌraɪtə/ n.	编剧
agent /ˈeɪdʒənt/ n.	代理人
blueprint /ˈbluːˈprɪnt/ n.	蓝图
studio /ˈstjuːdɪəʊ/ n.	制片厂
executive /ɪgˈzekjʊtɪv/ n.	主管
exclusive /ɪksˈkluːsɪv/ adj.	专有的

6 Listen to the passage and decide whether the following statements are true (T) or false (F).

_____ 1. According to the passage, movie ideas usually come from many sources.

_____ 2. The director is responsible for turning ideas into a story that will work as a movie.

_____ 3. The screenwriter creates the blueprint for producing the film.

_____ 4. When the blueprint is finished, the screenwriter usually shows it to producers personally.

_____ 5. Once producers buy the script, they have the exclusive rights to it.

7 **Listen to the passage again and answer the following questions.**

1. Where can the idea of a feature film come from?

_____

2. What is the screenwriter's job?

_____

3. Why does the screenwriter send an original script to an agent?

_____

Reading Tasks

Text A   Reading in Detail

Pre-reading Questions

1. Do you like Chinese movies or imported movies? Why?
2. Do you think it interesting to work in the movie industry? Why or why not?
3. How can a movie be considered a success?

Avatar, a Miracle in Film Industry

Avatar is a 2009 American science fiction epic film written and directed by James Cameron. The film is set in the year 2154, when humans are engaged in mining reserves of a precious mineral

5   on Pandora of the Alpha Centauri star system. The colonists' expansion threatens the continued existence of the Na'vi, a race which is indigenous to Pandora, as well as the moon's ecosystem. The film's title refers to the genetically

10   engineered Na'vi bodies used by several human characters to interact with the natives of Pandora.

Development on *Avatar* started in 1994, when Cameron wrote an 80-page script for the film. Filming was supposed to take place after the

15   completion of Cameron's 1997 film *Titanic*, for a planned release in 1999, but according to Cameron, the necessary technology was not yet available to portray his

vision of the film. Work on the language for the film's extraterrestrial beings began in summer 2005, and Cameron began further developing the script and fictional universe in early 2006.   20

Avatar was officially budgeted at $237 million. Other estimates put the cost between $280 million and $310 million for production, and at $150 million for promotion. The film was released for traditional two-dimensional projection, as well as in 3-D format. The film was viewed as a breakthrough in filmmaking technology for its development of 3-D viewing and stereoscopic filmmaking with cameras that   25 were specially designed for the film's production.

Principal photography for Avatar began in April 2007 in Los Angeles and Wellington, New Zealand. Cameron described the film as a hybrid with a full live-action shoot in combination with computer-generated characters and live environments. "Ideally at the end of the day the audience has no idea what they're   30 looking at," Cameron said. The director indicated that he had already worked four months on nonprincipal scenes for the film. The live action was shot with a modified version of the proprietary digital 3-D Fusion Camera System, developed by Cameron and Vince Pace, a cinematographer.

Motion-capture photography would last 31 days at the Hughes Aircraft stage in   35 Playa Vista, Los Angeles, California. Live-action photography began in October 2007 at Stone Street Studios in Wellington, New Zealand, and was scheduled to last 31 days. More than a thousand people worked on the production. In preparation of the filming, all of the actors underwent professional training specific to their characters such as archery, horseback riding, firearms, and hand to hand combat. They also   40 received language and dialect training in the Na'vi language created for the film. Prior to shooting the film, Cameron also sent the cast to the jungle in Hawaii to get a feel for a rainforest setting.

During filming, Cameron made use of his virtual camera system, a new way of

45 directing motion-capture filmmaking. The system displays an augmented reality on a
monitor, placing the actor's virtual counterparts into their digital surroundings in real
time, allowing the director to adjust and direct scenes just as if shooting live action.
According to Cameron, "It's like a big, powerful game engine. If I want to fly
through space, or change my perspective, I can. I can turn the whole scene into a
50 living miniature and go through it on a 50 to 1 scale. " Using conventional techniques,
the complete virtual world cannot be seen until the motion-capture of the actors is
complete. Cameron described the system as a "form of pure creation where if you
want to move a tree or a mountain or the sky or change the time of day, you have
complete control over the elements".

55   To film the shots where CGI (Computer Generation Image) interacts with live
action, a unique camera, a merger of the 3-D fusion camera and the virtual camera
systems, was used. While filming live action in real time, the computer-generated
images captured with the virtual camera or designed from sketch, are superimposed
over the live action images and shown on a small monitor, making it possible for the
60 director to instruct the actors how to relate to the virtual material in the scene.

        Composer James Horner scored the film, his third collaboration with Cameron
after *Aliens* and *Titanic*. Horner recorded parts of the score with a small chorus
singing in the alien language Na'vi in March 2008. He also worked with Wanda
Bryant, an ethnomusicologist, to create a music culture for the alien race. The first
65 scoring sessions were planned to take place in spring 2009. During the production,
Horner promised Cameron that he would not work on any other project except for
Avatar and was reported to work on the score from four in the morning till ten at
night throughout the process. He stated in an interview, "*Avatar* has been the most
difficult film I have worked on and the biggest job I have undertaken. " British singer
70 Leona Lewis was chosen to sing the theme song for the film, called "I See You".

        Avatar premiered in London on December 10, 2009, and was released

internationally on December 16, and in North America on December 18. It received
critical acclaim and achieved commercial success. The film broke several box office
records during its release and became the highest-grossing film of all time in North
America and worldwide, surpassing *Titanic*, which had held the records for the   75
previous 12 years. It also became the first film to gross more than $2 billion.
Following the film's success, Cameron stated that there will be a sequel. "I have had
a storyline in mind and even some scenes in *Avatar* are kept because they lead to the
sequel." He told *Entertainment Weekly*. Whatever Cameron imagines in the sequel,
he'll probably stick with a theme of environmental protection.   80

(958 words)

New Words and Expressions

epic /'epɪk/ *n.*   a long film, book, or other work portraying heroic deeds and
adventures 史诗般的电影(书籍、其他作品)

be engaged in   become involved in 从事于

reserve /rɪ'zɜːv/ *n.*   a supply of sth. not needed for immediate use but available if
required in future 储量

indigenous△ /ɪn'dɪdʒənəs/ *adj.*   originating or occurring naturally in a particular
place; native 当地的;土生土长的

refer to   describe or denote; have as a referent 指;参考

interact with△   act in such a way in order to have an effect on each other 与……
相互作用;与……相互影响

script /skrɪpt/ *n.*   the written text of a play, film, or broadcast 剧本

release /rɪ'liːs/ *vt.*   make a film or recording available for general viewing or
purchase 发行(电影)

portray★ /pɔː'treɪ/ *vt.*   depict sb. or sth. in a work of art or literature 描述;刻画

extraterrestrial△ /ˌekstrətə'restrɪəl/ **being** 外星人

promotion /prə'məʊʃən/ *n.*   the publicity of a product, organization, or venture
so as to increase sales or public awareness 推销;宣传

two-dimensional△ /'tuːdɪ'menʃənəl/ *adj.*   having or appearing to have length and
breadth but no depth 二维的;平面的

stereoscopic△ /ˌsterɪə'skɒpɪk/ *adj.*   of an impression of depth and solidity 立体的

principal /'prɪnsəpəl/ *adj.*   first in order of importance; main 主要的

hybrid▲ /'haɪbrɪd/ *n.*   a thing made by combining two different elements 结合
体;混合物

modify /'mɒdɪfaɪ/ *vt.*   make partial or minor changes to sth. 修改

proprietary△ /prə'praɪətərɪ/ *adj.*   protected by a registered trade name 专用的

• 141 •

digital/ˈdɪdʒɪtəl/ *adj.* relating to or using signals or information represented by discrete values of a physical quantity 数字的；数字化的

photography△/fəˈtɒgrəfɪ/ *n.* practice of taking and processing photographs 摄影

schedule/ˈʃedjuːəl/ *vt.* make arrangements for (sb. or sth.) to do sth. 安排；排定

undergo/ˌʌndəˈgəu/ *vt.* experience or be subjected to sth. 经历

archery△/ˈɑːtʃərɪ/ *n.* shooting with a bow and arrows 射箭

dialect/ˈdaɪəlekt/ *n.* a particular form of a language which is peculiar to a specific region or social group 方言；土话

prior to before a particular time or event 先于

cast/kɑːst/ *n.* the actors taking part in a play, film（戏剧、电影等的）一组演员

jungle/ˈdʒʌŋgl/ *n.* an area of land overgrown with dense forest and tangled vegetation, typically in the tropics（尤指热带的）丛林

virtual/ˈvɜːtjuəl/ *adj.* not physically existing as such but made by software to appear to do so 虚拟的

augment▲/ɔːgˈment/ *vt.* make (sth.) greater by adding to it; increase 增大；增加

monitor/ˈmɒnɪtə/ *n.* an instrument used for observing or keeping a continuous record of a process or quantity 监视器

counterpart★/ˈkauntəpɑːt/ *n.* a person or thing holding a position that corresponds to that of another person or thing in a different area 对应的人（或物）

perspective△/pəˈspektɪv/ *n.* a particular attitude towards or way of regarding sth.; a view or prospect 角度；视角

miniature★/ˈmɪnɪətʃə/ *n.* a thing that is much smaller than normal, especially a small replica or model 微缩模型；缩影

merger△/ˈmɜːdʒə/ *n.* a combination of two things 合并；结合

capture/ˈkæptʃə/ *vt.* record or express accurately in words or pictures; take into one's possession or control by force 捕捉；捕获

sketch/ˈsketʃ/ *n.* a rough drawing or painting, often made to assist in making a more finished picture 草图

superimpose△/ˌsjuːpərɪmˈpəuz/ *vt.* place or lay (one thing) over another, typically so that both are still evident 把……放在另一物上；叠加

collaboration★/kəˌlæbəˈreɪʃən/ *n.* the action of working with sb. to produce or create sth.（创造性劳动方面的）合作；协作

score/skɔː/ *vt.* compose the music for a film; gain points or marks in a game or test 配乐；得分

chorus★/ˈkɔːrəs/ *n.* a large organized group of singers 合唱团；合唱队

alien★ /ˈeɪljən/ *adj.*   belonging to a foreign country or nation 外国的；异族的

ethnomusicologist△ /ˌeθnəʊˌmjuːzɪˈkɒlədʒɪst/ *n.*   folk musician 民族音乐家

undertake /ˌʌndəˈteɪk/ *vt.*   take on; commit oneself to 承担

premiere△ /prɪˈmɪə/ *vt.*   present the first public performance of（电影）首映；首演

acclaim▲ /əˈkleɪm/ *n.*   enthusiastic and public praise 称赞

box office△ *n.*   ticket sales 票房

high-grossing△ *adj.*   of high ticket sales 高票房的

surpass★ /səˈpɑːs/ *vt.*   exceed; be greater than 超越

sequel△ /ˈsiːkwəl/ *n.*   a published, broadcast, or recorded work that continues the story 续集

Proper Names

Avatar /ˌævəˈtɑː/	《阿凡达》(电影名)
James Cameron /dʒeɪmz ˈkæmərən/	詹姆斯·卡梅隆(人名)
Pandora /pænˈdɔːrə/	潘多拉(电影《阿凡达》中的星球名)
Alpha Centauri /ˈælfə senˈtɔːriː/	阿尔法星系
Titanic /taɪˈtænɪk/	《泰坦尼克号》(电影名)
Wellington /ˈwelɪŋtən/	惠灵顿
Vince Pace /vɪns peɪs/	文斯·佩斯(人名)
Hughes Aircraft /hjuːs ˈeəkrɑːft/	休斯飞机制造公司
Playa Vista /ˈplɑːjə ˈvɪstə/	普雷亚维斯塔(地名)
Hawaii /həˈwɑːiː/	夏威夷
James Horner /dʒeɪmz ˈhɔːnə/	詹姆士·霍纳(人名)
Aliens /ˈeɪljən/	《异形》(电影名)
Wanda Bryant /ˈwɒndə braɪt/	万达·布莱恩特
Leona Lewis /liːəunə luːɪs/	利昂娜·刘易斯(人名)
Entertainment Weekly	《娱乐周刊》

Comprehension

8 **Choose the best answer to each question with the information from the text.**

(　　) 1. According to Cameron, the filming of *Avatar* was delayed because _____.

      A. the necessary technology was not yet ready

      B. the financial backing was not yet found

      C. the likely market was not yet assessed

      D. the script was not yet prepared

(　　) 2. *Avatar* was viewed as a breakthrough in filmmaking technology for _____.

        A. its special language designed for characters

        B. its creating a music culture for alien race

        C. its release in 3-D format

        D. its development of 3-D viewing and specially designed cameras

(   ) 3. Before the filming, all of the actors received the following training EXCEPT _____.

        A. archery   B. hand to hand combat

        C. physical exercise   D. dialect

(   ) 4. Cameron described his virtual camera system as a form of pure creation because _____.

        A. the filming would not be stopped until he was satisfied

        B. all the elements in the film would be under his complete control

        C. actors would feel easy in front of it

        D. it could create various settings

(   ) 5. According to the last paragraph, which of the following is NOT true?

        A. *Avatar* achieved great commercial success.

        B. *Avatar* was first released in Europe.

        C. *Avatar* broke the box office record previously held by *Titanic*.

        D. *Avatar* received criticism from critics because of its enormous budget.

9 **Complete the following summary with right words and expressions.**

    Avatar is a 2009 American _____ epic film written and directed by James Cameron. The development on *Avatar* began in 1994 when Cameron wrote an 80-page _____ for the film. Due to the lack of proper technology, film production was postponed. Besides the traditional two-dimensional projection, film was also _____ in 3-D format. And *Avatar* is touted as a _____ in filmmaking technology for its unique stereoscopic filmmaking camera. With the help of a modified version of the proprietary _____ 3-D Fusion Camera System developed by Cameron, _____ began in April 2007 in a way of blending live-action shoot and computer character generating. After completing the _____ and experiencing the atmosphere in Hawaii, motion-capture took place in Playa Vista, Los Angeles, California. By utilizing his _____ camera system, Cameron was able to adjust and direct computer-generated image _____ it were shot in live action. James Horner and ethnomusicologist Wanda Bryant completed the _____ work for the film. Following the film's success, Cameron stated that he would make a sequel.

10 Discuss the following questions with the information from the text.

1. What does the film's title *Avatar* refer to?
   (*genetically engineered*)

   _____

2. What did Cameron do in 2005 and 2006 before filming *Avatar*?
   (*develop, further*)

   _____

3. Why did Cameron send the cast to the jungle in Hawaii?
   (*rainforest setting*)

   _____

4. What is the advantage of Cameron's virtual camera system?
   (*display, allow*)

   _____

5. What did James Horner think of his scoring work for *Avatar*?
   (*difficult*)

   _____

Vocabulary & Structure

11 Fill in the blanks with the words given below. Change the form where necessary.

expansion	release	portray	promotion	principal
schedule	undergo	counterpart	undertake	surpass

1. The producer is reaping the rewards of a series of _____.
2. The singer's six singles and one album will _____ at the end of year.
3. Drinking is one of the _____ causes of highway accidents.
4. The newly-built factory is large, allowing enough room for _____.
5. Who will _____ the job of advertising the new product?
6. Foreign language learners often have difficulty translating terms with no direct _____ in the other language.
7. The difficulty I encountered in carrying out the plan _____ my expectation.
8. The explorer _____ much suffering in his walking across the desert.
9. In the story, he _____ as a self-serving careerist.
10. He _____ to be released from prison this spring.

12 Complete the following sentences with phrases or expressions from the text.

1. This company has been licensed to _____ export business.
2. The term can also _____ a conflict or disagreement, often involving

violence.

3. Experts are developing smarter, more mobile humanoid robots with the ability to _____ humans.

4. All the arrangements should be completed _____ your departure.

13 **Translate the Chinese sentences into English by simulating the sentences chosen from the text.**

Chosen Sentences	Simulated Translation	Chinese Sentences
Filming *was supposed* to take place after the completion of Cameron's 1997 film *Titanic*, *but* the necessary technology was not yet available.		这些新法令本应该起到防止犯罪的作用,但是目前的情况令人失望。
The film was *viewed as* a breakthrough in filmmaking technology *for* its development of 3-D viewing and stereoscopic filmmaking.		此次广告宣传被视作成功的,因为它带来了巨大的收益。(advertising campaign)
The director *indicated that* he had already worked four months on nonprincipal scenes for the film.		这些数据表明该公司陷入了严重的困境中。(figure)
The system displays an augmented reality on a monitor, allowing the director to adjust and direct scenes *just as if shooting* live action.		他目不转睛地看着我,就像第一次见到我似的。(stare at)
The computer-generated images are superimposed over the live action images and shown on a small monitor, *making it possible for* the director to instruct the actors how to relate to the virtual material in the scene.		对于干细胞的研究取得了巨大的进展,这使得医生有可能利用干细胞的自我更新功能治疗多种疾病。(stem cells, self-renewal)

14 **Rewrite each sentence with the word or phrase in brackets, keeping the same meaning. The first part has been done for you.**

1. Senior citizens have the right to receive free community health services.

   Free community health services _____. (available)

2. We can find a satisfactory way towards a solution of these problems by putting the application of physics and geological information together.

   The application of physics, _____, is a satisfactory

way towards a solution of these problems. (in combination with)

3. The hotel is most suitable for restaurant, bars and clubs.

   The hotel _____. (ideally)

4. This website reports world news on its unique standing.

   This website _____. (perspective)

5. The feeling of being invisible is accurately described.

   That description _____. (capture)

Text B   Skimming and Scanning

Film Production

Film production occurs in five stages. They are development, pre-production, production, post-production, and distribution and exhibition.

Development

In this stage, the project's producer finds a story, which may come from a book, play, another film, a true story, etc. After identifying a theme, the producer works   5
with writers to prepare a synopsis. (1) Next they produce an outline, which breaks the story down into one-paragraph scenes that concentrate on dramatic structure. Based on the outline, a description of the story, its mood, and characters is prepared. This usually has few dialogue and stage direction, but often contains drawings that help visualize key points. In the following step, a screenwriter writes a screenplay and   10
saves it over a period of several months during which the screenwriter may rewrite it several times to improve dramatization, clarity, structure, characters, dialogue, and overall style. Film distributors may be contacted at an early stage to assess the likely market and potential financial success of the film. They usually consider factors such as the film style, the target audience, the historical success of similar films, the   15
actors who might appear in the film, and potential directors.

The producer and the screenwriter prepare a film agenda, and present it to potential financiers. If the agenda is successful, the film receives a "green light", meaning someone offers financial backing: typically a major film studio, film council, or independent investor. The parties involved negotiate a deal and sign contracts.   20
Once all parties have met and the deal has been set, the film may proceed into the pre-production period. By this stage, the film should have a clearly defined marketing strategy and target audience.

Pre-production

In pre-production, the film is designed and planned. The production company is   25

created and a production office is established. The production is storyboarded and visualized with the help of illustrators and concept artists. A production budget is drawn up to plan expenditures for the film. The producer hires a crew. The nature of the film, and the budget, determine the size and type of crew used during
30 filmmaking.

Production

In production, the film is created and shot. More crew will be recruited at this stage, such as the property master, script supervisor, assistant directors, stills photographer, picture editor, and sound editors. These are just the most common
35 roles in filmmaking; the production office will be free to create any unique blend of roles to suit a particular film.

A typical day's shooting begins with the crew arriving on the location by their call time. Actors usually have their own separate call times. Since setting construction, dressing and
40 lighting can take many hours or even days, they are often set up in advance.

The grip, electric and production design crews are typically a step ahead of the camera and sound departments: for efficiency's sake, while a
45 scene is being filmed, they are already preparing the next one.

While the crew prepares their equipment, the actors put on their costumes and attend the hair and make-up departments. (2) The actors
50 rehearse the script and communicate with the director, and the camera and sound crews

rehearse with them and make final adjustments. Finally, the action is shot as many takes as the director wishes.

When the entire film is in the completion of the production phase, it is customary for the production office to arrange a party to thank all the cast and crew for their 55 efforts.

Post-production

Here the film is assembled by the film editor. The modern use of video in the filmmaking process has resulted in two workflow types: one using entirely film, and the other using a mixture of film and video. 60

There are two ways that film can be put together. One way is linear editing and the other is non-linear editing. Linear editing uses the film as it is in a continuous film. All of the parts of the film are already in order and need not be moved or any such thing. Conversely, non-linear editing is not subject to using the film in the order as it is taped. Scenes can be moved around or even removed. A better way to see it is 65 that non-linear editing is like a hodgepodge of video.

Once the picture is locked, the film is passed into the hands of sound editor of the sound department to build up the sound track. The voice recordings are synchronized and the final sound mix is created by the re-recording mixer. The sound mix combines dialogue, sound effects, background sounds, and music. 70

Finally the film is previewed, normally by the target audience, and any feedback may result in further shooting or edits to the film.

Distribution and Exhibition

This is the final stage, where the film is released to cinemas or, occasionally, to DVD, VCD, or direct download from a provider. The film is duplicated as required 75 for distribution to cinemas. Press kits, posters, and other advertising materials are published and the film is advertised.

Most advertising campaigns are designed to make their heaviest impact for the first two or three weeks of a film's release. If the campaign attracts the right audience and these viewers enjoy the film, they will tell their friends and thus sell the film to a 80 new audience. A second campaign is sometimes designed to appeal to a different portion of the public. (3) For example, the film may be an action movie with a star not usually associated with action films. The first campaign might reach out to take part of the public interested in action movies. The second campaign would be planned to attract that part of the public interested in seeing the star. 85

Film companies usually release a film with a launch party, press releases, interviews with the press, press preview screenings, and film festival screenings. The film plays at selected cinemas and the DVD typically is released a few months later.

90 The distribution rights for the film and DVD are also usually sold for worldwide distribution. The distributor and the production company share profits. (4) If the film can earn three times its budget in ticket sales during its domestic release, the producers and the investors will begin to

95 make a profit. The film will then be considered a commercial success.

Financial arrangements for exhibiting a film can be extremely complicated and may vary from film to film. In the simplest arrangement, the

100 distributor charges an exhibitor a flat fee or the exhibitor pays the distributor a percentage of the weekly box-office profits, often with a certain minimum payment guaranteed.

(1 095 words)

New Words and Expressions

theme /θiːm/ *n.*   the subject of a talk, a piece of writing, a person's thoughts, or an exhibition 主题

synopsis△ /sɪˈnɒpsɪs/ *n.*   a brief summary or general survey of sth. 提要;概要

assess /əˈses/ *vt.*   evaluate or estimate the nature, ability, or quality of 估算;估计

agenda△ /əˈdʒendə/ *n.*   a list or program of things to be done 备忘录;日程表

negotiate /nɪˈɡəʊʃieɪt/ *vt.*   try to reach an agreement by discussing with others 谈判;协商

strategy /ˈstrætɪdʒɪ/ *n.*   a plan of action or policy designed to achieve a major aim 战略;策略

storyboard△ /ˈstɔːrɪbɔːd/ *vt.*   make a sequence of drawings, typically with some directions and dialogue, representing the shots planned for a film or television production 制作(电影、电视的)情节串连图板

visualize★ /ˈvɪʒʊəlaɪz/ *vt.*   make (sth.) visible to the eye 使可见;使显现

expenditure★ /ɪksˈpendɪtʃə/ *n.*   the action of spending funds 费用;开支

recruit /rɪˈkruːt/ *vt.*   enroll someone as a member or worker in an organization 招募;征募

supervisor△ /ˈsjuːpəˌvaɪzə/ *n.*   a person who supervises a person or an activity 监督者;监管人

still /stɪl/ *n.*　a single shot from a cinema film 剧照

grip /grɪp/ *n.*　a member of a camera crew responsible for moving and setting up equipment（摄影队中负责移动和安放器材的）摄影助手

costume /ˈkɒstjuːm/ *n.*　a set of clothes worn by an actor or performer for a particular role 戏服；演出服

rehearse△ /rɪˈhɜːs/ *vt.*　practice（a play, piece of music, or other work）for later public performance 排演；排练

linear★ /ˈlɪnɪə/ *adj.*　arranged in or extending along a straight or nearly straight line 线性的

conversely /ˈkɒnvɜːslɪ/ *adv.*　introducing a statement or idea which reverses one that has just been made 反过来说；相反地

hodgepodge△ /ˈhɒdʒpɒdʒ/ *n.*　a confused mixture 大杂烩

synchronize△ /ˈsɪŋkrəˌnaɪz/ *vt.*　cause to occur or operate at the same time or rate 使同步发生

feedback /ˈfiːdbæk/ *n.*　information about reactions to a product, a person's performance of a task, etc. 反馈信息

duplicate★ /ˈdjuːplɪkɪt/ *vt.*　make an exact copy of 复制

poster /ˈpəʊstə/ *n.*　a large printed picture, notice, or advertisement displayed in a public place 招贴画；海报

appeal to　be attractive or interesting 对……有吸引力

flat fee△ *n.*　a regular payment 固定收费

Comprehension

15 Go over the text quickly and answer the following questions. For questions 1—7, choose the best answer from the four choices; for questions 8—10, complete the sentences with the information from the text.

(　　) 1. In development stage, an outline is made to break the story down into one-paragraph scenes which focus on _____.

　　A. dramatic compostion

　　B. dramatic style

　　C. story plots

　　D. dramatic characters

(　　) 2. Distributors assess the likely market of a film by considering the following factors EXCEPT _____.

　　A. actors and directors

　　B. whether a similar film has been previously made

　　C. film style

D. target audience

(   ) 3. A film agenda is successful, meaning that _____.

    A. actors and directors are decided

    B. the budget is made

    C. someone is willing to invest on it

    D. the schedule is made

(   ) 4. The size and type of the crew hired for producing a film is determined by _____.

    A. its budget

    B. its nature

    C. its potential market

    D. Both A and B.

(   ) 5. Filming crew usually arrive on the location earlier than actors because _____.

    A. actors must spend time rehearsing their performance

    B. their preparing work takes much time

    C. they have to send equipment to the location

    D. they must communicate with the director first

(   ) 6. Which of the following is NOT true on the ways of editing a film?

    A. There are two ways. One is linear editing and the other is non-linear editing.

    B. In linear editing, all of the parts of the film are already in order and need not be moved.

    C. In non-linear editing, scenes cannot be moved or cut.

    D. Generally, non-linear editing seems like a mixture of video.

(   ) 7. After being previewed, a film may have further shooting or edits due to _____.

    A. the target audience's feedback

    B. experts' remarks

    C. investors' suggestions

    D. advertisers' requirements

    8. In the final stage, a film is advertised through press kits, posters, and other _____.

    9. The distribution rights for the film and DVD are also usually sold for _____.

    10. Financial arrangements for exhibiting a film may _____.

Vocabulary & Translation

16 **Fill in the blanks with the words given below. Change the form where necessary.**

theme	assess	negotiate	strategy	expenditure
recruit	conversely	combine	appeal	commercial

1. Waterfalls are from very early times a favorite _____ for Chinese painters.

2. As time goes by, both of them are used to adopting the win-win _____.

3. You are supposed to write a notice to _____ volunteers for this international conference.

4. Critics pointed out that his new record was too _____.

5. The idea that both sides would share the profits _____ to Mary.

6. The local government should _____ industrial restructuring with reconstruction to achieve sustainable development.

7. He would have preferred his wife not to work, although _____ he was also proud of what she did.

8. The group is calling for higher _____ on primary education.

9. It is difficult to _____ where neither will trust.

10. The value of this villa was _____ at one million dollars.

17 **Translate the underlined sentences in the text into Chinese.**

1. Next they produce an outline, which breaks the story down into one-paragraph scenes that concentrate on dramatic structure.

   _____

   _____

2. The actors rehearse the script and communicate with the director, and the camera and sound crews rehearse with them and make final adjustments.

   _____

   _____

3. For example, the film may be an action movie with a star not usually associated with action films. The first campaign might reach out to take part of the public interested in action movies. The second campaign would be planned to attract that part of the public interested in seeing the star.

   _____

   _____

   _____

4. If the film can earn three times its budget in ticket sales during its domestic release, the producers and the investors will begin to make a profit. The film will then be considered a commercial success.

_____

_____

_____

Interactive Tasks

Pair Work

18 **Read the sample dialogues carefully, and then complete the interactive tasks that follow.**

Task 1

Sample dialogue

Mike: Hi, How is it going?

Jim: Not too bad, yourself?

Mike: Yeah good, I hear that there are heaps of new movies showing right now, will you want to see movies with me tonight?

Jim: Movies? Nah, I am not that into movies recently. I reckon the movies nowadays are simply the combination of three things: money, stars and commercials. I did go to few of so called "blockbusters", but I really don't like them. what was wrong with all those screenwriters and directors?

Mike: I get what you mean but going to movies is only for relaxing, as long as you enjoy its nice presentation and watch your favorite movie stars, that would be worth it.

Jim: No, I disagree. Movie should be close to real life and it should mean something. Anyway I will go through some movie with you tonight and see how it goes.

Interactive task

Role A invites Role B to the cinema. Role B, however, prefers to watch TV at home. In his eyes, present movie production aims much at commercial profits and most movies are disappointing. Role A doesn't think so.

Role A: What about going to the cinema with me?

Role B: I would rather watch TV at home. Most movies today are disappointing.

Task 2

Sample dialogue

Peter: Hi, what are you doing now?

John: I am working on choosing my future major now. Do you reckon that I should get into film academy to study performing arts?

Peter: Why are you interested in doing performing arts?

John: It's fun and challenging for me. Besides, I am hoping that I may have the opportunity to work with some movie stars.

Peter: Wake up, brother, performing is not what you think. As an actor, you will be working under constant pressure and you won't have a proper time schedule. To be honest with you, the chance of working with those famous actors is tiny, so is the possibility of becoming a star. It will be better off to choose a more realistic major and get a proper job.

John: What you say sounds right. There is always a gap between our dream and the reality.

Interactive task

Two young students are talking about their future major at university. It seems that Role A has great interest in performing arts while Role B reckons that this major is not so realistic.

Role A: A job in movie industry is attractive to me and I have a dream of becoming a movie star.

Role B: I plan to take a major in radio engineering and to be an engineer after graduation.

Group Work

19 Work in groups to design an interview.

In an interview on TV, the director, major actors and actresses of a movie are being interviewed by a host as the movie has recently achieved great success.

1. Form groups of 4 or 5 students.

2. Each group makes an outline as to the interview, which may cover the story, the performance, the tidbit, the advertising campaign, etc.

Story	
Actors and actresses	
Performance	
Tidbit	
Advertising campaign	

3. Each group rehearses the interview according to the outline.

4. All groups play the interview in front of the whole class.

Follow-up Tasks

Writing

正文段落的展开方法

1. 因果法。因果关系主要有以下几种：一果多因，一因多果，因果连锁。

People are learning English for different reasons. English is a required course for students in various examinations. Moreover, if someone wants to go abroad to pursue further study, English is helpful. Third, scientists know that English can help them to get information about the advanced science and technology all over the world. Finally, many businessmen are learning English because they often deal with import and export trades.

作者采用一果多因的写作方法从四个不同方面分析了学习英语的原因。

2. 例证法。例证法是以具体的事例来充实主题句，展开段落。请看四级考试 1999 年 1 月作文题正文段：

Of course, helping others is a virtue, but in some cases, we will have to say "no". For example, if what others want you to do is unreasonable or even illegal, you should say "no" without any hesitation. Everyone has his own principle of doing things, and we won't do anything opposite to the right principles. If we did, it would do nothing but harm both of others and us. In other cases, if the request from others is reasonable but beyond your ability, what you should do is just to say "no". Never promise others what you can't do. If you can't keep your promise, you will be considered dishonest and it will do you no good when dealing with other people.

3. 定义解释法。即通过对某个概念的解释和限定去展开段落。这种定义解释法多用于说明文,它对实际事物进行解说或对抽象事理进行阐释。例如:

Energy for the Life Processes

Energy is defined as the ability or capacity to do work. Associated with the idea of energy is the concept of movement. You lift an object and you say you have done work and that it took energy to lift the object. The object may fall to the ground and hit a nail a distance into the wood. Thus it did work.

这一段对什么是 energy 进行解释,并举实例说明,以便读者对"能量"有个具体印象。

4. 对照比较法。即通过对两个或多个事物的对照或比较,从中找出异同点,以此来阐明一个道理,从而展开段落。例如:

Punctuality

Punctuality is the main constituent of good appointment, shows real consideration for others. On the other hand, a person who is always late shows his selfishness and thoughtlessness and he is not worthy to be friend with.

这一段把守时和不守时的人做一番比较,这就使所阐明的道理更加令人信服。

Research Project

Work in groups of 4 or 5 students, and finish a research project based on the topic area of this unit. It involves lectures, seminars, team-based activities, individual activities, team presentation and a reflective summary.

Steps

1. Form a research group;
2. Decide on a research topic;
3. Work in groups to finish PPT slides;
4. Each member of the group gives oral presentation of his parts;
5. Hand in materials that include: Project Proposal (one for each team), Research Report (one for each team, 1 000 words), Summary (one for each person, 300 words), PPT (one for each team).

Research Methods

1. Field work: to generate the first-hand information
   - Questionnaires
   - Interviews (interpersonal, telephone, e-mail, door-to-door visit, etc.)
   - Observation
2. Desk work: to generate the second-hand information
   - Library: books and magazines
   - The Internet: Google the theme with the key words
   - Reading materials

Suggested Options

1. A review on the history of movie.
2. Comparison between Chinese movie and American movie with the same topic.
3. An introduction to a blockbuster movie.

Tips for Options

1. If you choose to review the history of movie, you need to collect a wealth of information by visiting relevant websites on the Internet. And your review will follow the chronological sequence.
2. If you try to make comparison between Chinese movie and American movie with the same topic, you are expected to choose the most well-known movies. Your comparison may focus on some of the following areas: story, character, theme, dialogue, music and overall style.
3. If you are interested in a blockbuster movie, your introduction may cover some of the following areas: background, plot, theme, character, actor and actress, director, promotion, box-office, comment and impact.

Unit Seven Photography

Highlight

Topic area	Structure	Skills
The power of photography The character and work of a wildlife photographer The essentials of photographic equipment Photographing the emotion of sports Light in shooting historic sites Preparing to shoot sports actions	define by provide ... for act as be reason enough to run out of in addition to plan for load ... with	Understanding the real power of photography Learning about the photographic equipment Describing and discussing the photography of sports emotions Discussing how to use light in shooting historic sites and how to prepare to shoot sports actions

Warm-up Tasks

1 **Listen to the following passage and try to fill in the missing words and expressions.**

We are a nation of photographers and (1) _____ technology. With a hugely growing market in digital photography, our lives and times are the most (2) _____ in history. Magazines and newspapers have the capability of going to press with photos shot only moments earlier. Television newscasts use viewers' digital (3) _____, sent in via the Internet, ranging from plane crashes to beautiful sunsets. At the click of a mouse and at a next-to-nothing cost, we send our relatives electronic photo (4) _____ of our vacation or the baby's first year.

Photography (5) _____ our history, linking us to our past and future. A small box known as the point-and-shoot camera, or affectionately as PHD (push here, dummy) camera is overtly doing the once mysterious tasks of (6) _____ and (7) _____. Today's young generation is (8) _____ bombarded with intelligent, well-composed, and compelling images hundreds of times a day. To put a weak image in front of this (9) _____ audience is almost unforgivable. We need to learn the power of photography and how it (10) _____ our lives. We have every reason to be an aspiring photographer and feel comfortable with the equipment and the people. Just do it.

2 Look at the following works of photography and discuss the following questions with your partner.

1. Try to appreciate the above photographs. Describe your impression at the first sight of each.

2. Think about the important moments in history and life, marked by these photo images. Analyze the impressiveness of such images in terms of photographic techniques and the significance or passion they represent.

3. Have you ever thought about becoming a professional or an amateur photographer? To become a good photographer of a certain field, what are the qualities that one needs to possess? Brainstorm and list them with your partners.

Listening Tasks

Micro Listening Skills

3 You will hear seven sentences. Each sentence contains one of the two words given to you. Listen carefully and choose the word you hear in each sentence.

1. A. hit   B. hid
2. A. preference   B. previous
3. A. formal   B. former
4. A. trial   B. trail
5. A. behalf   B. behavior
6. A. personalities   B. percentages
7. A. frustration   B. fascination

Dialogue

An Interview with Jeff Richter—An Awarding-winning Wildlife Photographer

Words & Phrases

prompt /prɒmpt/ *vt.*	促使
wildlife /ˈwaɪldlaɪf/ *n.*	野生动植物
gallery /ˈɡælərɪ/ *n.*	陈列室；画廊
capture /ˈkæptʃə/ *vt.*	捕获
trapping /ˈtræpɪŋ/ *n.*	（下套或设陷阱）诱捕
aspiring /əsˈpaɪərɪŋ/ *adj.*	有抱负的；积极的
freelancer /ˈfriːlɑːnsə/ *n.*	泛指非专职的自由职业者
guideline /ˈɡaɪdlaɪn/ *n.*	指导路线、方针
legwork /ˈleɡwɜːk/ *n.*	外出搜集情况，外勤（如前期准备中的收集信息、调查研究等）

4 **Listen to the dialogue and choose the best answer to the following questions.**

(　　) 1. The major reason for Jeff Richter's entering wildlife photography might be _____.

    A. his interest in nature and wildlife

    B. his decision to work in a gallery

    C. his impression about his friend's works

    D. Both A & C.

(　　) 2. The following statements about Jeff Richter's training and experience in photography are all true EXCEPT that _____.

    A. he didn't have much regular training in art

    B. he experimented a lot by taking photos

    C. he read publications about photography

    D. he directed a film about errors in nature

(　　) 3. According to Jeff Richter, he is different from other wildlife photographers majorly in that _____.

    A. he is more experienced and patient with wildlife so he could capture more excellent moments

    B. he used to be trapped in nature so he knows how to handle the harsh wildlife better than others

    C. he spends more time observing wildlife so he knows better the behavior of animals in the field

    D. he is an excellent specialist in trapping and hunting animals so he could capture more animals

(　　) 4. In Jeff Richter's view, all of the following should be included in the character of a good wildlife photographer EXCEPT _____.

A. a long-existing interest in nature and wildlife

B. a lasting persistence in finding good moments

C. enough patience in awaiting special sights

D. a quick mind in studying nature and wildlife

5 **Listen to the dialogue again and complete the following sentences with the information you have heard.**

1. You need never-ending stubbornness and patience to capture those special, _____ moments.

2. As a freelancer, you need to _____ your source of income first.

3. In self-promotion, I keep contact with publishers and editors to find _____ guidelines.

4. Always remember to keep learning and be _____ of yourself.

Passage

The Power of Photography

Words & Phrases

zoom /zuːm/ *n.*	(镜头)对目标的拉近/远离
Life magazine	美国《生活》杂志,以刊载有影响力的摄影作品闻名,曾多次停复刊,2007 年转为电子杂志

National Geographic	美国《国家地理》杂志
projector /prə'dʒektə/ *n.*	放映机；投影仪
clip /klɪp/ *n.*	电影或录像的片断
Vietnam War	特指美国干涉越南的战争(1961—1975)
Viet Cong /'vjet'kɒŋ/ *n.*	也作 Vietcong，越南共产党(人)
suspect /səs'pekt/ *n.*	嫌疑犯
execute /'eksɪkjuːt/ *vt.*	处决；处死
archive /'ɑːkaɪv/ *vt.*	存档
LCD *n.*	(liquid crystal display 的缩写)液晶显示屏

6 **Listen to the passage and decide whether the following statements are true (T) or false (F).**

_____ 1. Today everyone becomes a photographer for the lower equipment costs but few care to take efforts to improve photography.

_____ 2. An aspiring photographer knows what to record and he lets his camera work objectively without involving his mind's eye.

_____ 3. The author liked *Life* and *National Geographic* in his childhood because there was frequently no power for TV so he could only read with a candle at the time.

_____ 4. When we think of an important event in history and life, our mind scans our memory data the way we play a film clip.

_____ 5. Without a thinking mind, photography cannot possibly depict historical events well just by better lens and LCD.

7 **Listen to the passage again and answer the following questions with the help of words and phrases provided below.**

1. How do you understand the problem the author mentions about today's photography?

   (*prices, photographer, objective, mind, time and effort*)

   _____

2. What did the author do with *Life* and *National Geographic* when he was a kid? And why did he do that?

   (*race, moments, TV, power*)

   _____

3. What happens to our mind when we scan some key words about history and life, according to the author?

   (*grab, image, data bank, memory*)

   _____

4. How does the author describe Eddie Adams's photograph that often comes to mind when one thinks of the Vietnam War?

(*Viet Cong suspect, execute, gunshot to the head*)

Reading Tasks

Text A   *Reading in Detail*

Pre-reading Questions

1. What do you know about the equipment for a professional photographer?
2. What do you think are the essentials for the proper application and maintenance of photographic equipment?
3. Are there any special considerations about today's digital photography?

Choosing What's Inside the Camera Bag[①]

---

① This text is adapted from an article written by Jay Dickman in the book *Perfect Digital Photography* (2edn., McGraw-Hill Companies, 2009, pp. 170-173). He is the co-author of the book with Jay Kinghorn.

Since the invention of photography, two constants in the world of the photographer have been shutter and aperture. The equipment may become more and more technically sophisticated, but these two compatriots of the camera are still the core of the mechanical side of the camera. Here are a few ideas on using photographic equipment as your creative tool.

My camera bag is pretty well defined by years of travel and getting caught with too much or not having brought the correct equipment. On the plane or in the car, one medium-sized Domke camera bag, with two camera bodies and three or four lenses—depending on the shoot—will usually suffice for almost all conditions.

I carry two Olympus E-3 bodies, along with an Olympus E520 as a backup. I'll often carry a small point-and-shoot Olympus. The 5060 can go in a pocket and works in some situations where the larger bodies and lenses would broadcast "Photographer!" There are areas where someone shooting seriously may not be well received, and for those times, the 5060 looks more like a tourist's camera. But the quality from a camera like this is excellent and provides good quality files for printing. Another camera that resides in my pocket at all times, the Olympus 1030 is good to 33 feet underwater—and it's very small and compact.

Your camera choice may be a Nikon D300 with a second body, a D80, or a Canon 50D and a Canon 1Ds Mark Ⅲ. Having two bodies really makes the shooting process easier. I'll carry a wide zoom on one body, a medium-long zoom on the other. This way, I'm ready to shoot anything almost instantly. In many if not almost all situations, this camera setup can cover all your bases.

Lens choice is specific to the type of photography you are doing. In my "basic" bag I'll carry a 7 - 14mm (which, in the 35mm film world, is equivalent to a 14 - 28mm), a 12 - 60mm (24 - 120mm equivalent), and a 50 - 200mm (100 - 400mm equivalent). On shoots that require high-speed lenses, a 14 - 35mm f2 (28 - 70mm equivalent) and a 35 - 100mm f2 (70 - 200mm equivalent). If photographing sports or wildlife, a 150mm f2 (equivalent to a 300mm f2) would be extremely fast, with other choices such as a 90 – 250mm f2. 8 (180 – 500mm equivalent) and/or a 300 f2. 8 (a 600mm f2. 8 equivalent). These lenses, along with a 1. 4 or 2 power converter, which multiplies the focal length of lenses by a 1. 4 or 2x factor, give me just about all the lens power I need.

Always found in my bag is a TTL (through the lens) flash and a remote cord for that strobe so I can shoot off-camera with the flash. The cord allows me to hold the flash away from the camera so I can bounce or reflect the flash off of a ceiling or wall for a softer and more natural light. Today's flashes often use infrared or radio control, allowing the photographer to set up several wireless lights that are controlled from the camera. This is the official "Next Best Thing Since Canned Beer".

A Lexar wallet carries my assortment of Lexar CF cards, usually a couple of 8GB cards that reside in-camera, a few 4GB cards, and a 1GB card in the wallet.

In a second bag, I carry two 160GB WiebeTech pocket drives. These are configured, in my computer's operating system, to act as a RAID (Redundant Array of Independent Disks) device. When plugged into my laptop, the two drives appear as one on my desktop. When I drop images onto the drive icon, the images are copied to both drives, which mirror each other. Packed in that bag are enough CDs or DVDs to burn the number of images I think I may shoot on the particular assignment. *Before I erase/reformat a card, I make sure the files are in a minimum of two independent places.* This is a cardinal rule.

If you don't want to lug a laptop to Lithuania, several manufacturers make small and very portable hard drive viewing units. JOBO makes a beautiful unit, the GIGA Vu PRO evolution, which provides up to 160GB of space. Epson makes the P7000, and Apple offers the photo-capable iPod, iPod Touch, and photo-capable iPhone, now found in many photographers' bags. These units will hold a huge number of images and allow the photographer to view and share them. The one downside to using *only one* of these two units: will this be the only backup for your photos? This could be reason enough to carry a laptop or a portable CD or DVD burner.

One of the great benefits of shooting digital is the elimination of film and the problems of transporting the number of rolls needed for a trip. Now we carry a few CF cards that equal many rolls of film. One of the big issues with digital is power. We now have a technology that is 100-percent power dependent.

So, here are some power necessities for the road:

- As I mentioned earlier, use a camera system that uses the same batteries and charger.
- Always carry extra batteries. This includes rechargeable and non-rechargeable

types. In addition to two or three extra camera batteries, I also carry a small   65
bag with extra AA and AAA batteries. Nothing, and I mean *nothing*, is
worse than running out of power with no backup in the middle of a great photo
event.

- I always carry an extra charger, well worth the minimal weight increase since
  this provides 100-percent faster battery charging because you are charging two   70
  at once. It also provides a backup if one breaks. Not likely, but don't tempt
  Murphy's Law!

- I carry a small 12-volt power inverter (NexxTech Power Inverter model
  2218075), which can be found at Radio Shack. It's a 75-watt model that is
  small and light and provides charging time while on the road, plugged into   75
  your cigarette lighter.

- Keep appropriate adaptor plugs for the area in which you are traveling. I'll
  stop for lunch and ask to sit at a table by an outlet, so I can use my charger to
  top off the batteries. Steve Kropla's website (www. kropla. com/electric2.
  htm) not only lists the voltage availability worldwide, but it tells you the type   80
  of adaptor plug you'll need for that country. Take at least three adaptors.

- Brunton released the Solaris series of portable solar panels and Solo series of
  portable battery units that solves a lot of problems unique to digital—that
  need for power. I've been using the Solaris 26 solar panel, and with the Solo
  15 battery pack, I've been able to charge several of my E-3 camera batteries.   85
  This is an invaluable tool for today's traveling photographer. This gives you
  the ability to charge not only your camera battery, but your laptop battery,
  and your databank (JOBO, Epson, iPhone, whatever) in those powerless
  areas, as long as you have direct or indirect exposure to the sun for the
  charging process. These pack nicely, the battery being about the size of thick   90
  pocketbook and the panel folding up to similar size.

Travel and digital photography are natural and necessary partners, and
photographic equipment is the hammer and wrench of the photographer's toolbox.
The lighter and more efficient the toolbox, the easier it is for us to work in our
travels. Plan ahead for your photo outing, whether it is a Little League game down   95
the block or a month-long trip to Nepal. Take only what is necessary to get the job
done. Don't load yourself down with so much gear that it gets in the way of shooting
memorable showstoppers.

(1 289 words)

New Words and Expressions

constant /ˈkɒnstənt/ *n.*   sth. unchanging or invariable 不变的事物；常数；恒量

shutter /ˈʃʌtə/ *n.*   a mechanical device of a camera that controls the duration of a photographic exposure 照相机快门；遮光器

aperture /ˈæpətjʊə/ *n.*   a usually adjustable opening in an optical instrument 光圈

compatriot /kəmˈpætrɪət/ *n.*   a fellow countryman; a fellow part or person working closely together 同胞；同事；联系密切的部件

core /kɔː/ *n.*   the central, basic or most important part; the essence 核心

suffice★ /səˈfaɪs/ *vi.*   be sufficient; be enough 足够

backup△ /ˈbækʌp/ *n.*   a reserve or substitute 替代品；备份

point-and-shoot△ *n. & adj.*   (of, relating to, or being) a camera that adjusts settings such as focus and exposure automatically 能自动调节焦距和曝光的照相机（的）

broadcast /ˈbrɔːdkɑːst/ *vt.*   make widely known 散布；传播；使……广为人知

reside /rɪˈzaɪd/ *vi.*   live, be present 居住；存在

underwater /ˈʌndəˈwɔːtə/ *adv.*   being or used below the surface of the water 在水中或水下

wide zoom   any lens which is wider than about 28 mm with its varying capability for the focal length 广角变焦镜头

medium-long zoom   any lens with its focal length capable of varying from medium to long distances 中长变焦镜头

setup /ˈsetʌp/ *n.*   arrangement 设置；安排

converter /kənˈvɜːtə/ *n.*   a machine that converts electric current from one kind to another （用于调整镜头焦距的）变距镜   power ～ 逆变器

focal length /ˈfəʊkəlˈleŋθ/ *n.*   the distance from the surface of a lens or mirror to its focal point 焦距

factor /ˈfæktə/ *n.*   a given quantity about the exposure 曝光系数

TTL (through the lens) **flash**   a type of flash with its head working with the camera's internal metering system to determine flash output for proper exposure of the scene 测光闪光灯

strobe△ /strəub/ *n.*   a flash lamp that produces high-intensity short-duration light pulses by electric discharge in a gas 频闪闪光灯

bounce /baʊns/ *vt.*   reflect 反射

infrared▲ /ˈɪnfrəˈred/ *adj.*   of or relating to the range of invisible radiation wavelengths from about 750 nanometers, just longer than red in the visible spectrum, to 1 millimeter, on the border of the microwave region 红外线的

assortment /əˈsɔːtmənt/ *n.*   collection of various kinds 分类

CF card   short form for CompactFlash card, a mass storage device format used in portable electronic devices CF 卡, 标准闪存卡

configure★ /kənˈfɪɡə/ *vt.*   design, arrange, set up, or shape with a view to specific applications or uses 定制

redundant★ /rɪˈdʌndənt/ *adj.*   exceeding what is necessary or natural; superfluous 多余的; 冗余的

RAID   (Redundant Array of Independent Disks) 独立磁盘冗余阵列

icon /ˈaɪkɒn/ *n.*   [*Computer Science*] a picture on a screen that represents a specific command [计算机科学] 图标

mirror /ˈmɪrə/ *vt.*   [*Computer Science*] be a copy of, copy the data of [计算机科学] 成为……的镜像; 完全复制……的数据

erase★ /ɪˈreɪz/ *vt.*   remove (usually recorded or stored material) from one's mind or a magnetic tape or other storage medium 删除

reformat△ /rɪˈfɔːmæt/ *vt.*   remove the data on a storage body and determine the arrangement (of data) for new storage or display 重新格式化

cardinal★ /ˈkɑːdɪnəl/ *adj.*   of foremost importance; paramount 最重要的; 基本的; 首要的

lug△ /lʌɡ/ *vt.*   drag or haul (an object) laboriously 费力地拉拽

hard drive viewing units   硬盘数据显示器 (通常具有液晶显示屏供观看所存储图像文件)

photo-capable *adj.*   capable of viewing or taking photographs 拥有拍照功能的

downside△ /ˈdaʊnˌsaɪd/ *n.*   a disadvantageous aspect 不利方面

rechargeable /rɪˈtʃɑːdʒəbl/ *adj.*   able to be charged more than once 可重复充电的

minimal /ˈmɪnɪməl/ *adj.*   smallest in amount or degree (程度或数量上) 最小的

adaptor /əˈdæptə/ *n.*   one that adapts, such as a device used to effect operative compatibility between different parts of one or more pieces of apparatus 电源适配器

outlet /ˈaʊtlet, -lɪt/ *n.*   a receptacle, especially one mounted in a wall, that is connected to a power supply and equipped with a socket for a plug 电源插座

voltage /ˈvəʊltɪdʒ/ *n.*   electromotive force or potential difference, usually expressed in volts 电压; 伏特数

invaluable★ /ɪnˈvæljʊəbl/ *adj.*   of inestimable value; priceless 宝贵的; 无法估价的

panel /ˈpænl/ *n.*   a group of connected solar cells (太阳能) 电池板

wrench★ /rentʃ/ *n.*   a tool for exerting a twisting force 扳手

hammer and wrench△ (*slang*) necessary and routinely prepared elements 常规组

件;必备工具

gear /gɪə/ *n.*　equipment 设备;装备

memorable△/'memərəbl/ *adj.*　worth being remembered or noted; remarkable 值得纪念的;难忘的;值得注意的

showstopper△/ʃəu'stɒpə/ *n.*　a particularly arresting or outstanding person or thing worth much attention or applause 尤为引人关注的人或物

Proper Names

Domke	杜马克(美国知名摄影包生产商)
Olympus	奥林巴斯(日本知名光学器材生产商)
Canon	佳能公司(日本公司,主要生产光学、电子等产品)
Lexar	雷克沙,也作莱克沙(美国全球数码存储卡/闪存卡著名品牌)
WiebeTech	外接式硬盘品牌
Lithuania /ˌlɪθju'eɪnjə/	立陶宛(波罗的海沿岸国家)
JOBO	佳宝(德国公司,传统以制作摄影观片箱知名,现生产硬盘图像数据存储及显示设备)
GIGA Vu PRO evolution	佳宝生产的一款硬盘数据存储显示器
Epson	日本爱普生科技公司(主要生产与光学相关的数码设备)
Apple	美国苹果公司(生产电脑及相关数码产品)
iPod	苹果公司生产的袖珍数字音视频播放器
NexxTech	加拿大电器品牌
Radio Shack	美国购物网站
Brunton	美国户外作业用品品牌
Solaris	Brunton 生产的一种户外便携太阳能电池
Little League	美国的少儿棒球联赛
Nepal /nɪ'pɔːl/	尼泊尔(亚洲国家)

Comprehension

8 **Choose the best answer to each question with the information from the text.**

(　　) 1. According to the author, the two most essential mechanical considerations for photographic equipment have always been _____.

        A. power and storage   B. body and lens

        C. zoom and flash   D. shutter and aperture

(　　) 2. In choosing camera bodies, the author clearly stresses the equipment's different _____.

      A. qualities and types   B. sizes and functions

      C. zoom length and width   D. trademarks and situations

(   ) 3. The author's recommendation on lens choice shows that as a photographer he is _____.

      A. professional and experienced   B. careful and skillful

      C. efficient and exact   D. well-equipped and fully-loaded

(   ) 4. As the text shows, the author's "cardinal rule" about using storage device (cards, pocket drives, disks, driving viewing units, etc) is best represented by the word "_____".

      A. formality   B. portability

      C. reliability   D. particularity

(   ) 5. According to the text, all of the following choices could be included in the power necessities for a traveling digital photographer EXCEPT _____.

      A. solar panels and battery units

      B. databank and invaluable tools

      C. power inverter and adaptor plug

      D. batteries and charger

9 Complete the following summary with right words and expressions.

My choice of photographic equipment represents the constant technical consideration for photography. With the correct cameras and their accessories, my camera bag could provide the _____ equipment for almost all conditions. And usually the equipment choice is _____ to the type of photography I am doing. For example, wildlife or sports photography usually _____ high-speed lenses. And I always prepare a remote control cord so sometimes I can hold my _____ flash away from my camera to get the reflection of softer light. For a better guaranteed backup of my image files, my bag may contain the diversity of storage devices, including CF cards, _____ drives, CDs or DVDs as well as _____ hard drive viewing units.

With the _____ of film, the need for power comes up as a new _____ problem with digital photography. So, packed in my camera bag should definitely be the batteries and the necessities to keep them _____. Anyhow, good planning beforehand is always necessary for your photographic assignments. Never let the _____ bag get in the way of your efficient photography!

10 Discuss the following questions with the information from the text.

  1. Why does the author often carry a small point-and-shoot besides bigger Olympus types like the E-3 or E520?

    (*pocket, tourist camera, receive, larger body and lens, good quality*)

2. How could the author possibly copy the same files to two pocket drives at one time? Why does he do so?
(*configure*, *RAID device*, *icon*, *mirror*, *cardinal rule*)

3. What type of storage device are iPod and iPhone, according to the text? Why does the author describe them as photo-capable?
(*portable*, *units*, *images*, *view*, *share*)

4. What is the suggestion the author makes to largely if not entirely solve the problems occurring during the traditional charging process? What is special about the suggestion?
(*solar panels*, *solar battery units*, *as long as*, *exposure*)

5. The text gives a detailed introduction about the equipment for photography. And in the concluding paragraph, the author makes the statement "photographic equipment is the hammer and wrench of the photographer's toolbox". Yet he also reminds us that "the lighter and more efficient the toolbox, the easier it is for us to work in our travels". Try to analyze the author's view about photographic equipment, using the information from the text as well as whatever you know about photography.

Vocabulary & Structure

I Fill in the blanks with the words given below. Change the form where necessary.

sophisticated	compatriots	core	backup	minimal
broadcast	erase	transport	invaluable	memorable

1. The _____ of our concern is the protection of wildlife.
2. Before my luggage was _____ to South Africa, my return ticket had already been properly booked.
3. Harry and Sheila are _____ because they both come from the United States.
4. Usually it is not so easy to forget the painful experiences as it is to _____ files from computer disks.
5. Shanghai Expo 2010 has demonstrated the world's latest development of _____ technology in this field.

6. Hospitals and schools are equipped with the _____ generator in case there is a power failure.

7. The film was _____ for the fine acting of Ingrid Bergman.

8. Fortunately, the earthquake only did _____ damage to the stadiums under construction.

9. These photos taken in the war have proved to be _____ legacy to young people today.

10. Irresponsible sources of information tend to _____ rumors quickly.

12 **Complete the following sentences with phrases or expressions from the text.**

1. The vast desert land _____ rich material _____ the creation of the photographers.

2. Just as the plane was running _____ fuel, the pilot successfully landed it on the small ground.

3. Without the shelter of the spacesuit, astronauts would suffer from the _____ to harmful radiations.

4. If you don't carefully _____ your assignment, you will probably feel at a loss what to do in time of unexpected emergency.

13 **Translate the Chinese sentences into English by simulating the sentences chosen from the text.**

Chosen Sentences	Simulated Translation	Chinese Sentences
These are configured, in my computer's operating system, to **act as** a RAID device.		太阳能很多情况下可作为传统能源更清洁的替代品。(substitute)
In addition to two or three extra camera batteries, I also carry a small bag with extra AA and AAA batteries.		除了定期训练,长年的摄影实践对于成功者而言也是必要的。(essential)
This could **be reason enough to** carry a laptop or a portable CD or DVD burner		好奇心总能驱使年轻人进行野外摄影的历险。(wildlife)
Don't **load** yourself down **with** so much gear that it gets in the way of shooting memorable showstoppers.		没有积极的心理治疗,这些病人会长期为生活中的烦恼所困扰。(therapy, worries in life)

14 **Rewrite each sentence with the word or phrase in brackets, keeping the same meaning. The first part has been done for you.**

1. The new type of mobile phone meets a variety of needs in communication and entertainment.

The new type of mobile phone _____.
(suffice for)

2. With the persisting chaos in that country, there existed no sense of security in the guns people carried to protect themselves.

With the persisting chaos in that country, no sense of security _____. (reside)

3. They took efforts to be as fully prepared as possible to score high in the test.

They took efforts to _____. (cover all one's bases)

4. The dumbbells(哑铃) he used were characterized by the kind of muscles he intended to exercise.

The dumbbells he used _____.
(be specific to)

5. It would risk the dangers of his heart stroke to tell the old gentleman his daughter's misfortune.

It would _____. (tempt)

Text B   Skimming and Scanning

Photographing the Emotion of Sports[①]

Guess who won? Breck students celebrate winning the 2004 Minnesota high-school hockey championship in St. Paul. Jubilation shots tell the story. Canon 1D, ISO250, 35 – 350mm f3. 5/5. 6 lens at 135mm, 1/500 at f5. 6, electronic flash. Bruce Kluckhohn

---

① This text is adapted from an article in the book *Sports Photography: How to Capture Action and Emotion* written by Peter Skinner (Allworth Press in 2007).

Few endeavors bring out the range of emotions more than sport. (1) <u>Whether it's a group of biased, one-eyed, and very vocal supporters urging their side on, heckling an umpire, cheering in victory, or mourning a loss; or a nail-biting parent watching his or her Little Leaguer at bat with the score tied in the final game of the season, the opportunities to photograph raw emotion are there.</u> They present golden opportunities for memorable images.

5

Celebration, Excitement, and Jubilation

This Wayzata fan was really involved at the state high school hockey tournament in St. Paul. Shots like this help tell the story of an event. Canon 1D, ISO400, 35 – 350mm f3. 5/5. 6 lens at 90mm, 1/500, f4. 5, strobes. © Bruce Kluckhohn

A fan gets really excited at a Western Collegiate Hockey Association, final-five tournament, and Bruce Kluckhohn has brilliantly captured that excitement. Canon 1D, ISO200, 35 – 350mm f3. 5/5. 6 lens at 35mm, 1/500 at f4. 5, strobes. © Bruce Kluckhohn

There's no doubting the joy in this image as a U. S. fencer is tossed into the air after winning the 2004 Olympic gold medal. Canon 10D, ISO800, 70 - 200mm f2. 8 lens, pattern metering, 1/1000 at f2. 8. © Duane Hart

Excited fans cheering their team, going wild at a key play or the moment of victory are great
10 material for celebration shots. (2) <u>The photographer who can move in close, compose quickly, and fire off a series of images that truly capture the unbounded joy of the moment will come up with winning jubilation shots.</u> A great
15 advantage is that celebrating fans will usually be very happy, and cooperative subjects are, in most cases, willing to mug it for the camera. Fist pumping, the universal "we're number one" finger-raising, and other traditional gestures
20 made by fans celebrating are good subject matter. Similarly, players on the bench and team officials getting excited also provide excellent photo images. A shot of celebrating baseball players streaming from the dugout at game's end says it
25 all—we won! There is probably no better moment for the ultimate in jubilation images than

Pain and exhaustion from the extreme conditions during the North American RAID adventure sport championships are revealed in this tight portrait. Canon 20D, 17mm lens, ISO200, 1/160 at f4. Bob Woodward

the instant of victory—as that vital goal is being scored or the blast of the final whistle signals a win. Focus on the right people at that time and you'll have great shots.

Overall shots of large crowds of flag-and-banner-waving fans epitomize the   30 excitement that sweeps a stadium. Tens of thousands of people cheering, chanting, or doing a wave create an exciting spectacle, and images of this colorful mass of humanity can be just as exciting. Include a scoreboard or banner that symbolizes the venue or event to add interest. Hold the camera high above your head and take the shot—that little extra elevation can make a difference. An informal team shot of the   35 players and coaches holding a trophy aloft or the team sitting and sprawled around the trophy also shouts "victory and jubilation".

Tension and Strain

You can see tension and strain on the faces of players and fans alike, before and during an event. Often, this is when people like to be left alone—they probably won't   40 be as receptive to a camera as when they're celebrating—but if you take the photograph diplomatically—that is, don't simply thrust the lens into the subject's face—you could come away with a revealing portrait.

Heroics and Heroism

A great moment in sport is captured for posterity. USC head coach Pete Carroll congratulates senior quarterback Matt Leinart for his last appearance at the Los Angeles Memorial Coliseum where Leinart had never lost during his four years as a starter for the Trojans. Ben Chen knew the significance of the moment. Canon 1D MKII, 400mm f2. 8 lens, ISO1250, 1/1000 at f2. 8. © Ben Chen

45   Sport is all about heroes and their achievements. Look for photographs of sporting heroes whether in action or in quieter, more reflective moments. And while heroes for the sporting public at large might be NFL quarterbacks or major league baseball stars, your sporting hero could be your own son or daughter competing in Little League. Getting good shots of your sporting hero is simplified to some extent

50   because you can concentrate solely on them and their efforts rather than on the entire event. Access to professional sportsmen will not be as easy, but you can still shoot from the stands and occasionally there will be photo opportunities at spring training or similar events. On the other hand, photographing your Little Leaguer or high school athlete will be less complicated. You've still got to produce the images, but you'll

55   have a better chance of getting close to the subject.

Dejection and Disappointment

It's over! The faces of these dejected soccer players tell the story of a disappointing loss. Emotional moments like this are integral to sports.
Canon 1D, 400mm f2. 8 lens with 1. 4X extender, ISO200, /1600 at f4.
© Ben Chen

In any game, someone's going to lose. Images of dejected players, team officials, or fans are all part of the story. They can say as much about a game as the jubilation photographs. Look for the downcast player on the bench, head in hands or covered by

60   a towel, disappointed fans shaking their heads in disbelief, an exhausted player slumped over, dejection written all over his or her face. Pictures of these situations have a common message—we did our best, but lost! (3) A photograph of dejected players in the foreground with the all-revealing final scoreboard in the background has a poignancy about it that any viewer with an ounce of sporting empathy will

65   appreciate. Similarly, an image of jubilant victors in the foreground with the

vanquished in the background—or vice versa—is very telling.

Although not a pleasant subject, injury is a fact of sporting life. (4) <u>Don't set out to portray the pain of the injury—although a grimacing face does tell the story—but instead aim to depict the disappointment that a game, a season, or even a career has ended prematurely.</u> Photographing an injured player is a personal choice and   70 depends on your role at the game. The injury could have a major influence on the outcome, which makes it newsworthy. So, if you're photographing for a publication, take the shot and let the editor decide whether it runs or not.

Confrontation

Emotions can run high at MLB games. Los Angeles Dodgers pitcher Brad Penny wasn't too happy at being tossed out of a game. Canon 1D MKII, 400mm f2. 8 lens with 1. 4X extender, ISO 1600, 1/800 at f4. © Ben Chen

Many sports are about confrontation and in-your-face aggression. Shots of   75 competitors involved in face-offs can make great visuals. Similarly, athletes or coaches vehemently disputing an umpire's decision are good photographic material. These images might depict the less noble aspects of sports, including things such as bad sportsmanship and temper tantrums, but some confrontation shots can be humorous. Who could suppress a grin at a photograph of an irate Little Leaguer   80 glaring up at the umpire with a "How can you call that out?" expression on his or her face?

Encouragement and Support

Look for the shots that epitomize camaraderie and encouragement. The coach with an arm around the athlete's shoulder, giving words of advice or encouragement;   85 players in a huddle, listening to their captain's final instructions prior to a game; a Little League coach having a heart-to-heart with a youngster about to go to bat. Sports abound in images like these.

Planning to Capture Those Emotional Moments

"Come on ump! What was that?"Questioning decisions is universal to sport, and photographs portray the emotion. Canon EOS 3, ISO400 Fujicolor, 100 – 400mm f4.5/5.6 lens, maximum aperture. © Diane Kulpinski

A coach's pep talk becomes the focal point of the moment. Look for images like this when covering youth sports. Canon 1D, Mark II, 70 – 200mm f2.8 lens, electronic flash, 1/200 at f2.8. © Diane Kulpinski

90   You need to plan on capturing these moments of high drama and emotion. Professionals have a game plan to get what they need to fulfill their publication's needs. They work out ahead of time where they are going to be when emotions are likely to run highest—the end of the game is an obvious time, but there might be others such as when a legendary player is making a final appearance. Regardless of
95   what event you're photographing, plan ahead and put yourself in the right location to document the emotion. If you do it right, you'll have a collection of images that will complement the more typical action photographs that you make.

What Equipment to Use

Depending on your principal subjects, this type of photography could be ideal for
100   compact point-and-shoot cameras because much of the time you will be able to use

wide-angle lenses. And if you intend to isolate an individual, say on the bench, and can get reasonably close, a short-to-medium telephoto lens, equivalent to a 105mm lens on a 35mm camera, will be ideal. Watch professional photographers working at the end of a game. Invariably they will be shooting repeatedly at close range, using wide-angle lenses and fill-in flash. You should do the same—use a wide-angle lens and augment the ambient light with flash. This is one of those times in sports photography where probably you will be close enough to use flash. And if the winning team spontaneously gathers for an informal team shot with a trophy, have that wide-angle lens and flash ready. (Note: When you start using flash, if it's allowed, make sure you have changed the shutter speed to the correct synchronization speed. In the excitement of the moment, a basic thing like this can easily be overlooked.)

105

110

(1 282 words)

New Words and Expressions

endeavor★ /ɪnˈdevə/ *vi.*   attempt 尽力；努力

biased★ /ˈbaɪəst/ *adj.*   prejudiced 有偏见的

one-eyed△ /ˈwʌnˈaɪd/ *adj.*   unprofessional in skills and techniques; unfair and irrational in judgments 不在行的；不公允的

vocal★ /ˈvəʊkl/ *adj.*   full of voices; noisy 大声鼓噪的；喧嚣的

heckle△ /ˈhekl/ *vt.*   try to embarrass and annoy by questions, gibes or objections 诘问；责问

umpire△ /ˈʌmpaɪə/ *n.*   [Sports] a person appointed to rule on plays, especially in baseball 棒球裁判

mourn★ /mɔːn/ *vt.*   feel or express deep regret, grief or sorrow for 对……感到或表示遗憾或悲伤

raw /rɔː/ *adj.*   being in a natural condition, uncovered 自然的；未加掩饰的

fire off   finish (taking photographs) 拍摄完毕

unbounded△ /ˈʌnˈbaʊndɪd/ *adj.*   having no boundaries or limits; unrestrained 无边际的；无节制的；不羁的

mug /mʌg/ *vt.*   [Informal] make exaggerated facial expressions for photographing 做出表情供拍照

pump /pʌmp/ *vt.*   move or wave (usually. fists) up and down just like a pump with enthusiasm and strength 激昂地用力上下挥拳（作打气或压泵状）

gesture /ˈdʒestʃə/ *n.*   the act of moving limbs or other parts of the body to express or help express thought or to emphasize speech 为示意而做出的手势、姿态或表情

tournament▲ /ˈtʊənəmənt/ *n.*   championship series of games 锦标赛

subject matter theme，the major idea or matter to consider or express 主题；主旨

dugout△ /'dʌɡaʊt/ n.　[Baseball] either of two usually sunken shelters at the side of a field where the players stay while not on the field[棒球]球员休息处（通常为运动场边稍低于地面的两个掩体之一，球员不上场时在此处休息）

ultimate /'ʌltɪmɪt/ n.　the final part of a game 比赛终局；终场

blast /blɑːst/ n.　a sudden loud sound，especially one produced by a stream of forced air 巨响（尤指由一股受挤压的空气发出的响声，如哨音或汽笛声）

epitomize△ /ɪ'pɪtəmaɪz/ n.　be a typical example of 成为……的代表、缩影或典型范例

chant★ /tʃɑːnt/ vi.　sing or shout repeatedly in a monotonous and rhythmic way 有节奏的反复呼喊或歌唱

spectacle★ /'spektəkl/ n.　sth. that can be seen or viewed，especially sth. of a remarkable or impressive nature（尤指奇异或壮观的）景象

scoreboard /'skɔːbɔːd/ n.　a large board that records and displays the score of a game or contest 记分牌

venue△ /'venjuː/ n.　a place for large gatherings，as a sports stadium 会场；集会地点（如体育馆）

elevation★ /ˌelɪ'veɪʃən/ n.　the act of moving to a higher position 提升

trophy▲ /'trəʊfɪ/ n.　a prize or memento，such as a cup or plaque，received as a symbol of victory，especially in sports 奖品；奖杯（牌）

aloft△ /ə'lɒft/ adv.　high or higher up；in or into a high place 高高地；在高处

sprawl△ /sprɔːl/ vt.　cause to spread out in a straggling or disordered fashion 使……无序而又杂乱地向四周蔓延

tension /'tenʃn/ n.　tense mental condition 紧张情绪

strain /streɪn/ n.　excessive mental or bodily pressure （体力或精神的）过度压力

receptive▲ /rɪ'septɪv/ adj.　ready or willing to receive favorably 乐于接受的

diplomatically /ˌdɪplə'mætɪkəlɪ/ adv.　using tact and sensitivity in dealing with others 讲究技巧策略地；老练地

thrust /θrʌst/ vt.　force ... (into a unreceptive condition or situation)使……强行进入（不相容的地点或环境）

revealing /rɪ'viːlɪŋ/ adj.　enlightening or inspiring 有启迪作用的

reflective /rɪ'flektɪv/ adj.　thoughtful，characterized by careful consideration or profound meditation 深思的；富于思考的

quarterback△ /'kwɔːtəˌbæk/ n.　[American football] the backfield player whose position is behind the line of scrimmage and who usually calls the signals for the plays [美式橄榄]四分卫（后场运动员，位置在开球线后面，通常为比赛发号指令）

solely /'səʊ(1)lɪ/ adv.　singly；exclusively 单独地；专门地

stand /stænd/ *n.* (*pl.*)　tiered seats for watching sporting events 看台

integral★ /ˈɪntɪgrəl/ *adj.*　essential or necessary for completeness; constituent 必须的,不可或缺的

dejected△ /dɪˈdʒektɪd/ *adj.*　being in low spirits; depressed 沮丧的;情绪低落的

downcast△ /ˈdaʊnkɑːst/ *adj.*　low in spirits; depressed 垂头丧气的;沮丧的

slump★ /slʌmp/ *vt.*　cause ... to sink into a drooping posture, usually due to deep or sudden depression（常因极度消沉)使……呈萎靡颓丧的姿态

foreground▲ /ˈfɔːgraʊnd/ *n.*　the part of a scene or picture that is nearest to and in front of the viewer 前景(舞台或图画上位于观赏者前方且最靠近观赏者的部分)

poignancy▲ /ˈpɔɪnənsɪ/ *n.*　emotional or physical pain or distress 痛苦;辛酸

empathy△ /ˈempəθɪ/ *n.*　identification with and understanding of another's situation, feelings, and motives 移情作用(认同和理解别人的处境、感情和动机);感同身受的效应

vanquish△ /ˈvæŋkwɪʃ/ *vt.*　defeat in competition or conquer or subjugate in battle 战胜;击败;征服

vice versa /ˈvaɪsɪˈvɜːsə/ *adv.*　with the order reversed; conversely 反过来;反之亦然

telling /ˈtelɪŋ/ *adj.*　having force and producing a striking effect 效果显著而突出的

grimace△ /grɪˈmeɪs/ *vi.*　make a sharp contortion of the face because of injury or disgust（因伤痛或厌恶)脸部出现极端扭曲表情

prematurely★ /ˌprɪməˈtjʊəlɪ/ *adv.*　occurring too early because of unexpected reasons 过早地

outcome /ˈaʊtkʌm/ *n.*　a natural result; a consequence 结局;结果

newsworthy△ /ˈnjuːzwɜːðɪ/ *adj.*　of sufficient interest or importance to the public to warrant reporting in the media 有报道价值的

in-your-face△ /ɪnˈjɔːˈfeɪs/ *adj.*　marked by or done in a bold, defiant, or aggressive manner 挑衅的

face-off△ /ˈfeɪsɒf/ *n.*　confrontation 冲突;对抗

vehemently△ /ˈviːɪməntlɪ/ *adv.*　forcefully or strongly 激烈地

dispute /dɪsˈpjuːt/ *vt.*　question the truth or validity of; argue about; debate 就……进行争辩;质疑……真实或有效

sportsmanship△ /ˈspɔːtsmənʃɪp/ *n.*　conduct and attitude considered as befitting participants in sports, especially fair play, courtesy, striving spirit, and grace in losing 体育道德风尚或运动员精神(主要指适合参与运动的行为或态度,特别是公平竞争、礼貌谦逊、奋斗精神、胜不骄败不馁等内涵)

tantrum△ /'tæntrəm/ *n.*   a fit of bad temper 一阵坏脾气

grin★ /grɪn/ *n.*   the facial expression produced by drawing back the lips and bare the teeth, as in mirth or good humor （通常在高兴或情绪好时）咧嘴且露齿的笑容

irate△ /aɪ'reɪt/ *adj.*   extremely angry; enraged 极其恼怒的；勃然大怒的

glare★ /gleə/ *vi.*   stare fixedly and angrily 怒视

camaraderie△ /kæmə'rɑːdərɪ/ *n.*   goodwill and lighthearted rapport between or among friends; comradeship 友爱；同志之情

huddle★ /'hʌdl/ *n.*   a densely packed group or crowd, as of people or animals 聚拢的人群或畜群

heart-to-heart /'hɑːttə'hɑːt/ *n.*   an intimate conversation in private 私下的亲密谈话

youngster /'jʌŋstə/ *n.*   a young person; a child or youth 年轻人；孩子或青年

abound▲ /ə'baʊnd/ *vi.*   be great in number or amount 大量存在

fulfill /fʊl'fɪl/ *vt.*   carry out; satisfy 完成；达到要求

legendary△ /'ledʒəndərɪ/ *adj.*   extremely well known; famous or renowned 极其著名的；享有盛名的

complement★ /'kɒmplɪment/ *vt.*   serve as sth. that completes, makes up a whole, or brings to perfection to 补足；使完美；锦上添花

telephoto△ /'telɪ'fəʊtəʊ/ *adj.*   of or relating to a photographic lens or lens system used to produce a large image of a distant object 用于放大拍摄远距离景物的镜头或镜头系统的

invariably★ /ɪn'veərɪəblɪ/ *adv.*   without changing; constantly 不变地；始终如一地

fill-in△ /'fɪlˌɪn/ *adj.*   additional; extra 补充的；附加的

augment▲ /ɔːg'ment/ *vt.*   make (sth. already developed or well under way) greater, as in size, extent, or quantity 增强；增大

ambient△ /'æmbɪənt/ *adj.* *n.*   surrounding 周围的

spontaneously /spɒn'teɪnjəslɪ/ *adv.*   naturally without planning beforehand 自发地

synchronization△ /ˌsɪŋkrənaɪ'zeɪʃən/ *n.*   happening at the same time 同步性

posterity△ /pɒs'terɪtɪ/ *n.*   future generations 后世

Proper Names

ISO	感光度，即文中所指国际标准化组织（International Standards Organization）规定的胶片或数码感光器件的感光度
NFL	National Football League 的缩略语，即美

国国家橄榄球大联盟

MLB 　　　　　　　　　　　　Major League Baseball 的缩略语，即美国
职业棒球联盟

USC 　　　　　　　　　　　　University of Southern California 的缩略
语，即南加州大学

Los Angeles Memorial Coliseum 　　洛杉矶纪念体育场

Comprehension

15 Go over the text quickly and answer the following questions. For questions 1—7, choose the best answer from the four choices; for questions 8—10, complete the sentences with the information from the text.

(　　) 1. From the first paragraph we can get the general impression about photographing emotions in sports as being _____.

　　A. prejudiced and noisy

　　B. colorful and interesting

　　C. exciting and urgent

　　D. sad and immature

(　　) 2. In the second sentence in the "Celebration, Excitement, and Jubilation" part, what are mentioned about photographing the excitement of sports?

　　A. Attitude, responses and observation.

　　B. Distance, speed and imagination.

　　C. Movement, operation and courage.

　　D. Patience, creation and happiness.

(　　) 3. Compared with the players and fans in tension and strain, the subjects in jubilation might be more _____ with a photographer.

　　A. excited

　　B. fantastic

　　C. easy-going

　　D. diplomatic

(　　) 4. All of the following are true about photographing sporting heroes EXCEPT that _____.

　　A. they are stars or unknown athletes

　　B. they are either acting or thinking

　　C. they are available for closer shots

　　D. they are all professional athletes

(　　) 5. What techniques of art could be used in shooting dejection and disappointment, as revealed in the description about "scoreboards" and "foreground"?

   A. Contrast and symbolism.

   B. Irony and comparison.

   C. Romanticism and realism.

   D. Modernism and expressionism.

(   ) 6. According to the text, photographing confrontation depicts _____.

   A. decision disputes but also sportsmanship

   B. ill manners but also sometimes good humor

   C. aggression visuals but also noble temper

   D. sporting movements but also facial expressions

(   ) 7. The author believes that planning to capture emotional moments should involve the consideration about _____.

   A. drama, game and document

   B. height, appearance and images

   C. emotion, publication, and action

   D. time, people and place

   8. In sports photography, emotion is epitomized by subjects such as jubilation, _____, etc.

   9. For close shots of subjects, the author suggests using a _____ lens as a professional choice.

   10. Also necessary for shooting sports at close range are the use of _____ flash and the adjustment of the _____ speed.

Vocabulary & Translation

16 Fill in the blanks with the words given below. Change the form where necessary.

endeavor	biased	mourn	gesture	spectacle
reflective	dispute	integral	fulfill	spontaneously

1. The farewell between the rescue soldiers and local people was really a heart-moving _____.

2. The sense of responsibility and team work have always been _____ parts of our victory.

3. Shaking the head with a wavering (摇摆的) finger is usually a _____ of disapproval.

4. Shortly after the earthquake, the students from all over the school _____ gathered together and started their cooperation of searching for the missing.

5. It is very unfair and _____ for the media to always assume a background of the suspect whenever a crime happens.

6. They made their best _____ to break through the enemy line before the dawn.

7. For hours John and I _____ the feasibility of our journey across the tropical jungle for photographic experiments.

8. With tears in his eyes, the veteran slowly began the story of his guerrilla years, _____ the sacrifices of his fellow soldiers.

9. The girls _____ their assignments one hour earlier than the boys did theirs.

10. However urgent the war situation might be, the general always maintained his _____ manner while making quick and wise decisions.

17 **Translate the underlined sentences in the text into Chinese.**

1. Whether it's a group of biased, one-eyed, and very vocal supporters urging their side on, heckling an umpire, cheering in victory, or mourning a loss; or a nail-biting parent watching his or her Little Leaguer at bat with the score tied in the final game of the season, the opportunities to photograph raw emotion are there.

   _____

   _____

   _____

   _____

2. The photographer who can move in close, compose quickly, and fire off a series of images that truly capture the unbounded joy of the moment will come up with winning jubilation shots.

   _____

   _____

   _____

3. A photograph of dejected players in the foreground with the all-revealing final scoreboard in the background has a poignancy about it that any viewer with an ounce of sporting empathy will appreciate. Similarly, an image of jubilant victors in the foreground with the vanquished in the background—or vice versa—is very telling.

   _____

   _____

   _____

4. Don't set out to portray the pain of the injury—although a grimacing face does tell the story—but instead aim to depict the disappointment that a game, a season, or even a career has ended prematurely.

_____

_____

_____

Interactive Tasks

Pair Work

18 **Read the sample dialogues carefully, and then complete the interactive tasks that follow.**

Task 1

Sample dialogue

Tom： Linda, what's your impression of this photo of Taj Mahal(泰姬陵)?

Linda： Oh, it is fabulous(神奇的)! There have been a lot of Taj Mahal images, but I fell in love with this one at first glimpse(第一眼).

Tom： Me too. Look at the beautiful golden color here. There is a mysterious holiness all over the picture.

Linda： Yeah. The color effect comes from the good adjustment(调整) of light.

Tom： I agree, this is a perfect example of using natural light.

Linda: The only light source here was the sun, a little above the horizon. This is just a wonderful time to let in its golden and mild light.

Tom: You are right. As I know, the photo was taken right at dawn, when the sunrise was a little above the horizon. It was a National Geographic Expedition.

Linda: Taj Mahal this time was in the background on the right side, with a camel and its driver stepping into the Yamuna River from the left in the foreground, nearer to the lens, form a holiness of mystery. And the sun shines right in the middle from the still farther background with just the right mildness and strength to illuminate(照亮)the whole picture.

Tom: Sure. Light and shade is really the key of wonder here. As the photographer recalled later, he took advantage of the heavily-diffused(散射程度较高的) sunlight that day to bring about the wonderful effect.

Linda: That's true. But he also used the filter(滤光镜)to allow the exposure on the foreground to balance out(抵消)the brighter exposure value of the sky.

Tom: That should be the "Singh-Ray Galen Rowell Graduated Neutral Density filter". That's interesting. Let's have further analysis.

Interactive task

Two photographers are appreciating a photograph of the pyramids. The pyramids are small in the background with a local old gentleman in the foreground, taking up more than half of the frame(画面). The photo was taken at noon. Here light is still the key factor to create a masterpiece(杰作).

Role A: Is this photo about the pyramids in Egypt? It looks so special.

Role B: Right. It was taken near Cairo. I know the photographer took this photo in a hurry. But it is truly a meaningful masterpiece in many ways.

Task 2

Sample dialogue

Mary: What a breath-taking moment this photograph captured! This is an excellent work of sports action.

Bill: Also one of my favorites. I think we can read a lot of things from this split second, just like the beauty of strength, the struggling spirit and so on.

Mary: Sure. Look at his muscles and wide-open mouth. You can even hear the deep gasp for air at that moment.

Bill: This is Australian butterfly swimmer Pierce Hardy, powering to the end of the pool.

Mary: I really appreciate the splashes of water around him. What a beautiful sight of heated competition! This is the power of the camera, capturing the precious moments of life.

Bill: Yeah. But without good preparation the exciting moments could still slip away from the camera monitor. This is especially true with photographing sport action.

Mary: I know sports photographers follow their subjects all the year around, they even live and work with the athletes and coaches.

Bill: Absolutely, if they want to bring out excellent works. Here careful planning and preparation are the No. 1 issue for the photographer. This could include many things, such as the choice of time and location, and the familiarity with the subjects. For that they sometimes even work like the athletes, coming and going whenever and wherever they emerge.

Mary: And sometimes even like a spy, spotting every detail of the star's life and work.

Interactive task

Two students are talking about a photo of a downhill skier(高山滑雪运动员).

They are both attracted by the good photography of sports action here. And they both believe that good preparation and planning are quite essential for shooting sporting actions.

Role A: How amazing the photo is! I am a fan of winter Olympics but I've never noticed such a beautiful moment on my monitor.

Role B: This should be hard for the photographer. Downhill items mostly go on at a break-neck(危险的，极度高的)speed.

Group Work

🔟 **Work in groups to design your photographic evaluation.**

Type of photography（e. g. wildlife, sports, portraiture, or any other possible type）		
Evaluation of the photography		
Modules of techniques	**Merits in use or expression**	**Defects in use or expression**
Composition		
Exposure		
Lighting		
Focusing		
Color		
Choice of subjects		
Time and chance		
Creativity		
Others		

1. Form groups of 4 or 5 students.

2. Each group tries appreciating a photograph. Discuss and analyze its merits and defects(优缺点)by using the checklist below.

3. After the discussion, a representative from each group makes a presentation to summarize their analysis.

Follow-up Tasks

Writing

列举法

列举法是将数种因素一一列举出来以扩张主题句。主题句中一般有表示数量的词,如 many, some, several 等。例如:

There are some effective ways of losing weight. Physical exercise will be conductive to keeping people in good shape; proper diet is another useful method to protect them from getting fat; and still another way to lose weight is to be busy them selves with something else. What is more important, however, is to remove fat people's unhappiness rather than to remove the fat.

重复关键词法

即在主题句后的句中,以主题句为红线,采取后一句重复前一句中的关键词的方法,以保持整个段落在文字上和逻辑上的连贯和一致,这种方法多用于议论文。例如:

Moving Pictures

From moving pictures we can learn much about things and places that we can never see. Pictures about inventions and discoveries give us scientific knowledge. Pictures about life and adventures in foreign countries teach us geography. Pictures about historical events teach us history. Pictures based upon novels help us to appreciate literature. Newsreels tell us the news of the day. English moving pictures afford an excellent opportunity of learning spoken English for the students who study English.

上文中,主题句后的每句的开头,都重复使用了主题句中的关键词 pictures,使整段无论在内容上还是形式上,都一气呵成。

时空推展法

以事物发生、发展的时间和空间为依据展开段落的方法,称为时空推展法。这种方法多适用于描写文或记叙文。例如:

It grew dark before 7:00 o'clock. Wind and rain now whipped the house. John sent his oldest son and daughter upstairs to bring down mattresses(床垫) and pillows for the younger children. He wanted to keep the group together on one floor. "Stay away from the windows," he warned, concerned about glass flying from storm-shattered panes(窗格玻璃). As the wind mounted to a roar, the house began leaking—the rain seemingly driven right through the walls. With mops, towels, pots and buckets the Koshaks began a struggle against the rapidly spreading water. At 8:30, power failed, and Pop Koshak turned on the generator.

　　这是一段描写暴风雨袭击建筑物情景的文章。作者通过几个时间状语(before 7:00 o'clock, as the wind mounted to a roar, at 8:30)交代了暴风雨由弱到强的发展时序,描写有声有色、生动逼真而又井然有序。又如:

The asylum(收养院) has been abandoned for many years. The reddish bricks of the walls were probably shaped by local workmen, as we were told. The roofs were made of pieces of slate(石板), which had probably been plastered(紧贴) or mortared (胶粘) together to form the ridges that looked like terraced, thatched straw. And the bars that secured the door on the outside rested in the two V-shaped grooves(槽,沟) or notches(槽口). But they do not lock people in. These buildings now penned up horses.

　　这是一篇描写收养院外貌的文章,作者从最醒目的红砖开始,然后到石板屋顶、门,再对院内情形的推测,其描写犹如一幅浓淡分明的油画,远近层次非常清晰。

写正文段应注意的问题

　　古人把文章中间部分比喻为"猪肚",是要我们在写这一部分时应尽量做到内容充实丰富、论证有力。脸(开端)要漂亮,体(正文)也要健壮。写正文段具体应注意以下问题:

　　(1) 所写内容是否准确、清楚、具有说服力;

　　(2) 段落中有没有写出直接或暗含的主题句;

　　(3) 是否用了恰当手段使段落连贯;

　　(4) 段落内容是否完整、统一,有无说明不足之处或包括多余的细节;

　　(5) 所组织的材料是否以适当的顺序合理安排并表现出逻辑思维;

　　(6) 所运用的扩展方法是否得当,对段落中讨论的主要内容或相关的其他内容是否做到了主次分明,所用材料是否比例合适。

Research Project

　　Work in groups of 4 or 5 students, and finish a research project based on the topic area of this unit. It involves lectures, seminars, team-based activities, individual activities, team presentation and a reflective summary.

Steps

1. Form a research group;
2. Decide on a research topic;
3. Work in groups to finish PPT slides;
4. Each member of the group gives oral presentation of his parts;
5. Hand in materials that include: Project Proposal (one for each team), Research Report (one for each team, 1 000 words), Summary (one for each person, 300 words), PPT (one for each team).

Research Methods

1. Field work: to generate the first-hand information
   - Questionnaires
   - Interviews (interpersonal, telephone, e-mail, door-to-door visit, etc.)
   - Observation
2. Desk work: to generate the second-hand information
   - Library: books and magazines
   - The Internet: Google the theme with the key words
   - Reading materials

Suggested Options

1. An investigation about art students' greatest attention in their appreciation of photography.
2. What techniques may a young photographer use in shooting an old star?

Tips for Options

1. For option 1, properly design a questionnaire for your survey. Clarify and mark the control group to collect your data. For example, your survey may include such items as freshmen of art school in XX university, male students, female students, photography majors, etc.
2. For option 2, try to collect data by handing out a questionnaire or having interviews. Refer to concerned knowledge of statistics and try to maintain the validity and credibility of your investigation.

Unit Eight   Advertising

Highlight

Topic area	Structure	Skills

Advertising agency
William Bernbach and his
  advertising philosophy
Print advertising design
	there is no question that
	serve sb. well
	find oneself doing sth.
	be clear in the belief that
	be composed more of ...
	  than of ...
		Understanding modern advertising
		Describing and discussing advertising
		  design elements and principles
		Commenting on an advertisement

Warm-up Tasks

1 **Listen to the following passage and try to fill in the missing words and expressions.**

Advertising agencies offer a full range of advertising (1)_____ and advice based on market studies, popular culture and advanced sales techniques. They produce logos, (2)_____ effective and attractive color schemes to draw the consumer's (3)_____ to their clients' ads. They also prepare (4)_____ and brochures, and write descriptive copy for sales (5)_____. They may produce public service (6)_____ for charitable organizations and social programs as well, and (7)_____ press releases for new programs, events, and products. Advertising agencies use assorted forms of media to (8)_____ their clients' businesses or organizations, including magazine advertisements, newspaper ads, radio and TV (9)_____, websites, and even infomercials. Some also plan events, provide booths at conventions, and (10)_____ promotional items.

2 **Discuss the following questions about advertisements with your partner.**

1. How do you understand the messages in the following ads?
2. Which ad do you like best?
3. What do you think makes a good print ad?

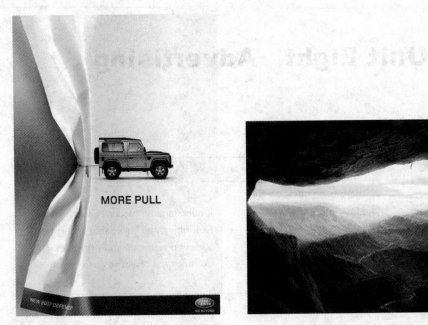

Land Rover UK—More pull

Pepsi—Dare for More

Apple—the iPod media player

Australia Post—If you really want
to touch someone, send them a letter.

Listening Tasks

Micro Listening Skills

3 You will hear five sentences. Each will be read three times. Listen carefully and write them down.

1. _____

2. _____

3. _____

4. _____

5. _____

Dialogue

An Interview with a Graphic Designer

Jon works as a moderator at Freelancegraphic. com. Now he is interviewing Linda, a graphic designer who currently lives in London.

Words & Phrases

graphic designer	平面设计师
moderator /ˈmɒdəˌreɪtə/ *n.*	主持人；版主
inspiration /ˌɪnspəˈreɪʃən/ *n.*	灵感
block /blɒk/ *n.*	障碍；阻塞
switch /swɪtʃ/ *vi.*	转换
take a power nap	打盹儿
come up with	想出；提出
illustration /ˌɪləsˈtreɪʃən/ *n.*	插图；图案
composition /ˌkɒmpəˈzɪʃən/ *n.*	构图
duplication /ˌdjuːplɪˈkeɪʃən/ *n.*	复制
scaling /ˈskeɪlɪŋ/ *n.*	缩放比例
Photoshop	图像处理软件
Illustrator	图形软件
deadline /ˈdedlaɪn/ *n.*	最后期限

visual /ˈvɪʒʊəl/ *n.*	视觉资料
passionate /ˈpæʃənɪt/ *adj.*	热情的

4 **Listen to the dialogue and choose the best answer to the following questions.**

(　　) 1. Linda came to London to study _____.

    A. fine art   B. fashion design

    C. industrial design   D. graphic design

(　　) 2. Which of the following does NOT inspire Linda's design work?

    A. Music.   B. Natural scenery.

    C. Artworks.   D. Talented friends.

(　　) 3. What is the first step of Linda's creation process?

    A. Making a little sketch.

    B. Painting shadows and light effects.

    C. Producing the theme.

    D. Drawing all things that will be inside the composition.

(　　) 4. Which of the following makes the greatest challenge to Linda?

    A. She has to find clients by herself.

    B. It is hard to get out of the "designer's block".

    C. She has to develop her own signature style.

    D. She always has a deadline to meet.

(　　) 5. How does Linda's job influence her life?

    A. She loves to observe people around her.

    B. When judging an artwork, she'll see its composition first.

    C. She has developed a natural sense for colors.

    D. She feels more sensitive to trends.

5 **Listen to the dialogue again and complete the following sentences with the information you have heard.**

1. Linda draws inspiration from many different forms of artworks, like _____, street art, _____ and music.

2. When Linda gets "designer's block", she will _____ something else. She will read design books or take a _____.

3. Linda usually uses Photoshop, Illustrator and some other 3-D software _____ of the designing process.

4. For Linda, the attractive part of being a designer is the fact that she can _____ and _____ by the way.

5. Linda thinks the most important thing for a designer is to _____ about what he/she does. Explore, _____ and be open to learn new things.

Passage

Out-of-home Advertising

Words & Phrases

susceptible /səˈseptəbl/ *adj.*	易受影响的
kiosk /kiːˈɒsk/ *n.*	亭;棚
format /ˈfɔːmæt/ *n.*	样式
fall into	分成
category /ˈkætɪɡərɪ/ *n.*	类别
billboard /ˈbɪlˌbɔːd/ *n.*	广告牌
transit /ˈtrænsɪt/ *n.*	交通系统
alternative /ɔːlˈtɜːnətɪv/ *adj.*	非传统的
booth /buːθ/ *n.*	亭;棚;展位
static /ˈstætɪk/ *adj.*	静态的
rack /ræk/ *n.*	支架;架子
address /əˈdres/ *vt.*	对……说话
predominant /prɪˈdɒmɪnənt/ *adj.*	占主导地位的
supplement /ˈsʌplɪment/ *vt.*	补充
revenue /ˈrevənjuː/ *n.*	财政收入
alongside /əˈlɒŋˈsaɪd/ *prep.*	在……旁边
stopping power	阻止力;令人驻足的力量
bold /bəʊld/ *adj.*	醒目的

6 Listen to the passage and decide whether the following statements are true（T）or false （F）.

_____ 1. Out-of-home advertising usually serves as a reminder to reinforce a creative concept employed in other media.

_____ 2. Transit advertising does not include airport advertising.

_____ 3. Alternative advertising provides a way to address consumers in places they may not expect.

_____ 4. Billboard advertising comprises 60 percent of total outdoor revenue in the US.

_____ 5. Billboard advertising plays a major role in the media strategy of an advertising campaign.

7 Listen to the passage again and answer the following questions with the help of words and phrases provided below.

1. How different is the out-of-home advertising from other media like newspaper, radio or TV?

   （*home, entertainment*）

   _____

2. What are the four formats of out-of-home advertising?

   （*transit, alternative*）

   _____

3. Where are billboards usually located?

   （*high traffic, busy roads*）

   _____

4. What elements are important to make effective outdoor advertisements?

   （*word, illustration, color, background*）

   _____

Reading Tasks

Text A　Reading in Detail

Pre-reading Questions

1. Have you ever heard of William Bernbach or any other advertising legend?

2. Do you know some famous adverting campaigns?

3. Is advertising an art or a science? How is it related to art and science

respectively?

William Bernbach—an Advertising Pioneer①

William Bernbach was born in New York City in 1911. As a child he enjoyed reading and writing verse and grew up with an appreciation of art. With the exception of a two-year tour of duty during World War II, Bernbach never strayed far from his roots in New York City. He attended New York University, receiving a bachelor's degree in literature in 1933. Bernbach also pursued studies in art, philosophy, and   5
business administration that would serve him well during his career.

During the Depression, Bernbach felt lucky when he found a mailroom job at Schenley Distillers. With his mind focused on an advertising career, the young man found himself   10
whiling away his hours creating ads for his employer. His creative spirit was appreciated by Grover Whalen, Schenley's chairman, who soon took the bright young man under his wing. When Whalen left to oversee the 1939 New York   15
World's Fair, Bernbach went with him as a staff writer. From this experience Bernbach learned a lot, but he was far more influenced by his subsequent job at William Weintraub agency.

At Weintraub, Bernbach's self-creation and self-promotion received an enormous   20
boost. He worked as a copywriter alongside modernist art director Paul Rand who greatly influenced his ideas about ad layout. They would visit art galleries and museums during lunch breaks, and talk about art and copy working in harmony. The pair's collaborative efforts resulted in an end-product that was more integrated and powerful. Bernbach understood how such collaborations could liberate agency creative   25
work.

With the onset of World War II, Bernbach put his career on hold to serve in the army. In 1945, he joined Grey Advertising, where he rose quickly from copywriter to creative director. As the company grew, Bernbach felt the constraints of market testing and research on creative advertising. In a 1947 letter to his bosses at Grey, he   30
commented, "I'm worried ... that we're going to worship techniques instead of substance." However, his bosses appear to have ignored the letter. And so Bernbach

---

① This text is adapted from materials at www. answers. com.

decided to "braze new trails" with his own agency.

He fulfilled the dream when he and Ned Doyle joined forces with Maxwell Dane
35 to establish their own agency. Among the three people, there existed a well-defined
division of labor. Doyle was the account executive; Dane took care of administration
and financial matters; and Bernbach was an idea machine that handled the creative
concerns. On June 1, 1949, Doyle, Dane & Bernbach (DDB) set up shop in the
shadow of the big Madison Avenue① Agencies. It wouldn't stay there for long.

40 In the 1950s Doyle Dane Bernbach displayed its style of advertising in four
notable campaigns for four unknown companies②. These companies, like Doyle Dane
Bernbach, were attempting to establish themselves in their respective markets. To
compensate for this lack of public recognition, the agency created a number of
strikingly different ads. Not only did the campaigns sell large quantities of cameras,
45 clothes, bread, and airline tickets, they sold Doyle Dane Bernbach advertising as
well.

One of Bernbach's best-remembered efforts was the campaign for Avis Rent a
Car. Putting Avis second next to the front runner Hertz was a stroke of genius.
"We're number two," said the ads, "We try harder. We have to." This strategy
50 worked as it appealed to the consumers' emotions towards an underdog who deserved
more. The Avis ad campaign was directly responsible for increasing Avis's market
share by 28 percent, and closing the gap with Hertz.

The Volkswagen advertising campaign was a similar story. These small German
cars were not what the American consumer wanted, or so it appeared. Again, DDB
55 converted a liability into a saleable asset. In 1959, the agency designed an ad for the
Volkswagen Beetle③, showing a small picture of the car against a sea of white space
and placing just two words at the bottom of the ad: "Think Small." Think small in
terms of price and energy efficiency. The self-deprecating headline presented the
Beetle in an offbeat manner. Not only did Americans purchase these "ugly"
60 Volkswagens by the thousands, but the car became a symbol for an entire "non-
conformist" generation.

As success built upon success, Bernbach helped DDB produce memorable
campaigns for myriad other clients. While much of the work coming out of DDB was

---

① Madison Avenue: an avenue located in the borough of Manhattan in New York City. The term "Madison
Avenue" refers to the American advertising industry.

② The four companies were Polaroid Cameras, Levy Bakery Goods, Ohrbach's Department Store, and El Al
Israel Air Lines.

③ "Think Small" for Volkswagen Beetle: recognized by *Advertising Age* as the top advertising campaign of
the twentieth century.

created by other writers and art directors, Bernbach is universally recalled as an inspirational mentor. He reviewed all work and created an atmosphere where creative personalities blossomed. Though his name came third on the masthead of Doyle Dane Bernbach, there was no question that Bill Bernbach was the impetus and direction behind the agency. The 1960s saw the golden age of advertising's "Creative Revolution" and Doyle Dane Bernbach was at the forefront of this movement.

Think small.

Bernbach's advertising philosophy went contrary to conventions. Above all he valued innovation and intuition. He frequently addressed audiences of advertising executives to explain that advertising is not formulaic. Creative advertising was, to Bernbach, composed more of intuition and a sense of artistry than of analytical prowess.

The Bernbach's concepts had a trademark simplicity that permeated both the copy and visual elements. His advertising philosophy revolved around the idea that persuasion was the purpose of advertising and that only a simple approach would "make crystal clear and memorable the message of the advertisement". His ads were always fresh and simple, yet exuded energy. Often self-deprecating, they were also frequently humorous and tasteful.

Bernbach's advocacy of advertising as art was grounded in the notion that the public had to be respected. He was clear in his belief that his audience was intelligent and literate. And the underlying respect would encourage favorable reactions to creative advertising.

Bernbach strongly believed that advertising success hinged on the quality of the product. One of Bernbach's most quoted lines is "Nothing makes a bad product fail faster than a great advertising campaign". This guiding principle led DDB to select only products that could live up to their advertising.

During his 33 years with DDB, when the agency achieved $1.2 billion in billings, Bernbach saw it change the dynamics of advertising and even America's cultural landscape. Krone① said, at Bernbach's death, "He elevated advertising to high art and our jobs to a profession." Sixteen years later, Bernbach's impact continues undiminished. And today he emerges as No. 1 on *Advertising Age's* 20th century honor roll of advertising's most influential people.

(1 061words)

New Words and Expressions

verse★ /vɜːs/ *n.*　a poem, or piece of poetry 诗；韵文

appreciation /əˌpriːʃɪˈeɪʃn/ *n.*　awareness of aesthetic qualities or values 欣赏；鉴赏

stray★ /streɪ/ *vi.*　move away from 走失；离群

pursue /pəˈsjuː/ *vt.*　apply oneself to studies or interests 追求

while away　spend（time）idly or pleasantly 消磨（时间）

take sb. under one's wing　help and protect sb. 庇护；照顾

subsequent /ˈsʌbsɪkwənt/ *adj.*　happening after sth. else 随后的

boost /buːst/ *n.*　push upward or ahead 增加；促进

layout /ˈleɪaʊt/ *n.*　schematic arrangement of parts 布局；版面设计

collaborative★ /kəˈlæbəretɪv/ *adj.*　accomplished by collaboration 合作的；协力完成的

collaboration★ /kəˌlæbəˈreɪʃən/ *n.*　act of working jointly 合作；协作

liberate /ˈlɪbəreɪt/ *vt.*　make free 解放；释放

put sth. on hold　stop the progress of sth. 暂缓某事

onset★ /ˈɒnˌset/ *n.*　beginning or start 开始；发生

copywriter△ /ˈkɒpɪraɪtə/ *n.*　person who writes the words for advertisements 广告文案编写人

creative director　head of the creative department at an advertising agency 创意总监

constraint▲ /kənˈstreɪnt/ *n.*　one that restricts, limits, or regulates 限制；约束

substance /ˈsʌbstəns/ *n.*　essential nature 要点；实质

braze new trails　do sth. different 开辟新道路

join forces with　come together for a common purpose 联合

well-defined△ /ˌweldɪˈfaɪnd/ *adj.*　having definite and distinct lines or features 明确界定的

executive /ɪgˈzekjʊtɪv/ *n.*　person responsible for the administration of a business

---

① Helmut Krone (1925—1996): a pioneer of modern advertising. He spent over 30 years at DDB and was the art director for the popular 1960's campaign for the Volkswagen Beetle.

经理;管理人

set up shop   establish a business or an organization 开始营业

respective /rɪsˈpektɪv/ *adj.*   considered individually 各自的

compensate /ˈkɒmpenseɪt/ *vt.*   adjust or make up for 补偿;弥补

strikingly /ˈstraɪkɪŋlɪ/ *adv.*   in a striking manner 醒目地

front runner△ person that seems most likely to win a race 领先者

stroke of genius very clever idea 天才的本领(主意)

underdog△ /ˈʌndədɒg/ *n.*   one at a disadvantage and expected to lose 失败者

convert /kənˈvɜːt/ *vt.*   change the nature, purpose, or function of sth. 转变;转化

liability★ /ˌlaɪəˈbɪlɪtɪ/ *n.*   weak point 不利条件

saleable /ˈseɪləbl/ *adj.*   possible to sell 适于销售的

asset /ˈæset/ *n.*   useful or valuable quality 优点;长处

self-deprecating△ /selfˈdeprɪkeɪtɪŋ/ *adj.*   having a tendency to disparage oneself 自贬的;谦虚的

offbeat△ /ˌɒfˈbiːt/ *adj.*   not conforming to an ordinary type or pattern 不寻常的;不落俗套的

non-conformist /nʌnkənˈfɔːmɪst/ *n.*   person who does not follow normal ways of thinking or behaving 不遵循传统规范的人

myriad▲ /ˈmɪrɪəd/ *adj.*   innumerable 无数的

inspirational★ /ˌɪnspəˈreɪʃənəl/ *adj.*   providing or intended to convey inspiration 启发灵感的;鼓舞人心的

mentor△ /ˈmentə/ *n.*   wise and trusted counselor or teacher 导师

blossom /ˈblɒsəm/ *vi.*   develop; flourish 发展;长成

masthead△ /ˈmɑːsthed/ *n.*   head or top of a mast 桅顶

impetus▲ /ˈɪmpɪtəs/ *n.*   impelling force 推动;推动力

forefront▲ /ˈfɔːfrʌnt/ *n.*   position of most importance; prominence 最前部;最前列

intuition★ /ˌɪntjuːˈɪʃən/ *n.*   instinctive knowledge or belief 直觉;直觉力

formulaic△ /ˈfɔːmjuˈleɪɪk/ *adj.*   characterized by or in accordance with some formula(根据)公式的;刻板的

artistry△ /ˈɑːtɪstrɪ/ *n.*   artistic quality 艺术性

analytical★ /ˌænəˈlɪtɪkəl/ *adj.*   of or relating to analysis 分析的

prowess△ /ˈprauɪs/ *n.*   superior skill or ability 高超的技艺

permeate★ /ˈpɜːmɪeɪt/ *vi.*   spread or flow throughout 渗入;渗透

revolve around center on 围绕;以……为主要内容

crystal /ˈkrɪstəl/ *adj.*   clear or transparent 透彻的;清澈的

exude△ /ɪgˈzuːd/ *vt.*　discharge or emit 缓慢流出；渗出

advocacy△ /ˈædvəkəsɪ/ *n.*　active support 拥护；提倡

be grounded in（on）sth.　be based on sth. 以某事物为基础；根据

literate /ˈlɪtərɪt/ *adj.*　knowledgeable or educated in a particular field or fields 有文化修养的

underlying★ /ˌʌndəˈlaɪɪŋ/ *adj.*　basic；fundamental 根本的；基础的

favorable /ˈfeɪvərəbl/ *adj.*　winning approval；pleasing 赞同的；有利的

hinge on depend on 取决于

live up to fulfil（an expectation，obligation or principle）符合；不辜负

dynamics△ /daɪˈnæmɪks/ *n.*　forces and motions that characterize a system 动态

elevate /ˈelɪveɪt/ *vt.*　raise from a lower to a higher position 提升

undiminished△ /ˌʌndɪˈmɪnɪʃt/ *adj.*　not lessened or diminished 未减少的

roll /rəʊl/ *n.*　list of names 名册

Proper Names

William Bernbach /ˈwɪljəm ˈbəːnbɑːk/	威廉·伯恩巴克（人名）
Schenley Distillers	施恩利酒业公司（美国）
Grover Whalen /ˈgrəʊvə ˈweɪlən/	格罗弗·惠伦（人名）
William Weintraub	威廉·温特劳布公司（美国）
Paul Rand /pɔːlˈrænd/	保罗·兰德（人名）
Grey Advertising	葛瑞广告公司（美国）
Ned Doyle	内德·道尔（人名）
Maxwell Dane	马克斯韦尔·戴恩（人名）
The Madison Avenue	麦迪逊大街（美国纽约）
Avis Rent a Car	艾维斯出租汽车公司（美国）
Hertz	赫兹公司（美国）
Volkswagen Beetle	大众甲壳虫汽车
Krone	克罗恩（姓氏）
Advertising Age	《广告时代》杂志

Comprehension

8 **Choose the best answer to each question with the information from the text.**

（　　）1. At which company did Bernbach learn the importance of art-copy teamwork?

      A. DDB.   B. Grey.

      C. Weintraub.   D. Schenley.

（　　）2. By saying that "It wouldn't stay there for long", the author implies that DDB would _____.

A. move to a new place

B. be challenged by the big agencies

C. have a rapid development

D. have big accounts

(   ) 3. What advertising appeal was adopted in the Avis ad campaign?

A. Emotional appeal.

B. Scarcity appeal.

C. Humor appeal.

D. Rational appeal.

(   ) 4. Which of the following is NOT true about Bernbach's ads?

A. Dramatic.   B. Humorous.   C. Offbeat.   D. Simple.

(   ) 5. What is true about Bernbach?

A. He created much of the work coming out of DDB.

B. He worked as a creative director at Weintraub.

C. He valued advertising rules over intuition.

D. He was regarded as a major force behind the Creative Revolution.

9 Complete the following summary with right words and expressions.

William Bernbach is considered to be a pioneer of modern advertising. When he was young, he pursued studies in literature, art, and philosophy that would _____ during his career. He once worked as a _____ with the art director Paul Rand who greatly influenced him. Bernbach understood how such _____ could liberate agency creative work.

In 1949, Bernbach and Ned Doyle _____ Maxwell Dane to establish their own agency. From 1950s to 1960, the agency displayed its unique _____ in many notable campaigns which took it to the _____ of advertising's "Creative Revolution" movement.

Bernbach's advertising philosophy went contrary to conventions. Above all he valued _____ and intuition. His concepts had a trademark _____ that permeated all his works. Bernbach believed that the respect for the public would encourage _____ reactions to creative advertising. He also believed that advertising success _____ the quality of the product. Even today, his impact on advertising remains undiminished.

10 Discuss the following questions with the information from the text.

1. Why did Bernbach decide to leave Grey?

(*constraints*, *favorable*)

_____

2. What kind of role did Bernbach play in DDB?

(*impetus*, *direction*)

_____

3. How did Bernbach influence American advertising?

(*unconventional*, *change*)

_____

4. Do you like the "Think Small" ad? Why or why not?

_____

5. William Bernbach once said, "Advertising doesn't create a product advantage. It can only convey it." How do you understand this statement?

_____

Vocabulary & Structure

11 **Fill in the blanks with the words given below. Change the form where necessary.**

appreciation	pursue	boost	liberate	asset
convert	blossom	prowess	favorable	elevate

1. They decided to _____ the first mate to the position of captain.
2. The self-willed young man _____ his college life into a long course of playing games.
3. The book received a _____ review after it was published.
4. He considered their military prowess an _____ for the democracies.
5. These reform measures _____ the villagers from poverty.
6. That holiday has been a _____ to our spirits.
7. Our village has _____ into a flourishing town.
8. She decided to _____ her studies after obtaining her first degree.
9. His _____ as a footballer makes it certain that he'll be chosen for the team.
10. Their proficiency in Chinese is inadequate for true _____ of Chinese culture.

12 **Complete the following sentences with phrases or expressions from the text.**

1. My old sister has to _____ marriage _____ because of her heavy work.
2. Some foreign missionaries _____ her _____ and gave her food and clothes.
3. The older boys _____ the younger ones to sing the school song.
4. She _____ as a bookseller in the High Street.

13 **Translate the Chinese sentences into English by simulating the sentences chosen from the text.**

Chosen Sentences	Simulated Translation	Chinese Sentences
Bernbach also pursued studies in art, philosophy, and business administration that would *serve him well* during his career.		他在那读了很多平面设计的经典书籍，这对他将来非常有用。(graphic design, classic)
With his mind focused on an advertising career, the young man *found himself whiling away his hours* creating ads for his employer.		玛丽一心向往着从事时装设计工作，她总发现自己在纸上画着时装草图来消磨时间。(fashion sketches)
Though his name came third on the masthead of Doyle Dane Bernbach, *there was no question that* Bill Bernbach was the impetus and direction behind the agency.		琳达虽然无法与玛丽相提并论，但毫无疑问，她是位很有才华的歌手和演员。(in the same league as, performer)
Creative advertising *was*, to Bernbach, *composed more of* intuition and a sense of artistry *than of* analytical prowess.		在玛丽看来，造就伟大艺术作品更多的是灵感和热情而非某些技巧。(inspiration, technique)
He *was clear in his belief* that his audience was intelligent and literate.		李院长清楚地认识到大学教育必须培养学生拥有开放的心态。(director, open mind)

14 **Rewrite each sentence with the word or phrase in brackets, keeping the same meaning. The first part has been done for you.**

1. My scores were not as good as I had hoped they would be.

   My scores didn't _____. (live up to)

2. He got ill after his wife died.

   His illness was _____. (subsequent to)

3. People gradually recognized him as the most powerful minister in the new government.

   He gradually _____. (establish)

4. They hold a leading position in global auto manufacturing, which is largely due to their flexibility and market knowledge.

   Their flexibility and market knowledge help put them _____. (forefront)

5. The exhibition contents centered on five main themes.

   The exhibition contents _____. (revolve

around)

Text B   Skimming and Scanning

Print Advertising Design[①]

Behind every effective advertisement is a creative concept. A creative concept implements the advertising strategy so that the message is attention-getting and memorable. In effective advertising, it is not just the words that need to communicate—it is the visuals, too. And they must work together to present the
5   creative concept.

In most advertising the power starts with the visual, and its primary function is to get attention. Designers have found that a picture in a print ad captures more than twice as many readers as a headline does. Ads with pictures also tend to pull more readers into the body copy. Furthermore, people notice ads and remember those with
10   picture more than those composed mostly of type.

The person who is most responsible for creating visual impact is the art director. One of the most difficult problems that art directors—and those who work on the creative side of advertising—face is to transform a big idea into words and pictures. During the brainstorming process, both copywriters and art directors are engaged in
15   visualization, which means they are imaging what the finished ad might look like.

(1) Various artists may create or develop specific parts of an art piece or scene, but it is the art director that unifies the vision. The art director is in charge of the overall visual appearance of the message and how it communicates mood, product qualities, and psychological appeals. Specifically, he makes decisions about whether
20   to use art or photography in print, and what type of artistic style to use. The art director's toolkit for print advertising includes the photos, illustrations, typefaces, color, and layout of the proposed ad. A good art director blends the visual elements of an ad into a powerful message that strongly resonates with the viewer.

When art directors use the word art, they usually mean photographs and
25   illustrations, each of which serves different purposes in ads. The decision to use a photograph or an illustration is usually determined by the advertising strategy and its need for realism or fanciful images.

Photography has an authenticity that makes it powerful. Most people feel that

---

① This text is taken and adapted from *Advertising Principles and Practice* written by William Wells, John Burnett and Sandra Moriarty(Beijing: Renmin University Press, 2009).

pictures don't lie. For credibility, photography is a good medium. Illustrations, on the other hand, eliminate many of the details you see in a photograph and retain the 30 "highlights" of the image. Because it abstracts, it can communicate faster and more pointedly than a photograph. It can also intensify meanings and moods, making illustrations ideal for fantasy.

Another important visual element in the design of print advertising is color. Color can be used to attract attention and stimulate interest. Generally, print ads with 35 color get more attention than ads without color.

Different color schemes create different visual effects. Some ads use full color, which helps convey realism. Some use black and white, which lends dignity and sophistication to a visual. Color works better when contrasted with non-color areas. Therefore, ads also use spot color, in which a second color is used in addition to black to highlight important elements. Take the Nike ACG boot ad for example. It uses red spot color to accent the feature of the product.

(2) The use of color in advertising design is also dictated by the need to communicate a certain mood and reflect a specific brand. For example, blue is a color that's commonly associated with clear thinking and intellect. It's no surprise that blue emerges as a favorite in the corporate world. Its implication of steadiness and reason continues to make it an effective choice for much company branding. IBM uses this color so extensively that the company is 55 often referred to as "Big Blue".

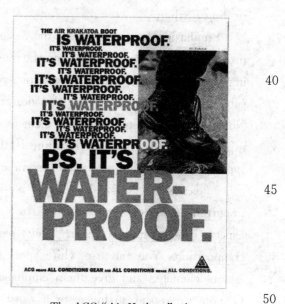

The ACG "Air Krakato" ad

40

45

50

The ad's typography is the appearance and arrangement of the ad's printed matter. In most cases, good typesetting does not call attention to itself because its primary role is functional. Type, however, also has an aesthetic role and the type selection can contribute to the impact and mood of the message. 60

Typefaces come in either serif or sans serif style. Serif means the end of each stroke of a letter has a little flourish. It is considered less "modern" in appearance. A sans serif typeface misses this detail and the ends of the stroke tend to be more block-like. Sans serif conveys a more modern image and looks best when surrounded by lots of white space. 65

Once art directors have chosen the images and typographic elements, they manipulate all of the visual elements on paper to produce a layout. A layout is a plan that imposes order and at the same time creates an arrangement that is aesthetically pleasing. Arranging all the elements so that they make sense and attract attention is a
70 challenge. Here are some design principles that help to arrange a layout.

Simplicity. The best layout is a simple layout. Generally, the more elements that are crowded into a layout, the more impact is fragmented. Too many elements create clutter rather than clarity. Ads that have a complex look will discourage people reading further.

75 **Emphasis.** The emphasis in design provides the focal point by making the most important element more prominent or eye-catching than the others in the design. Normally, the most emphasized element is
80 a picture, but it can be a headline if the type is big and bold enough to dominate other elements. (3) Emphasis is an important concept that touches on all aspects of graphic design and page
85 composition. You can use white space to isolate elements and give them emphasis. Or you can repeat an image or a word to establish its importance.

The Willie Garden Club brochure

Contrast. Contrast makes one element
90 stand out from another and indicate importance. It also adds interest to the layout and provides a means of directing the reader's eye. Contrast occurs when two elements are different. The key to working with contrast is to make sure the differences are obvious. Four common methods of creating contrast are by using
95 differences in size, value, color, and type.

Balance. Balance in design is the distribution of elements across the design. There are mainly two types of balance: symmetrical balance and asymmetrical balance. Symmetrical balance is achieved by placing elements in a very even fashion in the design. It generally lends itself to more formal, orderly layouts which often
100 convey a sense of tranquility or stability or elegance. It is used in more upscale product ads. (4) Asymmetrical layouts are generally more dynamic and by intentionally ignoring balance the designer can create tension, express movement, or

convey a mood such as anger, excitement, joy, or casual amusement. In the Willie Garden Club brochure, the off-balance design creates a sense of freedom and movement.

105

(1 127 words)

New Words and Expressions

implement /ˈɪmplɪmənt/ *vt.*   carry out; perform 实施；执行

body copy   main text part of an advertisement 广告正文

brainstorming△ /ˈbreɪnˌstɔːmɪŋ/ *n.*   a thorough discussion to solve problems or create ideas 集体研讨；集思广益

visualization△ /ˌvɪzjʊəlaɪˈzeɪʃən/ *n.*   the act or an instance of visualizing 形象化；想象

overall /ˈəʊvərɔːl/ *adj.* including or covering everything 全部的；全体的

unify /ˈjuːnɪfaɪ/ *vt.*   make or become one; unite 使联合；统一

specifically /spəˈsɪfɪkəlɪ/ *adv.*   speaking more exactly 具体地

toolkit△ /ˈtuːlkɪt/ *n.*   a set of tools designed to be used together or for a particular purpose 工具包；工具箱

typeface△ /ˈtaɪpfeɪs/ *n.*   the size and style of the letters used in printing 字体；字样

blend /blend/ *vt.*   combine or mix 混合；调和

resonate▲ /ˈrezəneɪt/ *vi.*   appeal to someone or cause someone to relate to 共鸣

fanciful /ˈfænsɪfʊl/ *adj.*   indulging in or influenced by fancy 幻想的；新颖奇特的

authenticity▲ /ˌɔːθenˈtɪsɪtɪ/ *n.*   undisputed credibility 可靠性；真实性

credibility★ /ˌkredɪˈbɪlɪtɪ/ *n.*   the quality of being believable or trustworthy 可靠性

eliminate /ɪˈlɪmɪneɪt/ *vt.*   remove or take out 除去；摆脱

pointedly△ /ˈpɔɪntɪdlɪ/ *n.*   in such a manner as to make sth. clearly evident 指向地；强调地

intensify★ /ɪnˈtensɪfaɪ/ *vt.*   to make intense or more intense 增强

fantasy /ˈfæntəsɪ/ *n.*   imagination unrestricted by reality 想象；幻想

stimulate /ˈstɪmjʊleɪt/ *vt.*   excite 刺激；使兴奋

color scheme   the choice of colors used in design 色彩设计

dignity★ /ˈdɪgnɪtɪ/ *n.*   formality in bearing and appearance 高尚；尊贵

sophistication /səˌfɪstɪˈkeɪʃən/ *n.*   quality of being sophisticated 精致

spot color   single mixes of ink used in printing 点彩色

highlight /ˈhaɪlaɪt/ *vt.*   make prominent; emphasize 强调；突出

accent /ˈæksənt/ *vt.*   stress; single out as important 强调；突出

dictate /dɪkˈteɪt/ *vt.* determine；command 支配

implication /ˌɪmplɪˈkeɪʃən/ *n.* meaning that is not expressly stated but can be inferred 含义

typography△ /taɪˈpɒgrəfɪ/ *n.* arrangement and appearance of printed matter 排印；印刷样式

typesetting△ /ˈtaɪpˌsetɪŋ/ *n.* arrangement of types for printing 排字（排版）

call attention to cause sb. or sth. to be noticed or observed 唤起注意

aesthetic★ /iːsˈθetɪk/ *adj.* of or concerning the appreciation of beauty 有关美的；悦目的

serif△ /ˈserɪf/ *n.* short line at the upper or lower end of the stroke of printed letters 衬线

sans serif△ /sænˈserɪf/ *n.* typeface that do not use serif 无衬线

stroke /strəʊk/ *n.* a single mark made by a writing 一画；一笔

flourish△ /ˈflʌrɪʃ/ *n.* embellishment or ornamentation 装饰曲线

manipulate★ /məˈnɪpjʊleɪt/ *vt.* handle skillfully 熟练控制；操作

impose /ɪmˈpəʊz/ *vt.* apply or make prevail by or as if by authority 推行；采用

fragment /ˈfrægmənt/ *vt.* break or cause to break into pieces (使)碎裂；分裂

clutter△ /ˈklʌtə/ *n.* confused multitude of things 零乱；杂乱

clarity★ /ˈklærɪtɪ/ *n.* clearness of thought or style 清晰；清楚

prominent /ˈprɒmɪnənt/ *adj.* noticeable 显著的；突出的

touch on be relevant to 涉及；提到

stand out be highly noticeable 突出；引人注目

value△ /ˈvæljʊ/ *n.* way in which light and shade are used in a picture（色彩的）浓淡；明暗

even /ˈiːvən/ *adj.* equally matched or balanced 相等的；均衡的

tranquility▲ /træŋˈkwɪlɪtɪ/ *n.* state of peace and quiet 平静；安宁

stability★ /stəˈbɪlɪtɪ/ *n.* quality of being free from change or variation 稳定；稳固

dynamic /daɪˈnæmɪk/ *adj.* characterized by action or forcefulness 动态的；充满活力的

intentionally /ɪnˈtenʃənəlɪ/ *adv.* in an intentional manner 有意地；故意地

off-balance△ /ɒfˈbæləns/ *adj.* not balanced 不平衡的

Proper Names

IBM	美国国际商用机器公司
Nike ACG(All Conditions Gears)	耐克全天候（耐克公司产品系列）
Willie Garden Club	威利园艺俱乐部

Comprehension

15 Go over the text quickly and answer the following questions. For questions 1—7, choose the best answer from the four choices; for questions 8—10, complete the sentences with the information from the text.

(　　) 1. What does "big idea" in Par. 3 refer to?

      A. Inspiration.　　　　　　　　B. Creative concept.

      C. Good idea.　　　　　　　　　D. Great plan.

(　　) 2. Which of the following is NOT included in the art director's responsibility?

      A. Deciding what type of artistic style to use.

      B. Working out the overall visual look of the message.

      C. Deciding whether to use illustration or photo.

      D. Producing specific parts of an art piece.

(　　) 3. Which is NOT true about the advantage of using an illustration in an ad?

      A. It simplifies the visual message.

      B. It helps focus attention on key details of the image.

      C. It makes an ad look more realistic.

      D. It conveys message faster.

(　　) 4. The main purpose of using spot color is to _____.

      A. add sophistication to an ad

      B. emphasize the important elements in an ad

      C. make an ad more appealing

      D. provide realism

(　　) 5. Type in a print ad is mostly used to _____.

      A. intensify the mood of the message

      B. convey the words of the message

      C. create an aesthetically pleasing effect

      D. reflect the artistic style

(　　) 6. Which of the following statement is true?

      A. A complex layout will encourage people to read further.

      B. Asymmetrical balance is often used to express elegance.

      C. Contrast is more than just how bright a color is compared to the background.

      D. White space can hardly be used to create emphasis.

(　　) 7. Which of the following is most likely to be created by using an asymmetrical balance design?

      A. Calmness.　　　　　　　　　B. Freedom.

C. Emphasis.   D. Contrast.

8. One of the greatest challenge that art directors face is to translate a creative concept into _____.

9. It is easier to understand an illustration because it usually calls attention to _____.

10. When dealing with contrast it is important to choose the elements which are _____.

Vocabulary & Translation

16 Fill in the blanks with the words given below. Change the form where necessary.

scheme	blend	eliminate	highlight	prominent
clarity	unify	overall	implement	arrangement

1. The house is in a _____ position on the village.
2. Professor Li asked Jack to _____ the unnecessary words from the essay.
3. The teacher laid out a perfect _____ for this team's work.
4. The _____ measurement of this room is 80 square meters.
5. The circular _____ of megaliths is called Stonehenge.
6. Those bridges and islets all _____ the garden scenery.
7. The government is _____ a new policy to help the unemployed.
8. All these small states were _____ into one nation.
9. The poem _____ the separate ingredients into a unity.
10. Belief in people should be accomplished with open eyes and _____ of judgment.

17 Translate the underlined sentences in the text into Chinese.

1. Various artists may create or develop specific parts of an art piece or scene, but it is the art director that unifies the vision.

_____

_____

_____

2. The use of color in advertising design is also dictated by the need to communicate a certain mood and reflect a specific brand.

_____

_____

_____

3. Emphasis is an important concept that touches on all aspects of graphic

design and page composition.

_____

_____

_____

4. Asymmetrical layouts are generally more dynamic and by intentionally ignoring balance the designer can create tension, express movement, or convey a mood such as anger, excitement, joy, or casual amusement.

_____

_____

_____

Interactive Tasks

18 **Read the sample dialogues carefully, and then complete the interactive tasks that follow.**

Task 1

Sample Dialogue

Mary: Hello, is that DOC Advertising Company?

Paul: Yes. What can I do for you?

Mary: We need to design a print advertisement which is to be shown in a magazine. Will you help us?

Paul: Sure. What's your product?

Mary: Watches. We are a watch manufacturer with a 120-year history. Our company is launching a new kind of sport watch. We need something to catch consumers' eyes.

Paul: Have you got any idea about the advertising message?

Mary: We want to highlight the watch's water-proof ability and its modern look. The product is aiming at people who love the outdoors.

Paul: Do you have some requirements for the design?

Mary: Maybe a simple yet dynamic layout is OK. We already have our logo. We need a compact slogan.

Paul: OK, will you please send us some detailed information about your company and your new product? We'll have a discussion later.

Mary: OK. I'll do it now.

Interactive tasks

A car manufacturer is launching a new kind of small family cars. Its marketing manager is calling DOC Advertising Agency about designing an ad put in the newspaper.

Role A: The car is comfortable, powerful and economical. We need an impressive and catchy slogan.

Role B: Do you have some requirements for the design?

Task 2

Sample dialogue

Susan: Bob, look at this ad for Dunham boot! It is so simple yet so impressive!

Bob: Yeah. I am pulled into it. It looks like a work of fine art. There are not so many elements in the layout. Only two simple illustrations with a few words at the bottom.

Susan: The layout and art shown here speaks of the beauty of nature. I guess it says these boots are for people who appreciate the nature.

Bob: That's just what I have in mind. I was most impressed by its use of white space around the boots and those created by snow. They help to make the boots stand out.

Susan: What about the balance used here? Is it an asymmetrical balance design?

Bob: I think so. You see this branch of the small tree. It is escaping from the left side and arching across the page.

Susan: And the lines of the shoelaces. They are bouncing above the shoes.

Bob: That's quite true. Both of them make the overall design dynamic.

Susan: I really love these ads that make you look twice.

Bob: So do I. That's the power of creativity.

Interactive task

Two young people are talking about the ACG boot ad (see Text B). The ad, with an asymmetrical layout, uses spot color to accent the product.

Role A: The ad is simple yet so striking! The layout effectively expresses the idea of tough boots for wet weathers.

Role B: I am most impressed by the repetition of the headlines. It uses spot color occasionally to produce the visual spice.

Group Work

19 **Work in groups to discuss about an advertisement.**

1. Form groups of 4 or 5 students.
2. Each group finds an ad that impress them most and discusses about its design. Fill in the following chart and make an analysis of the ad.

What is the ad's theme?	What makes the ad stand out?	What visual elements are used?	How is the layout arranged?

3. Each group gives presentation of their findings to the rest of the class.

Follow-up Tasks

Writing

结论段展开的方法

我们在前面说过：良好的开端是成功的一半。开端固然重要，但结尾也同样重要。否则就给人以"虎头蛇尾"之感觉。恰到好处的精彩结尾可给全文起到"画龙点睛"的效果，赋予全文以美感，令人百读不厌。结论段是通过归纳总结而得出最后结论，从而进一步深化主题。具体方法可因文体风格的不同而异。一般方法有如下几种。

1. 综合结论法。即通过总结全文的事实、论据及例证等做出合理的推断，最后得出结论。例如：

Why to Go to Graduate School

The life of a graduate student is often difficult. They are usually too busy studying to make a good living. Often they have to pay high tuition fees for their education. Some give up studying before they get their degrees. But most keep on working at their studies until they graduate. In today's world, most graduate students don't regret spending time with their studies. They are finding that things arc changing very fast. New developments are occurring in all fields. For many graduates, study has become a necessity.

该文讨论的是"为什么要上研究院去学习"。前两段讨论了美国绝大多数学生如何艰苦地完成学业,取得学位。在攻读学位时,他们不但要掌握所攻读的学术领域的发展和最新动向,而且在取得学位之后,还要学习另一个学术领域的知识。这是一个艰苦而又昂贵的学习生活。最后结论是:由于世界上所有的领域都在发生变化,不断出现新的进展,因此,艰苦而昂贵的研究生学习生活是值得的,是必要的。

2. 变换措辞,重申主题。所谓重复主题就是在文章结尾时,又回到文章开头所阐明的中心思想或主题上,再次肯定或强调。例如:

Automobiles in the U. S.

…

More car pools should be formed in order to put fewer automobiles on the road and to use less gasoline. Parking is a great problem, and so is the traffic in and around cities. Too many cars are being driven. Something will have to be done about the use of cars.

该文讨论美国车多为患的现象。汽车与美国人民的工作和生活结下不解之缘。但由于车多,城市出现交通拥挤、停车困难现象,随之就出现 car pool,就是合作用车互助组的办法。例如,有些家庭,他们自己组织起来轮流派车接送他们的孩子上学、放学,以减少交通拥挤。结论段中主题句"More car pools should be formed in order to put fewer automobiles on the road and to use less gasoline"就采用了归纳式语句,以建议的口气,把前段所谈的 car pool 的好处加以重申,引出对所讨论问题的最后结论。

3. 提出问题,引起思考,找出结论。虽然形式是问句,但意义却是肯定的,具有明显的强调作用,可引起读者思考。例如:

Homework

If there were no homework on weekends, students would come to school on Monday well refreshed and willing to work. Teachers, don't you agree?

文章讨论了关于周末不布置家庭作业的问题。在结论段,用反问句结尾,起到了强调和发人深思的效果。又如:

A Letter to the Youth

What is there to say about the position of a young scientist in our country? It is perfectly clear. Much is given to him, but much also is asked of him. And it is a matter of honor for the youth, as well as for all of us, to justify the great hopes which our fatherland places in science.

该文是巴甫洛夫给青年的一封信的结论段,一开头就用提问的方式,接着用回答问题的方式得出结论。

4. 重点摘述。即采取对全文进行简洁归纳的方法,使读者对全文的要点有个提纲挈领、简单明了的印象。例如:

Heart and Artery Disease

We can do something about this kind of illness. If some of the arteries are in a very bad condition, the surgeons can cut them open. They can take out the cholesterol and make the arteries wider; or take out a piece of artery and put in new piece. Besides, we have drugs that make the arteries wider, and medicines that stop the blood forming soiled clots. But the only real cure is to rest, and to have a healthy life.

该文讨论的是心脏与动脉的疾病。对付这种疾病的最好办法，就是前面段落所讨论内容的归纳：请外科医生做心血管手术，抽出胆固醇，或采取药物治疗的办法。而最好的办法，就是好好地调养、休息。

5. 引语法。引用名人名言、格言、谚语或故事中人的重要话语结尾，但所引用的名言警句一定要与前面的观点相符，以此让读者接受论点。例如：

In conclusion, I believe that opportunities are abundant in our society and everyone has an equal chance. We can acquire them only if we are prepared and qualified, just as a proverb says, "Opportunities are only for the prepared minds."

该结尾段通过引用谚语结尾，从而较好地表明了作者对 opportunities 的态度，深化了主题。

6. 建议法。通过展望未来、提出建议或措施来结尾也是一种很好的方法。例如：

Medical Care System

In my opinion, with the disadvantages outweighing its advantages, the medical care system in our country should be reformed. I think medical insurance system should be set up to replace the free medical care system.

结尾段应注意的问题

写文章最忌讳"虎头蛇尾"。所以，古人把文章的结尾比喻为"豹尾"，就是要我们收尾要响亮有力。脸（开端）要漂亮，体（正文）要健壮，腿（结尾）要有力。写结尾段具体应注意以下问题：

（1）照应引言段中的中心议题，且语气一致，内容为一整体；

（2）在开始时，应考虑运用一句具体的陈述或相应的连接技巧将正文段与结尾段的开头自然地连接起来；

（3）不要在结尾处出现新观点或包含文中未涉及的内容，一般所有新的论点在正文段出现；

（4）不要在结尾段写道歉式的句子；

（5）结尾处不要用"……"来表示；

（6）不要对结尾段的事实做过多的不必要的说明，以免使文章显得啰唆；

（7）不要过分夸张。

总之，要尽量避免结尾草草了事或画蛇添足，应做到意尽言止，恰到好处，并能呼应开头，给读者以想象和回味的余地。

Research Project

Work in groups of 4 or 5 students, and finish a research project based on the topic area of this unit. It involves lectures, seminars, team-based activities, individual activities, team presentation and a reflective summary.

Steps

1. Form a research group;
2. Decide on a research topic;
3. Work in groups to finish PPT slides;
4. Each member of the group gives oral presentation of his parts;
5. Hand in materials that include: Project Proposal (one for each team), Research Report (one for each team, 1 000 words), Summary (one for each person, 300 words), PPT (one for each team).

Research Methods

1. Field work: to generate the first-hand information
   - Questionnaires
   - Interviews (interpersonal, telephone, e-mail, door-to-door visit, etc.)
   - Observation
2. Desk work: to generate the second-hand information
   - Library: books and magazines
   - The Internet: Google the theme with the key words
   - Reading materials

Suggested Options

1. Make a study of public service announcements in China.
2. What are the secrets of successful ad campaigns?

Tips for Options

1. For Option 1, you need to narrow down the topic and decide the major points you're going to cover. For example, you may focus on the characteristics and problems of PSA in China and work out the solutions.
2. For Option 2, it is suggested that you firstly collect information about some successful ad campaigns, then analyze them and summarize the general principles that apply to the great ad campaigns.